CRACKING
HEADS

By
Benson S. Forbes

First printed in 2007, this is the second printing, revised and published by Shari S. Forbes in 2013.

ISBN: 061575516X
ISBN: 978-0615755168
(Shari S.\Forbes)

Published by Shari S. Forbes
PO Box 1424
Sherwood, Oregon 97140

Printed in the United States of America

CRACKING HEADS

MONDAY

7 a.m.

Harry Latter had been awake for some time. He lay rigidly on his back staring up at the ceiling from his railed hospital bed. He raked his long bony fingers through his shoulder-length thinning gray hair, and his brow creased in a frown as he struggled to remember, but as usual his mind was not cooperating. A hand grasped his wrist causing him to jump. He turned his head slowly and painfully and focused his watery pale blue eyes on the person standing beside his bed. The Hispanic woman dressed in a white nurse's uniform looked vaguely familiar, and he relaxed slightly.

"Good morning, Harry. I see you're awake," she said in a low voice with a slight Spanish accent. "You remember me. I'm Teresa, and this is Ozzie." She stepped a little to the side so he could see the young muscular black man who stood with his hands on the back of a wheelchair.

"Hey, my man, Harry," he said with a huge grin.

Harry smiled faintly. "Ozzie," he said.

"That's right, Harry," said Teresa as she stepped back into his view and smiled down at him. "We need to get you up now and into the wheelchair. Ozzie will help you."

Harry looked up at her blankly. "The square root of 64 is eight," he mumbled.

"That's right, my man," said Ozzie in a cheerful voice as he cranked a handle at the bottom of the bed and leveraged Harry up into a sitting position.

Teresa lowered the bed rail and grasped Harry's arm gently. "Now, can you swing your legs over the side of the bed, Harry?"

Harry slowly and shakily brought his legs around as he leaned heavily on Teresa. His emaciated body was clad in blue pinstriped cotton pajamas. He sat on the edge of the bed and looked down as Ozzie guided his feet into a pair of navy blue corduroy house slippers. "Seven times eight is 56," he muttered as Teresa and Ozzie helped him to his feet. They walked him forward a few paces, and Ozzie positioned the wheelchair behind him.

Teresa stood in front of him and grasped his shoulders. "OK, Harry, you can sit down now," she said.

Ozzie quickly shifted the wheelchair slightly when he saw Harry beginning to sit on the arm of the chair. When Harry was in the chair, Ozzie secured a safety strap around his waist. "Fifty-six divided by seven is eight, but that's not it," said Harry shaking his head.

"That's right. You've said that before," said Teresa smiling at him. "Now, Harry, today is a special day for you. Your niece is here, and she's taking you on a little trip. What do you think of that?"

"I have to get out of here. Have to get to the lab," said Harry in a slightly agitated tone.

"Yes, we know," said Teresa. "We'll help you get ready. First, I'm going to check your blood pressure and temperature, and then Ozzie will give you a shower and a shave and help you get dressed, OK?"

Harry frowned and shook his head. "The cube root of twenty-seven is three, and that's not it," he said sadly.

* * *

THURSDAY

6 a.m.

The sun had just risen in the New Mexico sky. Its first rays glinted off the windows of a low concrete building that served as the final security checkpoint for the National Security Agency's top-secret Advanced Spectrum Division housed deep inside a mountain about 100 miles northeast of Albuquerque. This checkpoint was one of many that the black Jeep Grand Cherokee had passed through on the rugged winding gravel road that was the only land access to Apparition Mountain.

The Jeep pulled to a stop between two armed guards who checked the papers of the driver and the sole passenger in the vehicle. When they had validated the papers, the guards opened the doors of the vehicle and stood back to allow the two occupants to step out. The driver, a tall, thin athletic-looking young woman with auburn hair, fell in behind the passenger, a man with silver-streaked dark hair who appeared to be in his early fifties. They followed the guards to the entrance of Apparition Mountain where one of them tapped a code onto a keypad beside a formidable steel door.

Almost immediately the door swung open where another guard waited. He nodded solemnly at the visitors and led them through a metal detector, then to a computer terminal where yet another guard scanned their facial features with a biometrics camera. Soon the guard smiled and handed them laminated identity cards attached to elastic cords, which they immediately hung around their necks. "Welcome to Apparition Mountain, Senator Goodman and Ms. Hoover," he said.

* * *

7:15 a.m.

Deep inside the Mountain, Dr. Daniel Graham had just finished checking Harry Latter's pulse, when his nurse, Betsy Mallory, walked into the small room where Harry lay on his back in a hospital bed. "We have a visitor," she began just as the tall young woman strode into the room. Betsy's mouth snapped shut and she looked at the Doctor apologetically.

Dr. Graham looked at the visitor with a slight smile and turned back to Betsy. "It's all right, Betsy. Would you please check on the other patient, and I'll be there in a moment."

"Certainly, Doctor." Betsy glanced curiously at the visitor as she left the room and quietly closed the door behind her.

After a few moments, the visitor approached the bed and looked down at Harry. Harry stared back at her out of his pale watery eyes. "And how is Harry today?" she asked in a low soothing tone.

"The cube root of 125 is five, AND THAT"S NOT IT!" Harry suddenly yelled at the top of his lungs. Both the Doctor and the young woman jumped at the sound.

"My, there's certainly nothing wrong with his voice, is there?" asked the young woman.

"No. Just his memory. Physically, he's healthy as a horse. That's not unusual for someone in his condition," said the Doctor. He leaned over and put his hand on Harry's forehead.

"The square root of 121 is 11, and that's not it either," Harry mumbled, shaking his head sadly.

"I have to get back," said the young woman. "I told the Senator I was going to the powder room. I just wanted to see if you think Harry's up for all this."

The Doctor nodded at her and leaned down over Harry again. "Harry, I'll be back in a little while. Try to sleep. It's still early," he said patting Harry's gnarled hand.

"Good-bye, Harry," said the young woman, as the Doctor held the door open for her. As they started to walk down the hall towards the Doctor's office, Harry's shrieking voice punctured the silence. "Cube root of 343 is seven! THAT'S NOT IT!"

They passed an open door, and the young woman saw a heavily bearded man lying in a hospital bed as Betsy, the nurse, adjusted the valve on an IV bottle hanging on a rack beside his bed. "Is that...?" asked the young woman.

The Doctor nodded. "Yes. They flew him in from Gitmo yesterday. He's sedated."

He closed the office door behind them and turned to look at her. "Well, Cyn, today's the big day. I'm confidant Harry's up for the experiment. I'm going to begin the sedative at 9:30, and I'll be monitoring everything throughout. We should soon know what Harry can't remember."

"Good, Dan. Just remember not to let on that you know me. The Senator doesn't know," she said, putting a finger to her lips as she opened the door to leave.

"All right, Cyn. I'll remember to call you Ms. Hoover, and you remember to call me Dr. Graham," he said.

"Yes, Dr. Graham," she said as she closed the door behind her.

* * *

Cynthia Hoover, or Cyn, as she had been called all her life, was thirty-six, a graduate of MIT, had never been married, and was the top aide for Senator Brian Goodman, chair of the Senate Intelligence Appropriations Committee. At least that's what nearly everyone believed, including the Senator himself. Only a couple of higher-

ups in the intelligence community knew who her real boss was, and there was no one higher than that except the President of the United States.

To those who knew her, it would not have been a surprise that she had achieved such status at so young an age in what was largely a man's world. From the time she was a small girl growing up on a ranch near El Paso, she had always possessed an uncanny ability to solve mechanical and mathematical problems. She just naturally seemed to know how things worked and how to fix them.

As the only child of parents who had married late in life, she was treated as an adult nearly from the time she was able to walk. Her father, Claude, had finally settled down and married when he was in his early fifties. He'd been a cattle broker and a colorful cowboy-type wheeler-dealer for many years in Southern Arizona. He was famous for his annual weeklong pit barbecues and for leading gold-prospecting expeditions into the Superstition Mountains. On one of his cattle-buying forays at a ranch south of El Paso, he had met Cyn's mother, Billy. She was a rancher's daughter and shared his passion for horses and gold prospecting. The twenty-year gap in their ages made not a whit of difference to Billy, and before long they sneaked off to Las Vegas for a three-day vacation and came back married.

Claude was fifty-eight when Cyn was born; Billy, thirty-eight. They were ready to get on with parenthood, and before Cyn could walk, she was riding horses, sitting in the saddle in front of one of her parents. By the time she could walk, she was panning for gold along with the adults who accompanied Claude and Billy on their treks into the wilds of Texas, New Mexico and Arizona. On her twelfth birthday, Claude and Billy gave her a newborn sorrel colt to raise and train. She named him Warrior because of his feisty spirit, and the two of them became inseparable.

By the time she was a teenager, she was fixing the hay bailer and the truck and any other piece of ranch equipment that broke down. She developed a passion for acquiring and restoring old broken down cars and if anyone had a problem with a computer, Cyn would have it fixed in no time at all. At the age of fifteen she achieved fame in quarter horse racing circuits as both the owner and jockey of Warrior who won every race from Ruidoso to Raton, New Mexico for three years running. It was in Raton when she was seventeen that she met the young Taos Indian, the flute player, so talented like herself.

In school she was a whiz, especially in physics and math. When she graduated as Valedictorian of her high school class and won a top scholarship to MIT, it was no surprise, and Warrior, by then happily retired, helped pay for her education with his stud fees.

7:30 a.m.

When Cyn opened the door to the small reception room, she saw that the Senator was engaged in conversation with a tall gaunt man wearing a lab coat. The men were sitting across a table from one another with coffee cups in front of them. As she entered, the two men stood up.

"Ah, here you are, Cyn," said the Senator. "I'd like you to meet Professor Karl Gregory Braun. Professor Braun is the mastermind behind the technology we're taking a look at today. Professor, this is my aide Cynthia Hoover. The two of you have something in common— you're both MIT grads."

As she reached out to shake the Professor's hand, Cyn quickly assessed his face—the thin lips, the gray eyes, and the short-cropped paper-white hair. She was certain she had never met or heard of him before. She found his handshake cold and rather limp. "Pleased to meet you, Ms. Hoover," he said in a frigid voice, and she noticed that the smile pasted on his lips did not reach his eyes.

"Likewise, Professor," said Cyn, taking in his appearance and trying to judge his age. She guessed he might be in his mid- to late-fifties. "And when did you attend MIT?" she asked.

"You can be assured it was before your time," he said with another thin smile. There was an awkward pause.

"Yes, well, we'd best get on with the business at hand," said the Senator. He glanced curiously from one to the other.

"Yes," said Professor Braun, abruptly turning away from Cyn and picking up a clipboard from the table. "If you'll follow me, Senator, I'll take you to the observation room where you'll be able to see the entire process. I believe you'll find my invention quite interesting."

"Well, Professor, you know why I'm here. I have to find out how the taxpayers" money is being spent and be able to justify how this new technology will benefit national security if we are to appropriate more funds."

"I'm confidant you'll be duly impressed, Senator."

"I understand you've come up with a way to revive that top-secret project that was abandoned at Los Alamos ten years ago."

"Precisely, Senator," said Professor Braun. "Now, if you will follow me, we'll show you how we're going to do that."

As the Senator and Cyn followed Braun out of the room, the Senator glanced at her with raised eyebrows. She simply shrugged and shook her head.

They followed Braun along a wide corridor until they reached a door marked "Restricted." Braun tapped a code onto a keypad, an electric lock clicked, and the door sprang open. They walked into a medium-sized room where one wall was completely taken up with a multiplex display panel showing various computer-generated standby patterns. Opposite this wall was a glassed-in balcony that overlooked a large room below where technicians huddled together in conversation or sat in front of computer terminals.

"That is the main control center," said the Professor as he gazed down through the thick glass.

"Looks like a NASA control center," said Cyn observing the activity below.

Braun nodded. "It is very similar, but this one has many times the computing power and four times the personnel."

"And you've already spent five times the amount NASA has spent on the Mars project," added the Senator.

"Going to Mars is easy compared to what we're about to do, Senator," said Braun.

"It's still a lot of money for one project," said the Senator.

"But this project is much more important to national security and besides…."

Braun was interrupted when the door sprang open and General Jefferson Allen Masters of the Air Force strode briskly into the room. He walked up to the Senator and clasped his hand. "Senator Goodman, glad you could make it to our little demonstration."

The Senator grinned. "Yes. I can't wait to see how all of you have been spending our taxpayers" money. By the way, Jeff, congratulations on your promotion." He pointed to the five stars on the General's epaulet.

"Totally unexpected, Senator," said the General. He winked and the Senator laughed.

"This is my aide Cynthia Hoover, General," said the Senator, turning to Cyn who was standing slightly behind him. "She has a Ph.D. in Quantum Physics from MIT."

The General looked at Cyn and nodded his head. "I'm impressed. Pleased to meet you, Ms. Hoover."

"The pleasure is mine," said Cyn. "Congratulations on your promotion. I've heard a lot about you."

"All good, I hope," said the General with a teasing smile and a glance in the Senator's direction.

"But of course," said Cyn grinning back at him.

* * *

What she had heard was indeed good. General Jefferson Allen Masters had risen quickly through the Air Force ranks because of his leadership skills and his ability to articulate military tactics for public consumption. After his time in Iraq, whenever the news media wanted to interview an expert on Air Force strategy, he was the one they trotted out.

The media loved him and often referred to him by the nickname his men had given him: "Jammin' Jeff"— "When you're in a jam, get JAM!"

Now at the age of 58 General Masters had achieved the top rank of five-star general and had no visions of retirement. He currently commanded the Roca Grande Air Force Base in New Mexico, which was publicly known. What was not publicly known is that he also headed up the NSA's top-secret Advanced Spectrum Division at Apparition Mountain.

He had been the much doted-on youngest child and only son of Jack and Maureen Masters who were fairly prosperous farmers in Southeastern Nebraska. He had twin sisters, Tara and Cara, who, being eight years older, doted on him also.

Ever since anyone could remember Jeff had always been fascinated with planes and aerospace. When they asked him throughout his school years, "What do you want to be when you grow up?" he unswervingly answered, "An Air Force pilot." When they asked him what he wanted to do after he graduated from high school, he always replied, "I want to attend the Air Force Academy in Colorado Springs." And that's exactly what he did.

Later he led bombing missions in Viet Nam and came home a much decorated war hero. Following that, he went home to Nebraska where he served as a colonel with the Strategic Air Command based in Omaha. He met and married an Omaha girl, Janet Clark, but after two years and no children they divorced. He did not remarry, and before long he was at the Pentagon and promoted to general.

During the Gulf War he helped plan Air Force strategy, and in the Iraq War, he not only was in charge of the Air Force efforts, but also physically led key bombing missions. He did not believe in sitting behind the scenes directing while his men were at the front. On one such foray after the fall of Baghdad a land-to-air missile brought down his plane. American ground forces found the wreckage of the plane but no sign of him. They feared the worst: that terrorists had captured him and that they would soon witness a televised beheading on Al Jazeera.

Weeks went by with no word of General Masters. Then one day as American troops were probing houses in a village near the Syrian border, a man dressed in Arab garb hobbled up to them speaking in English. It was Jeff Masters. He told them he had been held prisoner, moved from village to village, as his captors eluded the Americans. They had treated him fairly well. The only injuries he had suffered were from the plane crash—a number of cuts and bruises, and a broken leg that they had set and was now healing. He said he had pretended not to understand their language and had consequently overheard a great deal. He gathered that they were holding him for a strategic moment when they could make a dramatic demand in exchange for his life. Finally, with the troops getting closer and closer, his captors had become increasingly nervous. He overheard them talking about beheading him and then fleeing across the border. So, when they came to bring him food, he managed to overpower them and escape.

His capture and subsequent release had made top news in the States for over a month. After several weeks of medical treatment and debriefing in Frankfurt, Germany, General Masters again came home a decorated war hero.

8 a.m.

Braun was looking down into the control center with a frown. "I'd better check in with my team before we start," he said. "I'll let General Masters brief you on the fundamentals if you will excuse me?"

"Sure, Karl. You need to be down there," said the General. "Please sit over here," he said to Cyn and the Senator as Braun quickly exited. General Masters sat down at a computer terminal as the two guests settled themselves in comfortable armchairs facing the large split-screen display on the wall opposite the viewing balcony.

"This should be quite interesting." Cyn smiled at the Senator.

"Yes, indeed," said Senator Goodman. He looked over at the General. "We've both read the brief. I understand you've come up with a way to access the formula for the E5 Weapon. Believe me, if we can revive that project and make it work, it'll be the biggest breakthrough in defense since the invention of the Atom Bomb."

"I couldn't agree with you more," said General Masters.

"Refresh my memory," said Cyn playing dumb. "What exactly is the E5 Weapon? I understand from what I've read that it was a top-secret project abandoned ten years ago because of a fire at Los Alamos?"

The General smiled and nodded. "That's right. Actually there was a massive explosion followed by a raging fire when they pushed the button to test the E5. No one has been able to figure out what caused the fire because all records of the formula were destroyed and the head scientist was so severely injured that he's never been the same."

The General swiveled in his chair and tapped a command on the computer keyboard. Instantly an image filled the screen on the wall. He glanced back at Cyn. "Since you're an MIT grad, I'm sure you know what this is."

Cyn smiled. "Of course. It's the Electromagnetic Spectrum."

The General nodded. "And, as you know, various technologies operate on various wavelengths. The concept of the E5 Weapon is based on the theory of Selective Induced Radiation and is really quite simple. It would allow us to select what we want to shut down prior to an invasion. We could choose to knock out some or all of the systems that work within the Spectrum. For example, we could shut down all communications, including radio, television, land-based phones, cell phones and computers—even laptops. It would virtually make it possible to take over an entire country without firing a shot—without loss of life or destruction of property."

"Wow!" said Cyn. "What an idea! It's much better than the earlier E-Weapons that simply fried everything in their path. But it's beyond me how you'd ever develop something like that. The technology behind it would be enormously complex."

"Exactly," the General agreed "As I said, the concept is simple, but developing it is another matter altogether. However, there is one human being on this planet who figured it out, and that person is Professor Harry Latter who was the head of the project at Los Alamos."

The Senator leaned forward in his chair. "Harry Latter," he said with a frown. "But isn't he totally incapacitated with Alzheimer's?"

The General nodded sadly. "That's right. As I said, he was so severely injured in the fire that he's never been right since. His condition is similar to Alzheimer's. He has severe memory loss. Unfortunately, he's the only one who knew the entire formula for the E5 and therefore would be the only one who could figure out what went wrong."

"So, of course, the big question is: How do you plan to revive the project?" asked the Senator.

"Yes, indeed, that is the big question, and today you are going to see how we're going to do that." The General smiled mysteriously, swiveled around in his chair and tapped another command on the keyboard. The image of a human brain appeared on the screen. Dozens of animated arrows darted about. "I'm sure you know what this is," he said, turning back to them.

"A human brain?" asked the Senator.

"That's correct," said the General. "Today we're going to explore the brain of Professor Harry Latter."

"What?" the Senator cried. "You mean you've come up with a way to repair the damage in his brain so he can remember the formula for the E5! Amazing!"

The General shook his head. "No, unfortunately, we have not found a way to restore his mind, but we have found a way to download his memory."

"You're kidding!" gasped the Senator. He slumped back in his chair, his mouth open, unable to say anything further. Cyn just stared at the General.

"I know it's hard to believe, but Karl Braun has perfected a formula to calculate the size of a person's memory and has built a computer system capable of storing it. We're going to try it for the first time today with Harry Latter."

"But...but, isn't that some sort of invasion of privacy...or something?" stammered the Senator. "He's incapable of giving his consent, I assume, unless he had assigned Power of Attorney for Health Care Directives to someone."

"For a while, we couldn't find any close relatives—no wife, no children, no living parents or siblings, but then we managed to unearth a niece who lives in Vermont. We contacted her and explained the situation—that we wanted to transfer Harry to our Alzheimer's Care Unit at the Air Force Base in Roca Grande where he could benefit from the latest in Alzheimer's care, all courtesy of the government. She agreed, and we flew her down to Palm Springs where Harry was confined in the Desert Villa Nursing Home. She signed the papers to release him from the nursing home, and we flew him here. She got a complimentary week's vacation in Palm Springs on us for her efforts."

The General paused, looking from the Senator to Cyn. The Senator wore a frown, but Cyn's face was expressionless.

"Well…but you didn't tell his niece what you were going to do?" asked the Senator after a bit.

The General shook his head. "No, of course not. This is top-secret, as you well know. If it makes you feel any better, be assured that Harry would have definitely given his consent to this if he'd been capable of doing it. The poor man is constantly shouting math equations, and appears to be stuck in his own quagmire of trying to figure out what went wrong with his project. We're only going to help him resolve the issue. Besides, he was working for us when the accident happened, and the government's been paying for his nursing home care. We also have all the authority we need under the Patriot Act."

"I see," said the Senator. "It is, after all, in the interests of national security."

"Exactly! I also remind you that the E5 Project and Braun's invention will remain top-secret. You and Ms. Hoover, of course, have clearance in order to persuade your committee to recommend the necessary funding and get it passed by Congress. You do understand that?" asked the General looking intently at the Senator.

"Yes, of course. If the mission goes well today, I'll get the job done without revealing any details about what sort of weapon it is or how we were able to retrieve the formula. Cyn's job will be to draft the proposals without revealing the secrets. She's very good at that, and we've done this many times over the past three years."

The General nodded and his expression relaxed. "Good. Now, I'm prepared to answer questions about the technology we're going to be using today to download Professor Latter's memory. Just remember I won't be able to give you all the technical details. For purposes of security, only Professor Braun knows the entire process, and he has a personal technical assistant who knows only enough to be able to correct problems with the computer system."

The Senator sat back in his chair and frowned. "Well, I assume Braun has come up with a way to hook up a computer to a human brain and somehow download and store the memory contained therein on said computer. I'm no techno-whizz, and I can't even begin to think of what questions to ask. On the other hand, that's why I have Cyn. She *is* a techno-whizz, and I'm sure she has plenty of questions." He looked at Cyn and smiled. "Right, Cyn?"

"You bet!" said Cyn. She was sitting on the edge of her chair, wide-eyed with anticipation.

"Then fire away," said the General.

"Well, first and foremost in my mind is how on earth Professor Braun is able to compute how much memory is stored in the brain in order to come up with a system capable of downloading it."

"Good question. As you may know, the brain stores everything that we perceive throughout the course of our lives. In fact, even at the time of birth, the brain is not „empty." We have data stored there from the time of conception—data passed along through DNA and genetics." The General paused and brought up another image of the brain subdivided into its various segments.

"Actually the brain is a super, super-duper computer capable of processing and storing more information than the biggest system we've invented up until now," he continued, gesturing toward the image on the screen.

"I assume you're referring to the National Security Agency's super computer?" asked Cyn.

The General smiled. "That's right. NSA's system has thirty-two central processing units all linked together, and that's still not enough. Professor Braun's calculations call for nine times that amount—two hundred eighty-eight CPUs—and that's just for downloading only the long-term memory."

"Incredible!" Cyn jumped to her feet in her excitement. "And what about storage capacity? That would have to be well into the petabyte range!"

"Petabyte? What's that?" interrupted the Senator.

Cyn turned to him with an apologetic expression. "Sorry, Senator. I didn't mean to talk in techno-babble. You know that computer storage capacity is measured in terms of bytes?"

The Senator nodded. "Yes. I've heard of bytes, megabytes and gigabytes…."

"Right. Then after gigabytes are terabytes and beyond that are petabytes."

"You mean far bigger than the national debt?" asked the Senator with a straight face.

Cyn and the General laughed. "That's right, Senator, but not much bigger," quipped the General.

"Oh, now that you put it in that perspective, I think I understand how big this storage system would have to be," said the Senator with a chuckle. "Go ahead, Cyn."

Cyn turned to the General again. "You mean Braun has come up with this system?"

"Yes, indeed he has. After he worked out the formula, his technician worked with NSA's techies to put the system together. Needless to say, it was a huge undertaking, but they managed to get it done in a little under ten months."

"And has it been tested prior to today?"

The General nodded. "Yes. We know it works even though they had to iron out a couple of glitches."

"Good," said the Senator glancing at his watch. "Looks like it's almost time for the procedure with Professor Latter. Tell us a little more about how you envision using this technology to benefit national security beyond today's mission to retrieve the formula for the E5."

"For intelligence gathering, of course," said the General in a hushed tone. "Just think of the possibilities. This would take interrogation methods to a whole different level and would be much more humane than torture. If a prisoner is not cooperating and telling us what we want to know, we can simply download his memory and find out what he knows and be assured he's telling us the truth. This is much more reliable than the so-called truth serum the CIA tried using back in the 1950s. In fact, now that we've made this breakthrough, it may even be possible in the very near future to plant a microchip on a suspect and read his mind."

"Good grief! The ultimate invasion of privacy," muttered the Senator as he slumped back in his chair.

* * *

9:30 a.m.

A sedated Harry Latter dressed only in a cotton hospital gown sat silently in a stainless steel wheelchair. Dr. Graham hovered over him taking his pulse and checking his blood pressure while his nurse Betsy stood by. The Doctor looked up and nodded, and Betsy pushed the wheelchair into the open elevator where an armed guard stood. The Doctor followed and took up a position next to Harry's wheelchair. The guard checked their identifications before the elevator door closed. After descending eight floors the elevator stopped, and the door slid open. Betsy wheeled Harry into a magnetically shielded room lined with beryllium copper. Karl Braun was waiting for them.

"Is our patient comfortable?" he asked as he walked over to them.

"All vital signs are good," said Dr. Graham, placing a hand on Harry's shoulder. "I have administered the four-hour sedative as specified."

"How was he early this morning? Still talking in math equations?" asked Braun as he gazed down on Harry's shaved head.

"Same as always, except that he seemed more agitated this morning. He still thinks he has the wrong answer when he is right."

"Splendid. At least we know he can compute correctly, which is a good indicator of long-term memory functionality. It's his short-term memory that is the problem, and we are not interested in that."

Dr. Graham frowned. "I hope you have a high level of confidence in the experiment today."

"There is no question about that," said Braun somewhat huffily. "I can assure you that no harm will come to him. The experiment is fully controlled, and we have briefed you on the medical parameters many times. You should be aware that all precautions have been taken."

"Yes, I am aware of that, Professor Braun, and you should be aware that my patient's well-being is of more concern to me than your experiment, especially after what happened in the first trials."

"Well, there is no reason to be concerned. He will not be in any pain." Braun glanced at his watch. "Now, let's get the patient hooked up." He turned abruptly and led them toward a small magnetically shielded chamber in the center of the room.

Dr. Graham grasped the handles on the back of Harry's wheelchair, indicating to Betsy that she should remain where she was. He wheeled Harry to the door of the chamber. Two technicians dressed in pale blue protective suits were waiting. Portable fiber optic floodlights cast concentrated beams on a table in the center of the chamber. The technicians carefully lifted Harry from the wheelchair and lowered him onto the table. Dr. Graham and Professor Braun looked on in silence from the door as one of the technicians scanned Harry for signs of static electricity. When none was found, the technician lifted Harry's head while the other one fitted him with multi-sensor headgear that resembled an Astronaut's helmet. When they had finished adjusting the straps under Harry's chin, Dr. Graham looked at Braun with a raised eyebrow.

Braun smiled in his tight-lipped way. "The very latest. This helmet is much improved over what we used before. It has ten times more sensors, and each of them can detect less then one billionth of a volt."

The Doctor looked at Harry with a frown. "You're absolutely certain these sensors will pick up all the medical data as well and won't cause any harm?"

Braun shrugged impatiently. "You should have no doubt about that, Dr. Graham. All aspects of bodily function are channeled through the brain, and as you should know from your briefings, the sensors pick up signals but don't emit any, thereby causing absolutely no harm. Perhaps *you're* experiencing a short-term memory lapse?"

His icy gray eyes lasered into Graham. The Doctor refused to look at him. He just grimaced and watched the technicians who were now connecting the helmet to a shielded fiber optic cable.

Braun turned his attention to another technician who was sitting at a computer terminal just outside the door to the chamber. "Are you receiving a signal?"

The technician nodded. "Yes, Professor, but there is sixty-cycle static and other background noise."

"Good. All you're hearing is background noise from the lights, our own body signals and the radiation coming through the door." He turned back to the chamber and spoke to the technicians inside. "You can strap the patient to the table now and put on the oxygen mask."

Dr. Graham stood silently by Braun, watching as the technicians strapped Harry's body to the table with anti-magnetic belts. Then they secured Harry's head to the table with a rigid plastic chinstrap. Having completed that, they looked at Braun, and he gave them a thumbs-up approval. The technicians hurriedly removed the portable lights and exited the chamber.

Dr. Graham sucked in a deep breath as he had a last glimpse of Harry bathed in the white light coming from the doorway. He closed his eyes and offered up a silent prayer. Suddenly his eyes snapped open. He peered anxiously at the chamber, but all he saw was Braun standing in the doorway with the two technicians. "Did you hear or see something just then, Professor?" he asked.

Braun looked at him curiously. "Hear what? No. I was just waiting for the technicians to clear the room. We'll have to leave now." He nodded at the technicians. "Seal it up."

As Braun walked over to the technician at the computer terminal, the two at the door of the chamber strained against the heavy radiation-proof door and it clanged shut with a finality that made Dr. Graham shudder.

Braun was leaning over the technician peering at the computer monitor. "Do we have the background noise under control?" he asked.

"We're still zeroing it out, Sir. These new sensors are even picking up heat radiation in the chamber."

"All right, then. Increase the heavy water circulation until it stabilizes.

Then maintain the flow, but under no circumstances let the temperature in the chamber rise above 71.55 or fall below 71.5 Fahrenheit."

"Yes, Sir." The technician tapped the keyboard, sending the command to Central Control.

Braun checked his watch and plucked a cordless phone from its cradle on the desk next to the computer. He clicked a button and waited for a couple of seconds. Then he said, "Yes, Jeff. Everything is on schedule. We are finishing last-minute adjustments right now. In just a couple of minutes we'll calibrate the computer to the patient's biofunctions."

* * *

9:45 a.m.

"That was Professor Braun. He is just about ready to begin the countdown," said General Masters. He got up from the computer terminal and took a seat next to the Senator.

Cyn sat gazing up at the multiplex screen where wavy lines and blips were dancing and blinking. The date and time were displayed in the upper right hand corner.

"If all goes well the computer will communicate with Harry's brain and once that happens, we'll be able to see his short-term memory as it downloads," remarked the General.

"What will we see on the display?" asked the Senator. "I hope it's not gonna be just a bunch of waves and dots."

"Karl has taken care of that. His computer system is not only capable of storing the memory as data, but also of translating it into visual form from any part of the magnetic spectrum."

"Incredible!" said Cyn. "That's well beyond what they were able to accomplish at USC Los Angeles back in 2003."

"That's true," said the General. "I don't thoroughly understand it, but Karl Braun somehow adapted Harry Latter's theories of magnetic filtration and quantum imaging that he developed years ago and applied them to decoding brain signals."

The Senator raised a hand. "Whoa! Hold on there. I'm in the dark. What happened at USC? I assume you mean the University of Southern California?"

Cyn grinned at him. "Sorry again, Senator Goodman. Actually, back in 2003, scientists at USC were able to recreate the hippocampus area of a rat's brain. This was all in the interest of being able to restore short-term memory that had been impaired by some trauma such as injury to the head. One of the scientists claimed he was actually able to see the rat's dream."

The Senator snorted. "Ha! What do you suppose a rat dreams about?"

The General laughed. "Probably about the world's largest chunk of Swiss cheese, or in the case of a nightmare, about being chased by a giant pussycat with murder on its mind!"

They all chuckled at this image. Then Cyn's brow furrowed again. She looked at the General with narrowed eyes. "OK, General Masters. If Professor Braun was able to develop Professor Latter's theories about magnetic filtration into this particular practical application, then why do you need to get into his memory? It seems to me that his theories would also apply to the E-Weapon."

"That's a very good question, Ms. Hoover," said the General nodding in approval. "You are absolutely right. Harry Latter's theories on magnetic filtration certainly serve as the keystone for the E-Weapon, but only Harry knows how to generate a radiation blanket to cancel out selected magnetic frequencies."

"Ah, yes, I see," said Cyn. "That's the key to shutting down a frequency without destroying the infrastructure."

They sat silently contemplating this information. Suddenly a ten-second-countdown clock appeared on the screen before them and a voice boomed over the loudspeaker. "All systems go. Ten, nine, eight, seven, six, five, four, three, two, one. Matrix sensors seeking circuits. Computer in transfer mode."

The various screens on the display panel flickered and then each display came to life. Each identified its function. The one displaying Harry's biofunctions was the only one with graphics: "EKG—normal; Respiration—normal; Blood Pressure—normal; Temperature—normal." The rest were in standby mode.

"Zeroing out background noise and zeroing in on multi-circuits," continued the voice over the loudspeaker.

Another display came to life with the image of a brain in color graphics similar to the one that Cyn and the Senator had seen earlier. Then four more screens showed graphics of different parts of the brain. Each described the function it performed—short-term memory, long-term memory, optic nerve translation and auditory translation.

"Contact made with short-term memory," announced the voice excitedly. "Data transfer in progress."

"Fantastic!" exclaimed the General raising a fist in the air.

"Right on!" exclaimed the Senator, catching the General's excitement.

Cyn remained silent as she concentrated on the short-term memory display. It was currently flashing and pulsing in a rainbow of colors.

"Downloading STM begins now," said the voice on the speaker. "Time shown is memory time, not real time."

A loud cheer came over the loudspeaker from the Control Room where technicians were glued to their computer screens.

The clock on the display began rapidly counting backwards: Minus 30 minutes, minus 60 minutes, minus 2.0 hours. When it reached minus 60 hours Cyn looked at the second hand of her watch and pulled a calculator out of her bag.

"What are you doing?" asked the Senator, noticing Cyn tapping in numbers on her calculator.

"Calculating the rate at which we're downloading the short-term memory." She held up her calculator and peered at it. "According to my calculations, we're downloading 269.66 hours of memory time per minute."

They glanced back up at the screen and saw that the clock had now gone past minus 3,000 hours and was still counting.

"Good grief! How many hours are in the memory?" asked the Senator.

"When was the last time you met the President?" asked the General.

The Senator frowned. "Let me think…it was on his birthday."

"Let's see. The President's birthday is on March 17, so that was…."

"Two hundred sixty days and ten hours ago," said Cyn tapping on her calculator. "That's 6,250 hours ago."

"Wow!" said the Senator. "So, how many minutes would it take to download that?"

Cyn was about to do the calculation when the clock abruptly stopped and a voice boomed over the loudspeaker, "STM download complete."

A loud cheer went up from the Control Room as the technicians relaxed for a moment.

"What happens now?" asked the Senator. "Will we be able to see what's in Harry Latter's memory?"

"Yes, Senator. The computer is now arranging the data so it can be understood. It is going through the algorithms right now, and that may take a few minutes or even an hour before we see the result."

"Look at that, General Masters," cried Cyn pointing to the bio display. "Harry's blood pressure and pulse are above normal!"

The General grabbed a cell phone and tapped a number. "What's going on with Professor Latter's vital signs, Dr. Graham?" he asked. "Is anyone paying attention to them?"

Cyn and the Senator watched anxiously as General Masters listened to the reply. As he clicked off his cell phone, he nodded toward the bio screen where the pulse and blood pressure were back to normal.

"What was that all about?" asked the Senator.

"According to Dr. Graham, Professor Latter is doing fine and his vital functions are handling the experiment well. Apparently, the sudden rise in blood pressure and pulse was caused by a lowering of the oxygen supply, but it has now been adjusted."

"Well, that's a relief," said the Senator, mopping his forehead. "You know, I've just realized that if the Professor's memory is played back in real time, it could take many months, even years, to see all of it."

"Yes, you're right," said the General. "However, we're only interested in certain time zones in Harry's long-term memory. Downloading his short-term memory is just to quantify the experiment and establish the operating parameters so that when the long-term memory is downloaded it should go faster and retrieval will be quicker."

"Standby for short-term memory datum point," said the voice over the speaker.

Cyn looked intently at the display as the clock spun to minus one hour, forty-five minutes and ten seconds. The display screen flickered violently and suddenly thousands of star-shaped pixels and other geometric shapes in a wide range of colors appeared, spinning and swirling at random.

After watching this brilliant display for some time, the Senator began to fidget. "What's going on? It doesn't seem to be working."

The General started to answer, but at that instant, the door swung open and Professor Karl Braun marched into the room and stood between his audience and the multiple screen display.

"Any minute now we will see what Professor Harry Latter had on his mind at eight o'clock this morning," he announced.

Cyn thought his tight-lipped smile looked more like a smirk as he looked from one of them to the other. Then he looked up at the display where the star-shaped pixels continued to twist and turn in an erratic fashion. No one said anything as they watched the screen in anticipation. After a few more moments, Braun frowned and walked over to the window that looked down into the control room. The General got up and followed him. Below technicians were huddled in groups deep in conversation, while a few sat in front of their terminals still looking at the whirling pixels on their monitors. Braun reached into his lab coat pocket and pulled out a cell phone. He punched in a number. Down below a technician seated at a computer terminal elevated above the rest of the room picked up the cell phone beside his computer and looked up at the glass wall where Braun and the General stood.

"What is the problem, Jake? What is causing the delay?" asked Braun in a hushed tone.

"It appears the computer cannot decipher the memory code, Sir. All we have is a random pixel display made up of stars and triangles," said the technician into the phone as he continued to look up at Braun.

"I know that already, Jake," hissed Braun impatiently. "Switch to Algorithms E, F and G, and if they don't work, go to the next sequence."

Braun and the General watched as the technician spoke excitedly to several others who were standing around him. They, in turn, shouted something to the others in the room, and all the technicians rushed back to their computers.

Cyn and the Senator had been watching Braun from across the room and they saw him turn and whisper something to the General.

"Just a slight delay," said the General as he walked back to where Cyn and the Senator were seated. "It appears there is a small glitch in one of the programs, and it will take a few minutes to iron it out."

"Sorry for the delay, but these things happen," said Braun. "How about a coffee break? I'll call the cafeteria and order coffee and pastries."

"Sounds great. It's been a long time since breakfast." The Senator stood up and stretched his back.

Cyn was oblivious. She was concentrating on the whirling shapes on the screen.

"Coffee, Ms. Hoover? Or would you rather have something else—cranberry juice, perhaps?" asked Braun frowning down at her.

"What?" mumbled Cyn without taking her eyes off the screen. "Oh, sure, that's fine…whatever."

Braun looked at the Senator with a raised eyebrow.

The Senator chuckled. "What she means is, she'll have coffee, too— black, no sugar."

Braun shook his head and pulled out his cell phone to place the order.

The General placed a hand on the Senator's arm and pulled him aside. "She's OK, I hope?" he asked, motioning with his head toward Cyn. "She appears to be in a trance."

"Oh, she's in a trance, all right—a trance of concentration. Can't you almost see all those wheels turning inside? It wouldn't surprise me if Cyn has the glitch ironed out before the Control Room. That's her problem-solving mode. I've seen it many times," said the Senator with a grin.

When the coffee and pastries arrived, Cyn was still fixated on the screen. The General placed a cup of coffee and cherry Danish on a small table beside her chair, but they went untouched.

* * *

10:30 a.m.

Dr. Graham and Betsy were sitting in front of their medical diagnostic terminals watching Harry's vital signs. They were unaware of the computer glitch that was creating havoc in the control room.

"I can't see anything wrong," remarked the Doctor. "Harry appears to be doing all right."

"Yes, everything seems normal," said Betsy. She glanced at the Doctor with a concerned look. "You've been very quiet since the experiment began. Is something wrong?"

Dr. Graham leaned back in his chair and ran his hands through his hair. "I don't really know, Betsy. There is something that happened, but I'm not sure that it wasn't just a figment of my imagination."

"Do you feel all right?" she asked. She reached over and felt his forehead. "You don't feel as if you have a temperature."

"No, it's nothing like that. I have to tell you something, Betsy. You'll probably think I'm crazy, but I'll tell you anyway."

Betsy's eyes grew wide as she looked at his pallid face. "What is it, Doctor?"

"It happened when I was just about to leave the door of the chamber. I was saying a silent prayer like I always do when I heard a voice or at least I sensed one."

"Whose voice was it?"

"I don't know, but it was the most soothing voice I've ever heard. It made me feel light, as if all my worries had suddenly been lifted off my shoulders."

"What did the voice say?" asked Betsy in a hushed tone, watching him carefully.

"Just four words… *It will be OK.* That's all."

",,It will be OK?" Perhaps it was Professor Braun or one of the technicians," murmured Betsy.

"No. It was definitely not someone in the room. I can"t really describe it, but I'm sure it was not an earthly voice."

Betsy leaned over and touched his arm. "Perhaps it was an answer to your prayer," she said with a gentle smile.

Dr. Graham ran a hand through his hair again and sighed. "Perhaps, Betsy. I just don't know. And there was something else…"

"Something else? Please tell me."

"I heard the voice when my eyes were closed, and when I opened my eyes and looked at Harry on the table, he was surrounded by an aura of colored lights, sort of like a rainbow. The aura didn't touch him, but seemed to float around him. Then suddenly it was gone. I asked Braun if he saw or heard anything unusual, but he said he didn't. I don't know, Betsy. Maybe it was my imagination, but it was all too real to me, and I just can't shake this feeling that I have—sort of a premonition, I guess." He took off his wireless glasses and wiped a hand across his eyes to brush away the tears that had formed in the corners.

Betsy observed this with great concern. "What sort of premonition?" she asked in a hushed, almost reverent tone.

Dr. Graham put on his glasses and looked directly at Betsy. "I have this feeling that Harry is not going to survive this experiment. I am convinced Harry is about to die."

Betsy's hands flew to her mouth and she jumped to her feet. "Then you must stop the experiment, Doctor! Pull the plug now!"

Dr. Graham shook his head sadly. "They won't do that, Betsy. They won't shut it down because I heard a voice and have a premonition. I can just hear them. They'd want to know what solid medical data I have. Then they'd tell me I'm just imagining it—that I'm under stress and should take some time off. Don't worry. Doctor Snider can take over."

He looked back at the monitor and waved a hand at it. "See? There's nothing wrong with Harry's vital signs. Everything is normal. Except for that short incident with the oxygen, his vital signs have been good throughout."

Betsy looked at the monitor and frowned. "Well, if his vital signs go out of the normal range again, can't you shut the experiment down then?"

The Doctor shook his head again as he continued to stare at the monitor. "I wish I could, Betsy. The General and Professor Braun are the only ones who can make that decision, and by the time I'd convince them to do it, I"m sure it would be too late."

Betsy and Dr. Graham sat staring helplessly at Harry's heartbeat on the EKG monitor. It was quite normal.

* * *

11 a.m.

Senator Goodman sipped his coffee and listened to General Masters talking about his war adventures in Iraq. Professor Braun pretended to listen as he kept glancing at the screen and at the clock. Cyn had not touched her coffee. She was still staring at the five-pointed stars and triangles swirling on the screen.

The Senator drained his coffee cup and looked at Braun. "Professor, how long do you think this is going to take? I have to be back in D.C. by early this evening."

Braun shrugged. "The problem should be fixed by now. I'll check in with the head technician again."

As Braun walked over to the window that looked down into the control room, General Masters reached over and patted the Senator's arm. "Don't worry, Senator. The plane is standing by at the Air Base, and, if necessary, I'll order a helicopter to take you to the Base. This problem should be straightened out soon. We still have plenty of time."

Braun looked down into the control room and spotted Jake standing in the midst of a technicians" huddle talking animatedly and stabbing a finger at his computer terminal. Braun took out his cell phone and pressed a key. Almost immediately, Jake picked up his cell phone and looked up at Braun.

"What's going on?" asked Braun in a low voice so the others couldn't hear.

"We're running the Q, R and S algorithms now and getting ready to switch to T, U and W." Jake's voice was agitated. "So far nothing's worked, and we're about to run out of algorithms."

"Well, we're up the creek if the T U W doesn't work, because the X Y Z are the same, and the computer will automatically shut down," hissed Braun.

Jake mopped perspiration from his brow as he continued to stare at Braun. "I know that, Sir. I can override the auto shut down if I have to. Should I go ahead and do that now to give us more time?"

"How much time do you want, Jake? The Senator has to get back to D.C., and if he has to leave before we have any results, we may not get the funding we need and have to sack the whole damned thing. Then you and I will be looking for another job."

Jake gulped. "I'm trying my best, Sir. Another twenty minutes should be enough."

"All right, Jake, but twenty minutes max, you hear me?"

Jake nodded up at Braun and slammed down his cell phone. Braun could see him yelling orders as he ran back to his computer. The control room became a madhouse as technicians scattered in all directions.

Braun placed his cell phone back in his pocket and took a second to compose himself before walking back over to where the Senator and the General were on their third cups of coffee.

"There's been another small glitch, but my technician assures me that everything will be straightened out in twenty more minutes. I apologize for the delay," said Braun, trying his best to be humble.

The Senator scowled. "Oh, all right, Professor Braun, but this is getting annoying. General Masters assured me last week that the project was ready to demonstrate after I told him that further funding has become a major issue with the committee. I'm sure you're aware that the budget for this project will run out shortly, and I need something substantial to present to the committee if I'm going to recommend further funding. All I've seen so far is a bunch of stars twirling around."

"Yes, I am aware of that," snapped Braun.

Both the General and the Senator glared at him.

"I'm truly sorry for the delay," he continued in a softer tone of voice.

"Another twenty minutes, Senator Goodman. If we can't solve the problem by then, I will concede defeat." He clasped his hands in front of him and looked down at them in a penitent fashion.

After a moment the Senator's features softened. "Sorry to be so hard on you, Professor. I do understand how new technology has glitches that need to be worked out. I guess we're all on edge here with anticipation. Believe me, no one wants to see this work more than me."

The General cleared his throat. "Yes, well, as I said, we'll make sure you get back to Washington on schedule. I'm sure Karl and his team will have this straightened out soon."

The Senator opened his mouth to speak, but stopped short when he heard Cyn suddenly shout, "Aha!"

They all looked in her direction and saw that she was leaning forward in her chair looking even more intently at the jumble of whirling pixels on the display.

"What is it, Cyn?" asked the Senator as he got up and walked over to her. The General and Braun followed.

"I think I just figured something out," she said excitedly, not taking her eyes off the screen. "Professor Braun, can you isolate one of each of those shapes and magnify them?"

Braun looked at her curiously, and then he walked over to the computer terminal. He hesitated for a moment, tapped on the keyboard and stood back to look at the display. After a few seconds, the thousands of pixels disappeared, and enlarged pixels of each shape emerged.

"It's only a star and some triangles," said the Senator, shrugging his shoulders. "So what's the big deal?"

"I think they're tiles that make up a mosaic," said Cyn.

"Tiles?" asked Braun with a puzzled expression.

"Yes! I see it now!" cried Cyn. "They're Penrose tiles, and they're part of a pattern. I think this has to do with the way the brain stores information—in layers, each layer representing an instant in time. If you can arrange the tiles in the proper pattern, we'll be able to see a visual presentation of what's in Professor Latter's memory."

"What about that, Karl? Does that make sense to you?" asked the General.

Braun frowned. "No. It makes no sense at all. First of all, I fail to see what Penrose tiles would have to do with the brain, and, secondly, even if they did, how would you ever put them together to form the pattern?"

"That's easy," said Cyn looking at Braun with a curious expression. "You form the pattern by applying the Fibonacci Sequence."

Braun looked at her with a blank expression.

"You know...Fibonacci. One plus one is two; two plus one is three; three plus two is five; five plus three is eight, and so on," said Cyn.

"Oh, that. I'd forgotten what it was called," said Braun after a pause.

The General tapped him on the arm. "How about getting your technician to try Ms. Hoover's idea? It's been almost fifteen minutes now, and they don"t seem to be getting anywhere." He pointed at the display where the pixels continued to swirl in a random pattern.

"Well, I don't know...." Braun frowned at Cyn.

"Come on. What have you got to lose? We're running out of time. At least ask your tech if he can do it," said the General impatiently.

"Oh, all right, but I think it will be a waste of time." Braun turned on his heel and marched over to the window. He whipped the cell phone out of his pocket and pressed the key. He saw Jake pick up the phone and look up at him.

"Listen, Jake. Do you know anything about Penrose tiles or the Fibonacci Sequence?" he asked in a hushed tone.

"Sure," said Jake, nodding affirmatively. "What about it?"

"Do you think you could program the computer to arrange all those pixels into a mosaic by applying the Fibonacci Sequence?" he asked.

"Sure thing. I can do that in no time at all."

"Good. Do it right away, then."

"Sure, but I need to know which part of the Fibonacci Series you want me to use."

Braun rolled his eyes upward and rubbed a hand over his eyebrow. "Just a minute, Jake. Hold on," he said. Braun put a hand over the phone and turned around. "Ms. Hoover, would you come over here for a moment, please?" he asked.

Looking surprised, Cyn quickly strode over to him.

"My top technician is on the phone, and he knows all about Penrose tiles and Fibonacci. He says he can program the computer, but he needs to know what part of the Fibonacci to use. Would you please advise him?"

"You want me to advise him? I thought you'd want to do it. I wouldn't want to interfere and have something go wrong with your project," she said.

"Precisely my point. You think you have the answer, and for some reason General Masters thinks you have the answer, so you go ahead and try it, and if anything goes wrong it will be your doing, not mine. Do I make myself clear?" Braun"s frigid gray eyes bored into her.

Cyn was stunned by his antagonism. She could only nod.

"Good. Here. You talk to him. His name is Brent Jacobson. We call him Jake."

Cyn's hand involuntarily flew up to her throat as she caught her breath. *Jake? Oh, my God, it can't be.*

Braun was talking on the phone. "Senator Goodman's aide is going to tell you what needs to be done, Jake. Her name is Ms. Hoover."

He thrust the phone into Cyn's quivering hand. She held it up to her ear and looked down into the control room. "Ms. Hoover?" She saw him grinning up at her from the control room. She couldn't answer for a moment. It *was* him.

"Ms. Hoover, what part of the sequence do you want me to use?" he asked in a serious tone. She glanced down again and saw that he was still grinning wickedly up at her.

She turned her back to the window and heard him chuckle. "Begin the sequence at five with a star in the center and build around it until the next star fits. Do this with each piece of datum as it comes in," she managed to say in an all-business voice.

"Right. I know exactly what you mean. I can do it right from the keyboard without having to burn in a new algorithm."

"Good," said Cyn. She quickly handed the phone back to Braun.

"Come quick! Something different is happening on the display," called out the General.

Cyn and Braun rushed back over to where the General and the Senator sat gazing at the multiplex screen.

The twirling pixels had disappeared, and a mosaic was slowly forming in the center of the screen and growing outward. First a star appeared and then triangles. Then another star appeared and more triangles laid themselves next to those already there. The larger the mosaic grew, the quicker the pieces appeared. Within seconds the screen was filled with a completed mosaic with blotches of colors.

"What is it, Professor?" asked the Senator, squinting at the screen. "What are we seeing?"

Braun didn't answer. He was staring in amazement at the display. Cyn looked at him with a raised eyebrow and quickly jumped in. "The computer has arranged the information according to a mathematical series and what we see is the short-term memory at the instant of time shown on the clock," she explained.

"It just looks like a blurred photograph," said the Senator. "Can't you sharpen it up?"

Braun's cell phone rang. He listened for a second and then held out the phone to Cyn. "It's for you Ms. Hoover," he said. "It's Jake."

Cyn put the phone to her ear. "Yes?" she asked somewhat apprehensively.

"Good job, Ms. Hoover!" exclaimed Jake. "Fibonacci seems to be doing the trick. What's next?"

"Blend in the mosaic and reduce the magnification," said Cyn as she stared at the screen.

"Right," said Jake. He disconnected, and Cyn handed the cell phone back to Braun.

As they all stared intently at the display, a picture began to take shape. A cheer went up from the control room over the loudspeaker.

"It's a picture, for sure," said the Senator bolting upright in his chair. "But of what?"

"Remarkable," commented the General. "Do you realize this is a first? This is the first time in the history of the human race that we are able to actually see what's in a person's mind!"

"Brent Jacobson should be promoted and given recognition for this technical breakthrough. Don't you agree, Professor Braun?" asked Cyn.

Braun simply scowled.

"Yes, I think that's a great idea. I'll see to it," said the General. He was still staring at the screen and hadn't noticed Braun's expression.

"I don't get it, Cyn," said the Senator. "There's a picture there for sure, but what are we looking at?"

Cyn thought for a moment and reached out to Braun. "May I borrow your cell phone to speak to Jake again?" she asked with a pleasant smile.

Still scowling, Braun pulled the cell phone out of his lab coat pocket and handed it to her. "Press the star key," he said when she looked at him questioningly.

"Jake, it's Ms. Hoover again. Do you have any way of knowing what Harry Latter was doing at 8:15 this morning?"

"Sure. I have his activity log on the computer. Hang on a sec. I'll bring it up."

Cyn listened for a second and then she chuckled. "It makes sense now. Thanks, Jake."

She clicked off the cell phone and announced, "Mystery solved. At 8:15 this morning, Professor Latter was having a shower."

"What? I don't see Professor Latter at all. It just looks like blotches on a camera lens," said the Senator shaking his head.

"No, of course you don't see Professor Latter, because we are inside his head looking out. We are seeing what Professor Latter saw at 8:15 this morning," explained Cyn.

"Yes, I see it now. Those blotches—that's water spray from the shower head," said the General.

"Yes! Yes! I see it now! And look! Those are white tiles lining the shower, and there's a liquid soap dispenser hanging on a stainless steel rack in the corner!" shouted the Senator, clapping his hands together. "Wow! This is something else! I don't think we'll have any problem getting your funding, Jeff."

The General breathed a sigh of relief and grinned at Braun. "Thanks, Senator. That's really good to hear, isn't it Karl?"

Braun nodded, but didn't say anything.

"Now, can we look at another point in time in his short-term memory?" asked the Senator.

Cyn glanced at Braun. He rolled his eyes and muttered, "Be my guest."

Cyn hit the star key on the cell phone. Jake quickly picked up. She squinted at the digital clock on the screen for a moment. "Jake, could you please go to 7:15 a.m.?"

"Sure thing," came the reply. "Stand by."

The clock ran back to 7:15. The screen flashed and switched to another mosaic.

"Who's that?" asked the Senator.

"That's Dr. Graham leaning in close, and that's his nurse Betsy Mallory further back towards the door," said the General.

"Looks like there's someone else coming in the door behind the nurse," said the Senator.

"Quick, Jake. Go to 7:45," murmured Cyn into the cell phone.

"Done," said Jake.

The mosaic scene quickly shifted again, and this time, they saw a view of Harry's legs and arms. He was apparently sitting in a wheelchair, and a woman's hand was clasping his right wrist.

"That must be the nurse taking his pulse," said the Senator.

Braun glanced at his watch and cleared his throat. "Have you seen enough of the short-term memory, Senator Goodman? Now that we're convinced we can decode the memory, I'd like to get on with downloading the long-term memory."

"By all means," said the Senator. "At this rate, it looks like you'll soon be able to find out what went wrong with the E5."

"May I have the cell phone, Ms. Hoover?" asked Braun.

Cyn handed him the phone, and he spoke into it. "Jake, are you still there?"

"Yes. Sir."

"All right. I want you to start downloading the patient's long-term memory as quickly as you can. Follow the same procedure as you did for the STM."

"Right, Sir. What about the algorithms?"

"Never mind the algorithms, Jake. Let's just get the LTM downloaded." Braun switched off the cell phone and turned his attention to the multiplex display.

Cyn returned to her seat next to the Senator.

As they all focused on the clock, they saw it begin to move, slowly at first, and then it gradually gained speed. Soon the clock was moving so fast the digital numbers became a blur.

Ten minutes later the clock was still spinning, and the Senator got to his feet and stretched his back again. "How long is this going to take?" he asked.

"I'm not sure, Senator, but it shouldn't be very long now. We should be able to complete the process by two o'clock as we had planned," said Braun.

"Well, while we're waiting, I'll call the cafeteria and order something for lunch," said the General, rising to his feet. "Cold cuts and potato salad OK with everyone?"

"Sure. That would be fine," said the Senator. "Meanwhile, I'm going to adjourn to the Men's Room for a moment."

He strode over to the far side of the room where the toilets were located.

Cyn got up from her chair and walked over to the window. She looked down at the scene in the control room below. Technicians were glued to their computers, some speaking rapidly into cell phones. She saw Jake sitting rigidly in front of his computer, concentrating on the monitor. He did not look up.

Cyn slowly paced back over to the multiplex display. The clock was still spinning. The only screen that had anything on it was the one that displayed Harry Latter's biofunctions. Cyn observed that all his vital functions were normal. She looked around and saw that Professor Braun and General Masters were engaged in conversation over near the door. The Senator had not returned from the Men's Room.

She walked over to where the Professor and the General were standing. When they saw her approaching, they suddenly stopped talking and looked at her with solemn faces.

"Well, Ms. Hoover, what do you think?" asked the General after an awkward pause.

"It all seems to be going well now," said Cyn. "General Masters, I was wondering if it would be all right for me to go down and look around the control room. I find all this highly fascinating."

"I don't see why not," said the General. "OK by you, Karl?"

Braun shrugged. "Fine, just as long as you don't get in the way."

"I'll call security and tell them you're cleared to go in. Just go on out to the elevator, and a guard will take you down," said the General as he reached for a phone hanging on the wall near the door.

* * *

11:35 a.m.

Cyn walked past banks of computer terminals where technicians were monitoring segments of the experiment. Occasionally she would stop to look over the shoulder of a technician at a display. "I'm just interested," she would say when the technician noticed her presence.

At last she had casually wandered up to where Brent Jacobson presided at his computer overlooking the control room. As she stood behind him, hands clasped behind her back, he did not look around at her. Instead he reached up and tugged on his right earlobe—a gesture all too familiar to her. He knew she was there. This was an ability he had that had always amazed her. There was no sneaking up on Brent Jacobson, "Ms. Hoover," he said, still not looking at her. "Having a look around?"

"Yes. I find this all quite fascinating," she said staring at the nape of his neck where his thick black hair was tied back in a long braid wrapped at various intervals with leather thongs. He hadn't changed much. He was still drop-dead gorgeous.

"Well, then. Take a look at this," he said, motioning for her to lean in closer. He pointed at his monitor with his left hand, but his right hand hovered over a small cell phone directly in front of him.

When Cyn leaned in close over his shoulder, he took his hand away from the cell phone, and she saw a message on its screen written in their old code. She quickly deciphered it. It said: "Do you have a safe cell phone with text messaging?"

She nodded. "Yes. That's fascinating technology."

He tapped rapidly on the cell phone keypad as Cyn continued to lean over his shoulder, both of them staring at the computer monitor. When he finished, she glanced down. The coded message said, "This is my private cell number. Send messages in the old code. We can communicate that way."

She straightened up and smiled. "Well, I won't bother you any longer, Mr. Jacobson. You've certainly done an outstanding job here."

"Thanks," he said. "And thanks for the help in figuring out how to read the STM."

"Think nothing of it. I'm sure you would have figured it out yourself given some time. It's just that the Senator is on a tight schedule and is impatient to see the end results."

Cyn turned to walk away. As she did so, she glanced up at the viewing window and saw Karl Braun glowering down at her. She waved at him casually and moved on through the banks of computers. Braun watched her for a moment, scowling, and then turned away from the window.

Cyn ambled back towards the entrance where she had noticed a high bank of computers that blocked the view from the upper room. Behind the bank she found an empty cubicle. She quickly ducked into the cubicle, pulled out her cell phone and sent a text message to Jacobson. Almost instantly, he replied.

"Hello, Cyn. It's been a long time."

"Yes, it has," Cyn wrote back. "You're the last person I expected to run into here."

"Well, you just never know where a 'good' penny's going to turn up, do you?"

"So, you're working for Professor Braun? What's the scoop on him? He doesn't seem to understand the ins and outs of his own project."

"Be careful about Braun. There's much more to him than meets the eye. Be careful what you say."

Cyn raised an eyebrow remembering Braun scowling down at her. "Ok, Jake. I think I'd better get back now. They might wonder why it's taking me so long. I'll be back in touch when I get the chance."

"Right. I'd like to see you, Cyn. I never really got over you, you know."

Cyn's face reddened when she decoded this message, and she was surprised to feel tears springing up in her eyes. She paused for a moment and took a deep breath before writing back. "We'll see," she wrote. She quickly clicked off her cell phone and put it back in her pocket.

* * *

12:30 p.m.

When Cyn walked back into the viewing room, no one noticed her. The three men were standing in front of the multiplex screen staring at it in rapt concentration. Cyn saw that the clock was still spinning so fast it was a blur. As she walked up to join them, the bio monitor began to flash a warning. Harry Latter's pulse and blood pressure had suddenly risen far above normal again.

Karl Braun whipped out his cell phone and hit a button. "What's going on with the patient now?" he asked in a gruff voice.

"All right. See to it then. We're almost finished with the download," he said after a moment. He clicked off his cell phone and faced the others who were looking at him with great concern.

"Everything is fine. Dr. Graham says the oxygen supply decreased, and he is leveling it out now. There, you see." He pointed to the bio screen where Harry's vital signs had once again returned to normal.

"That's a relief," said the Senator. "Any idea what's causing the oxygen problem?"

Braun shrugged. "We'll have to look into that when we do our post-op analysis. At any rate, we're nearly finished with the download, and the patient's sedative is good for another hour. Dr. Graham will have him back in his hospital bed long before he wakes up."

Braun's cell phone rang, and he put it to his ear. "Just a moment," he said into the phone. He looked at General Masters. "Jake says we've got eleven years of long-term memory downloaded. Do you want to take a look at it?"

"By all means," said the General. "Can you continue with the download while we're looking at a point in time?"

Braun nodded. "No problem."

"Let's take a look then," said the General.

Braun spoke into the cell phone and then clicked off.

"Look at the screen!" shouted the General.

The display sparkled with brilliant greens, purples and yellows as scores of pixels twirled chaotically.

"These are different from the stars," said the Senator, his eyes wide with amazement.

"That's right. They're pentagons," said the General.

"Of course, you'd know that, being in the military," said the Senator, jabbing the General with an elbow. Everyone laughed politely at his little joke, but they didn't take their eyes from the screen.

After a bit, Cyn said. "You're right, General Masters. They are pentagons, having five equal sides, and if you connect all the points, they form five-pointed stars—the same as the ones we saw in the short-term memory."

"Yes, I see that now." The General stood with his arms crossed, leaning back slightly, concentrating on the screen. "What do you think, Karl?"

Braun nodded. "Yes, I agree. That's exactly what they are."

"So it should be easy to arrange them into an image, just like with the STM, shouldn't it? Then we can access the point in Professor Latter's memory that we are interested in." The General was looking intently at Braun now.

Braun dropped his eyes and appeared to be studying his feet. "Well, yes, I suppose so." Suddenly he looked up at Cyn. "What do you think, Ms. Hoover?"

Cyn was somewhat startled that he would ask her opinion. "It would be pretty much the same, except with a slight variation. You know what I mean?" she said.

"Of course," said Braun. "Why don't you confer with Jake on the process? I need to check in with Dr. Graham about the patient's stability."

"I'd be pleased to do that…that is, if it's OK with everyone else." Cyn looked at Senator Goodman and the General for confirmation.

"Sure, sure. Anything to speed this up and find out what Professor Latter knew," said the Senator rubbing his hands together.

"Fine with me," said the General. "Let's get on with it. Here, you can use my cell phone. See, Senator, I told you we'd have you back in D.C. in plenty of time."

Cyn took the cell phone from his outstretched hand and pressed the key for Jake. He answered immediately.

"Jake, this is Ms. Hoover again. Professor Braun has asked me to confer with you about getting those pixels rounded up into a visual image. These are slightly different than the ones for the STM. Do you know what to do?"

"Spiral to the ratio of 1.618?" he asked.

Cyn chuckled. "That's exactly what I had in mind. How did you guess?"

"Oh, it has something to do with taking some of the same classes as you at MIT, I suppose."

Cyn rolled her eyes. She glanced at the General and the Senator. They were in avid conversation in front of the screen and not paying attention to her. Out of the corner of her eye she saw Braun over at the computer terminal with his back to the room, a cell phone to his ear.

"Ms. Hoover?" asked Jake. "Are you still there?"

"Yes. Just thinking for a moment is all."

"OK. I'm going to arrange the pixels. What point in the memory should I go to?"

Without lowering the cell phone, Cyn looked over at the General. "Excuse me, General Masters. What date in Professor Latter's memory do you want to access?"

The General looked up from his conversation with Senator Goodman. "Oh, yes, that would be April 10, ten years ago," he said.

"Did you hear that, Jake?" asked Cyn, speaking into the phone.

"Sure did," came the reply. "You should be able to see a visual image in just a few minutes."

"Good," said Cyn. She clicked off the cell phone and joined the General and the Senator in front of the screen.

Braun finished his conversation with the Doctor and walked over to them. "We've disabled the vital signs display up here," he announced. "The patient is fine, and Dr. Graham is monitoring him from his station. There seems to have been a problem with our display up here."

"Oh?" asked the General with a raised eyebrow, but he was quickly distracted by what was happening on the screen in front of them. The clock stopped on the target date. The screen flashed and then a spiral began winding from the center of the screen out forming a matrix of colors. When the spiral was complete, the screen flashed again and an image appeared.

"Wow! Bomb's on target!" shouted the General over the cheers coming through the loudspeaker.

No one else said a word. They stood mesmerized, eyes glued to the image on the screen.

Braun was the first to speak. "I believe what we are seeing is Professor Latter's computer monitor. He appears to have been working at his computer at Los Alamos on the day of the fire, but I don't understand what he has entered."

"Nor do I," said the General, squinting at the image on the screen.

"Looks like just a bunch of random letters," commented the Senator.

"Oh, I think I know what it is," said Cyn. "I'll bet he encrypted everything he entered on his computer due to the top secret nature of the project."

"Of course. That's it," said Braun. "We do the same thing here."

"Well, does anyone know how to decode it?" asked the Senator.

"No. Remember everything was destroyed in the fire," said the General crestfallen.

"That's true," said Braun. "But we don't need the code. All we have to do is turn the clock back a bit to read the message before he encrypted it."

"Of course! Why didn't I think of that!" said the General, slapping himself on the forehead. "Ms. Hoover, would you tell Jake to go back about five minutes and let it run forward? It is possible to view events in the memory as they move through time rather than just a still frame, isn't it, Karl?"

"Yes, I'm sure that can be done," said Braun. "Ms. Hoover, just tell Jake what we want. He'll know what to do."

Cyn frowned as she pressed the key on the cell phone. Now, the General and Braun seemed to be acting as if she were their secretary. She transmitted the request to Jake and thought briefly about saying something to them, but decided against it for the moment. The importance of the moment seemed to outweigh her offended feelings. She would deal with it later if it occurred again.

Within seconds the image changed and came alive. They were still looking at a computer monitor, but now it was blank except for a blinking cursor. As they continued to watch, letters and words began to appear as Harry typed them in.

Kelly Renfrow
Customer Service Department
K Mart
Santa Fe Trail Road
Santa Fe, New Mexico 87501

Dear Kelly:

As we discussed on the phone, I recently purchased five pairs of underwear from your Men's Clothing Department. I washed the underwear according to instructions on the label, but when I did, it shrank to a size fit for an infant. I am therefore returning the merchandise and receipt for a full refund.

Sincerely,

Harry Latter
15 Atom Drive
Los Alamos, New Mexico 87545

"What! Nobel Prize winner Harry Latter is writing about underwear on the day of the big test?" cried the Senator. "What time of day is that?"

The General pointed to the upper right of the screen where a clock read 6:15. "He must have just arrived at his office and was taking care of some personal business before getting on with the order of the day."

As they continued to stare at the screen, they saw Harry's hand reach forward on the keyboard and push a function key. Instantly the K Mart letter became a scramble of meaningless letters and numbers.

"Look! He encrypted it," said Cyn. "Why would he do that?"

"Probably out of habit," said Braun. "I do that all the time."

"Well, all I can say is there must be a lot of dirty laundry classified as top secret!" said the Senator. He laughed heartily at his own joke.

"*Touché!* That's a good one, Senator," said General Masters with a chuckle.

On the screen, Harry's hands were now opening a desk drawer and pulling out a day timer notebook. He leafed through some pages until he came to April 10. Then his right hand reached out and plucked a roller ball pen from a dark blue coffee cup that was inscribed in gold: "*Pi are not Squared. Pi are Round.*"

The Senator laughed again. "Looks like our Professor had a sense of humor."

Now Harry was writing in the day timer, and they watched, fascinated, as the words took shape:

Tuesday, April 10

10 a.m.	*Magnetic Frequency Converter*
11 a.m.	*Review tests on filters using new alloy*
Noon	*Lunch with Adams*
2 p.m.	*Review tests on circuits*
	Pick up milk, eggs and bread on way home.
7 p.m.	*Meet George for dinner at Palo Verde Grill*

"This is incredible," commented the Senator. "It's as if *we're* Harry Latter. I'm truly impressed with the technology, and I can promise you there will be no trouble with the committee approving the budget."

"That's good news, Senator," said the General. "After a little fine tuning, we should be able to put this technology to work for intelligence gathering within a couple of months, wouldn't you say, Karl?"

"Yes, I think that's a reasonable time frame."

"Well, congratulations to you both for the great work," said the Senator. "There's still one thing that bothers me, though, and that's the issue of privacy. We've already had a glimpse into Professor Latter's private affairs. Are you going to look at his after-work hours?"

General Masters nodded and folded his arms across his chest. "Yes, we'll look at everything until we find the information we need to revive the E5. We view it as a matter of national security."

"Well, I understand how you could take that stance with a terrorist or even a suspected criminal, but I don't see how you can do it with one of our own scientists who was never suspected of a crime," said the Senator with a frown.

"It's all legit, Senator. We're technically holding Harry Latter under the rights accorded us by the Patriot Act."

"The Patriot Act! But Harry Latter surely can't be deemed a threat to national security! The man has Alzheimer's!"

"Alzheimer's is precisely the reason Professor Latter is a threat to our national security, Senator. The disease has rendered him incapable of telling us what went wrong with the testing of the weapon. What he has in his head is crucial to our security, don't you see?"

The Senator cupped a hand under his chin and frowned. "Well, I see what you mean, but I still think it's a stretch. I doubt if it would hold up in court, but then nobody's really going to find out about it I suppose."

"That's right, Senator," said the General. "There are only a handful of us who know who the patient is and what information we're seeking. All those technicians down there and the other mid-level staff just think this is some poor old duff who has Alzheimer's and his relatives have given consent to try this out and see if we can restore his memory."

"Well, who all knows besides those of us in this room?" asked the Senator.

"Sorry, Senator. I can't tell you that. Just rest assured that it's only those who have the highest level of security clearance."

The Senator glanced at his watch. "Well, what say we take a look at the first item on Harry's agenda—ten o'clock, I think it was. Maybe that will tell us what we want to know. I won't have much more time to look at anything else."

"Good. Karl, tell Jake to advance to ten o'clock, please."

"Yes, General. Right away."

Cyn gave him the cell phone, and he called Jake. Almost immediately the clock spun forward, and a new image came into view. A pasty-faced man with sandy-colored eyebrows and a shaved head was looking directly at them. In the background, laboratory tables were topped with a maze of wires and electronic equipment.

The man smiled crookedly revealing a gap between his upper front teeth. "Right on time as you ordered, Sir. The new batch of filters is ready to test."

There was silence for a moment, and then the man said, "Yes, Sir. These filters now cover the complete spectrum from the I-Red."

Silence.

The man nodded. "Yes, that's right. The test chamber contains all the magnetic frequencies except for Gamma and above."

"What's going on? Why can't we hear Professor Latter?" asked the Senator.

"That seems to be an aberration of the memory storage process," said Braun. "Apparently, the brain does not store that which comes from within—only what you hear, see, feel and taste. At least that's what we currently believe. It's possible that what you say is stored in a different manner and we haven't figured out how to play it back yet. We plan to do more research in that area, but in the meantime, we should be able to find what we need to know by seeing what Professor Latter saw and hearing what he heard."

"Ah-ha. So, in other words, we can't *really* read Professor Latter's mind, *per se*," said the Senator. "That is, we can't see what he is thinking, other than what we see him actually write, or what we hear others say in response to him. That gives me a small bit of comfort on the privacy issue.

Could it be that our brains don't store our words or our thoughts as a protection against invasion of privacy?"

"It could very well be," said Braun. "However, I believe the brain does store everything and possibly has some sort of protective device to keep outsiders from accessing that part of the memory. Sort of like a firewall on a computer. I think we'll eventually be able to crack it."

"Jeez, you mean just like those computer hackers?"

Braun smiled. "Something like that."

The Senator shook his head and turned his attention back to the display. Electronic circuit boards now filled the screen. Hands reached out and lifted a circuit board connected to cables and tilted it in various directions before placing it back on the table.

The pasty-faced man appeared in front of them again. "That is the visual wavelength filter," he said. Silence. Then he said, "Yes, Sir. I'll see to it right away."

Now, they were viewing the room through Harry's eyes as he moved through it and stopped outside an elevator door. The door slid open and a guard dressed in a military uniform smiled at them. "What floor, Sir?" they heard him ask as Harry walked into the elevator. Then they were looking at the guard's back as he pressed a button, and then they were watching the numbers on the elevator display as they counted down from four to one.

"Well, that didn't tell us anything," said the General shaking his head in disappointment. "Let's move on to two o'clock, right before the fire. Maybe that will give us some insight."

"Right," said Braun. He communicated with Jake again on the cell phone, and instantly the clock moved forward.

Now they were looking at a bank of oscilloscopes displaying a series of wavy lines in various colors. Then the view zeroed in on one of the oscilloscopes, and Harry Latter's hand reached out and began turning a small knob, which increased one of the numbers on the oscilloscope's screen.

"He's increasing the magnetic frequency," said Braun. "He must be testing the magnetic filters."

Slowly, the number increased and then without warning they heard a deafening bang and everything went blank.

"What's happening?" asked the Senator as they stared at the blank screen in bewilderment.

No one answered. A few minutes passed, and then they were looking up at an acoustically tiled ceiling. Billowing clouds of black smoke soon concealed it from view. Harry was apparently lying on the floor, and now he slowly began to look around and get up. They saw tangles of electrical cables, smashed electronic equipment and other debris scattered everywhere. Now, thick black smoke filled the screen, obscuring everything from sight.

"That's enough," said the General. "We know what happened after that, but we still don't know what caused the explosion and the fire. We're obviously going to have to go back and review every moment in Harry's memory throughout that day and possibly even several days before the fire."

"But we don't have enough time to do that before Harry's sedative wears off, do we?" asked Cyn.

"I remind you that we are recording and storing the patient's memory as it downloads," said Braun. "There is still about a half hour left before the sedative wears off, and we'll continue downloading to make sure we have enough going back through the time that Professor Latter developed and worked on the project."

"Good," said the Senator. "I've seen enough to justify the funding. I need to be on my way back to Washington now. Good work, Professor Braun."

He walked over to Braun and shook his hand and then turned to the General. "I assume I'll be included in your report about the E5, Jeff?"

"Yes, of course," said the General with a smile as he clasped his hand.

"Well, Cyn, are you ready to go?" asked the Senator.

Cyn nodded and began to collect her things.

"Um, Senator Goodman, may I have a word with you in private?" asked the General.

"Sure," said the Senator. He walked over to the far side of the room with General Masters.

Braun looked at them curiously, shrugged his shoulders and went back to studying the multiplex screen. The clock was again spinning backwards in a blur as they attempted to record as much of Harry"s memory as possible before the sedative wore off.

"Cyn, would you please come over here for a second?" asked the Senator.

Cyn walked over to where the Senator and the General were standing.

"Cyn, General Masters is impressed with your knowledge of the technology, and he has asked me if I can spare you for a few days. He'd like you to stay on and assist them with fine-tuning the technology and searching the memory download for the information about the E5. I've told him it's OK by me if you're willing."

Cyn caught her breath. "Sure, Senator. It would be an honor, but I don't have any change of clothes or anywhere to stay."

The General grinned. "That will be no problem, Ms. Hoover. We'll arrange everything. There's an inn in Roca Grande and a General Store. You can keep the Grand Cherokee to drive while you're here. My aide, Captain Denton, will get everything together that you'll need. Report to him on Level One next to my office at fourteen hundred, and he'll have everything ready for you."

"Well, all right, then, but who's going to drive the Senator back to the Air Base?"

"That's all taken care of, too, Cyn. One of the General's drivers will take me. No problem. I'll get back to Washington and start drafting the proposal for the committee. You can look it over and do the rewrite when you get back," said the Senator.

"OK, but I have another question," said Cyn, looking at the General and then back over her shoulder at Professor Braun who was still intent on the screen. "Does Professor Braun know I'm staying on?" she asked in a low voice.

"Yes, he does. I spoke to him about it earlier," said the General. "He agreed, but it's not really his decision anyway. I'm the head of the project, you know."

"Well, I've got to get going. Give me a call on the secure line about once a day, Cyn," said the Senator.

"Sure thing, Senator Goodman. I'll keep you posted, and thanks for your confidence in me."

"It's well-earned. You be good now, you hear?" he said with a chuckle. He left through the door that the General held open for him. His driver was already standing at attention outside the elevator door.

The General closed the door and turned to Cyn. "OK, Cyn, you're in," he said in a low voice. "Just remember to pretend you're working for me."

Cyn gave him a tight smile. "Of course. Thanks, Jeff. I'll keep you posted through the secure system."

The General nodded. "Carry on, then."

* * *

1:15 p.m.

Cyn stood a few feet behind Brent Jacobson and stared at his computer monitor. Now the screen was filled with thousands of light blue hexagonal pixels that seemed to form a mosaic, but there was no definable picture.

"What do you make of this, Ms. Hoover?" asked Jake without turning around.

Cyn smiled. He had sensed her presence again, but this time it was not as amazing. She had adjourned to the women's room and sent him a text message on her way to the control room. She walked forward and placed a hand on his shoulder as she leaned forward to look at the screen.

"Mmmmm," he murmured, flexing his shoulder slightly and sending an electrical current up her arm. She quickly withdrew her hand.

Cyn caught her breath and pointed at the upper right hand portion of the screen. "Look at the clock," she said.

"Yes, I noticed that," he said. "We're on real time, so supposedly that's what Professor Latter is seeing right now, but that doesn't make sense. He shouldn't be seeing anything except complete darkness. There's no light in the chamber."

"Are you still downloading?" asked Cyn.

"Yes. At least I thought I was until the clock suddenly reverted to real time and these pixels popped up."

"Possibly the sedative has worn off and Professor Latter is awake…."

Suddenly Dr. Graham's voice boomed through the loudspeaker. "Medical Emergency! Code One!"

"Oh, God! Look at the bios!" shouted Jake.

Cyn saw that Harry's heartbeat was nearly flat. She looked up at the viewing room and saw General Masters and Professor Braun gesticulating wildly at each other. Then the General grabbed the cell phone from Braun's hand and Jake's phone rang. When Jake picked up, Cyn could hear the General's voice loud and clear. "Stop the downloading NOW!" he shouted. "I'm ordering them to get Professor Latter out of the chamber right now. His life is in danger!"

"Yes, Sir!" said Jake as he began pushing a series of function keys and yelling orders to the other technicians around him.

* * *

1:30 p.m.

Dr. Graham and several technicians ran to the chamber followed by paramedics pushing a medical trolley. A technician slid the bolt back and tried to pull the chamber door open without success. Two other technicians rushed forward to lend assistance. As hard as they pulled, the door did not budge.

"We need more help!" yelled one of the technicians as he continued to heave on the door handle.

Others rushed forward and strained at the door, but still it would not open.

"I'll bring that forklift over! That's the only way we're going to get this open!" shouted one of the technicians as he sprinted toward the machinery. He climbed onto the forklift and started it up. As he pulled up close to the door another technician grabbed a thick steel cable and chained one end to the door handle and the other to the forklift.

"Easy does it," said the technician as the driver began to back up. The tension in the cable gradually increased until it was taut.

The driver revved the engine and eased off the clutch.

"Stand back!" yelled the Doctor as he saw the wheels beginning to spin.

Plumes of white smoke and the smell of burning rubber filled the room. The driver coughed and his eyes began to stream. The wheels continued to spin, and the cable squealed as it stretched and took the strain.

"Watch out!" yelled the driver as the door handle began to bend.

Everyone in the room ran for cover behind anything they could find just as the door handle popped free and the cable whipped around.

The driver cut the engine on the forklift. He climbed down and stood looking at the cable lying on the floor with the door handle attached to it. "We'll have to bring in the special saw and cutters to get through that magnetic shielding plus the six-foot wall of lead."

"How long is that going to take?" asked Dr. Graham as he came out from behind a partition and dusted himself off.

The driver shook his head sadly. "It will take at least an hour, I'm afraid."

Dr. Graham planted his hands on his hips and stared at the floor. "Damn! I'm afraid Harry doesn't stand a chance."

* * *

1:45 p.m.

In the control room technicians milled about taking a break. All computer monitors were frozen on the last image that had come through—the light blue hexagonal pixels that formed a fuzzy mosaic. Suddenly a hush fell over the room when Professor Braun burst in with a grim expression on his face. He strode quickly through the room headed for Jake's command post.

Cyn and Jake had been exchanging a few text messages in their secret code while they waited for further orders. Cyn quickly pocketed her cell phone when she saw Braun approaching.

"What's up, Sir?" asked Jake as Braun walked up to them. He quietly slid his cell phone under a pile of papers at the side of his computer keyboard.

"They can't get the chamber door open, and Dr. Graham thinks Professor Latter may be dead," said Braun in a low voice.

"Oh, no! Not again!" said Jake without thinking.

Braun glared at him for a moment, and Jake hung his head. "They're going to have to cut through the walls of the chamber and that's probably going to take at least an hour," Braun continued. "I have to be there, so here's what I want you to do."

"Yes, Sir?" said Jake looking back up at Braun.

"You know that General Masters has assigned Ms. Hoover to work on the project?" he asked, acknowledging Cyn's presence for the first time.

Jake nodded. "Yes, she told me, Sir."

"All right, then. I want you to dismiss all the technicians here. Give them the rest of the day and tomorrow off. Shut down the control room. Then, you and Ms. Hoover can go to your office and start reviewing what we've got. See if you can find the reason for the fire on the E5 Project. Got it?"

"Yes, Sir. We'll get on it right away," said Jake.

Braun looked at Cyn and she nodded. "All right, then. I'll check in with you later. In the meantime, if you find anything, be sure to page me."

"Yes, Sir," said Jake as Braun turned to leave. He waited until Braun had left the room and then he turned on the microphone to the loudspeaker. "Professor Braun says the project is a success, folks. Good show. We have what we need, and we're closing down the control room and giving you the rest of today and tomorrow off. Enjoy your long weekend and report for work as usual on Monday morning. Congratulations!"

A cheer went up as technicians shook each other's hands and then scurried to shut down their equipment and gather their belongings. Within five minutes Jake and Cyn were the sole occupants of the control room.

"Ok, Ms. Hoover. Follow me," said Jake as he scooped up his cell phone and some paperwork.

Cyn followed him out of the control room and down a long corridor. At last he paused in front of an unmarked door and tapped a code onto the keypad next to the door. Cyn heard a metallic click and Jake opened the door. He held the door back for her to pass through. The minute the door closed, he put his things down on the desk and came over to her. Before she had time to react he had his arms around her and his forehead pressed up against hers. She found herself staring once again into the depths of those lapis eyes.

"We can talk freely in here, Cyn. My God, it's been a long time, and I've missed you," he murmured.

Cyn forced herself to reach up and remove his arms from around her shoulders. "Not now, Jake," she said firmly, stepping back and shaking her head. "We have work to do, and no one here must find out that we know each other, OK?"

He leaned back and studied her. "Hmmm, I take it you're still working for the NSA. I thought you were Senator Goodman's Aide."

"I *am* Senator Goodman's aide, and I can't tell you why I'm here, so don't ask," she said sternly. "You should know better, being in the NSA yourself."

Jake raised an eyebrow in amusement. "You're right. I won't ask. I'm just glad you're here and we're working together again, like old times."

They stared at each other for a second. Cyn was the first to blink as usual. "All right. Let's get on with it, then." She turned away and took a deep breath to calm herself.

After a second Jake turned away and walked over to his oversized desk. He booted up his computer and drew up a second chair to the left of his own. He motioned for Cyn to sit there as he took his own seat. When his computer had loaded, he tapped a few keys and an image came on the screen. "Well, well, what have we here?" he asked.

Cyn froze halfway down into taking her seat as she stared at the screen.

Spinning on its axis in the center of the screen was a three-dimensional five-pointed star that resembled a Christmas tree ornament.

Cyn sat down and looked at her watch and then back at the monitor. "The clock is still showing real time," she said, pointing at the display.

"I see that," said Jake frowning. "But I shut down, and all we should be seeing is what we saw when we were in the control room."

"And the clock should say 1:30, instead of 1:50," added Cyn.

"Maybe I accidentally loaded the wrong program," muttered Jake. He closed the screen and then tapped in the commands again. The same thing came up. The star continued to spin, and the clock read 1:51.

"Somehow we're still getting a signal," said Jake.

"Look at the EKG," said Cyn. "It's totally flat now, indicating Harry Latter is dead!"

They sat staring at the display in amazement for a minute, and then Cyn said, "It must be some sort of background noise."

Jake shook his head. "No, it can't be that. We zeroed out all background noise from every frequency when we began the project. Just a minute. Let me check something." He tapped in a series of commands and various charts came up. After peering at them for a bit, he said,

"Whatever this is, it has a very high frequency, and it is coming from inside the chamber."

"Could it be coming from the bio monitors?" asked Cyn.

"I doubt it, but I'll check," said Jake. Again he tapped in commands on the keyboard and looked at the graphs that came up. "Nope. The EKG sensors are fine. This high frequency signal is not coming from them. There's no latent energy."

"This is baffling," said Cyn. They both leaned back in their chairs and stared at the graphs for a moment.

Suddenly, Jake leaned forward and began tapping on the keyboard again.

"What are you doing?" asked Cyn.

"I just had a hunch," said Jake. "I'm going to plot this high frequency signal against the EKG and see if that tells us anything."

"But I don't see what that has to do with. ..." Cyn began and stopped abruptly when a new graph appeared on the screen.

"Ha! Just as I suspected!" exclaimed Jake. "This signal began at the same time the EKG line went flat. In other words, this signal began the instant Professor Latter's heart stopped beating at exactly 1:35 p.m.!"

Suddenly there was a brilliant flash on the screen and the monitor went black.

"Now what?" asked Cyn, frowning at the black screen.

"I don't know," said Jake as he tapped keys on the keyboard. Nothing happened. "It's weird."

"Let's try going back to 1:35 and see if we can bring up that star again," said Cyn.

Again Jake entered commands and the clock and spinning star reappeared on the screen. "What do you want to do now?" he asked.

"Let's see if we can translate that star into an image before we go forward in time."

"How do you propose to do that?" asked Jake, squinting at the spinning three-dimensional object.

Cyn thought for a moment and then said, "Can you see if there are any smaller frequencies attached to this larger one?"

"Oh, you mean pairing," said Jake. "Sure. It will be easy to check."

After a bit, a series of numbers appeared in a separate window on the monitor. "Well, would you look at that," said Jake. "They're not pairs at all. They're in fives."

"Fives? I've never seen that before, but I guess it makes sense because there are five points on the star," said Cyn. "Can you rearrange the signals so they are parallel to each other?"

"What distance apart do you want them?" asked Jake, his fingers poised over the keyboard.

"I'm not sure," said Cyn frowning. "How about trying one, two, three, five and eight?"

Jake grinned. "Fibonacci again. OK. Just a moment. I'll have to change magnetic filters."

He performed that function and then typed in a series of commands on the keyboard. The three-dimensional star continued to spin on its axis. He tapped on the keyboard again and then shook his head. "Sorry, Cyn. Fibonacci doesn't do the trick this time."

Cyn thought for a moment as she continued to stare at the star. "I know!" she said suddenly with a smile. "How about trying 1.618 to twenty thousand decimal places?"

Jake grinned at her. "Of course! Phi, the Divine Proportion! Why didn't I think of that?" He turned back to his keyboard and rapidly began typing again.

"It's working!" said Cyn. The star began to spin faster and faster until it was a blur. Then, as if by magic, it disappeared, and an image came on the screen.

They were looking down from ceiling height at Harry Latter strapped to a table. He was wearing something that resembled an astronaut's helmet.

"Where's that image coming from?" asked Cyn. "Is there an overhead camera in the chamber?"

Jake shook his head. "No. Anything like that would interfere with the downloading."

"Start the clock moving forward in real time, and let's see what happens," said Cyn.

"Right," said Jake.

He hit a function key and the image began to move quickly back and forth over Harry's body. They saw his body from every conceivable angle, still from above. Then the image became still, hovering directly over Harry again. Suddenly, a brilliant flash obscured the view and the screen went dark.

"Where on earth did that image come from?" asked Cyn.

"It's definitely coming from Professor Latter," said Jake quietly. "There are no other frequencies in that chamber, remember?"

"What! Do you mean Professor Latter's brain was still emitting signals after death, and that is what we saw?" cried Cyn.

Jake crossed his arms and leaned back in his chair, smiling slightly. "No, Cyn. I don't believe it's Professor Latter's *brain* that emitted the signal. I think it was his *spirit*."

Cyn started to object, but when she looked into Jake's eyes, she saw the hawk circling lazily above the Rio Grande Gorge, heard the haunting notes of the flute, and remembered what he had told her those many years ago.

* * *

Brent Jacobson was three-quarters Taos Indian. He was one of a handful of his people to have been born and raised in the Taos Pueblo. In fact he still had a home there that he returned to whenever he had vacation time. His lapis blue eyes and last name were hand-me-downs from his English grandfather.

William Barclay Jacobson immigrated to America from Sussex, England in 1910 at the age of twenty-two and found his way to New Mexico and then to Taos in the 1920s. He was an artist, and the unspoiled beauty of the land and the freedom of the way of life drew him. He soon discovered and became enamored with the local Indians and their crafts.

He became friends with Chief Red Willow and was invited to visit at the Pueblo. When he fell in love with the chief's only daughter, Red Willow made a rare exception and allowed them to marry and take up residence in the Pueblo. A proud and fiercely independent people, the Taos had for centuries enforced a strict policy forbidding marriage outside the Pueblo.

While there was some grumbling at first, the Taos soon forgot that W. B. Jacobson was not one of them. He adopted their Tiwa language, their ways and religious beliefs as if he had been born into them. Inside the tribe he was known as Singing Wind, the Indian name given him in recognition of his artistry. He carved flutes from wood and played them at tribal ceremonies.

He had a son and a daughter, both of whom lived and married within the Pueblo. His son, Barclay Allen Jacobson, known as Running Wolf, carried on the tradition of flute making, and bred quarter horses. He had married Susannah Fleetdeer, and in 1969 they had a son. They named him Brent Barclay Jacobson.

From the time he was able to speak, it was clear that Brent possessed special talents. He seemed to have been born with knowledge that it takes most people years to acquire through experience and education. He simply knew how things worked and how to improve on them.

When he was only four he picked up one of his father's flutes, put it to his mouth and began to play as if he'd been doing it for years. Amazed, Running Wolf quietly placed some sticks, gourds, paint and feathers within reach to see what Brent would do with them. A couple of days later he found Brent sitting on a rock out by the horses happily playing a melody on the flute he had constructed. The horses hovered near him, and as Running Wolf watched, one of the horses reached down and nuzzled Brent's ear.

Running Wolf smiled. It was not the first time he had noticed that his son had a knack with horses. Having this gift himself, Running Wolf was quick to recognize it in Brent. When Brent was seven Running Wolf gave him a black colt to raise. Brent named him Black Thunder. The colt grew into a fine stallion that eventually won many races in the quarter-horse circuits, but he would allow no one to ride him except Brent. He followed Brent everywhere, like an adoring dog, but for other humans he had little use.

When he was old enough Brent joined the other men in the Kiva to participate in the ancient tribal ceremonies. It was there that he was given his Indian name Soaring Hawk because he had the ability to transport himself above the earth and see things one only sees from a great height, such as through the eyes of a hawk or an eagle. In a number of these sessions, he astounded the other men by describing terrain he had never visited. On one occasion, he was able to locate a missing goat when he "saw" it down in a ravine a half mile away.

As the years passed and Soaring Hawk grew into manhood, the tribal elders noted his growth and did all they could to promote him as an emissary for Native American culture. They recorded his music and sold it in the gift shop at the Pueblo. He became a popular performer at various cultural events and tourist attractions throughout New Mexico. He wrote a small book of vignettes about growing up on the reservation—all of this before he had reached the age of eighteen.

But because of his "visions" in the Kiva ceremonies, Brent Jacobson developed a passion to be part of the world outside the confines of the Pueblo. He wanted to learn much more than what the reservation schools could offer. A horse race in Raton showed him the way.

In the summer before his senior year in high school, Brent entered the quarter horse race in Raton, riding Dark Fury, a three-year-old filly sired by Black Thunder. He came in second in a photo finish against the circuit champion Warrior ridden by Cyn Hoover of El Paso, Texas.

After the race Brent went to congratulate Cyn and something happened to him that had never occurred before. He fell deeply and profoundly in love.

From that time forward Brent and Cyn spent as much time together as possible. She visited him in Taos. He visited her at the ranch near El Paso. They met in between. About mid-way through their senior years, Cyn encouraged Brent to apply for a scholarship and acceptance at MIT. For him it was a piece of cake, and the next fall they moved in together in a small apartment near the MIT campus in Cambridge, Massachusetts.

1:55 p.m.

Professor Braun joined General Masters and Dr. Graham who were watching a crew of technicians attempting to break into the chamber. They were cutting a hole in the inch-thick outer magnetic shield composed of copper alloy. Plumes of white smoke rose from the diamond-tipped Skill saws, and the acrid smell of saw blade lubricant permeated the room.

"How is it going?" asked Braun.

General Masters shook his head. "They're making good progress, but the Doc here thinks it's too late for Harry."

Braun looked at the Doctor questioningly. Dr. Graham shrugged his shoulders in resignation. "According to the EKG monitor, his heart stopped beating at 1:35. Not much chance of us being able to revive him at this point."

"What do you think happened?" asked the General.

"I don't want to speculate. We won't really know for sure until we do an autopsy," said the Doctor with bitterness in his voice. "We should have stopped the downloading when we had that emergency with the oxygen earlier, rather than running it right down to the time the sedative was due to wear off."

A loud clanging noise echoed through the room causing them to jump. They looked around and saw that the technicians had cut out a large panel of the shield and had dumped it on the concrete floor in a corner of the room.

The General motioned to the technician in charge. "How long now?" he asked as the supervisor came over to them.

"I'm not really sure, Sir," said the technician. "We still have to get through that six-foot lead wall. It's very soft and presents some difficulties. As I see it, we have two options. We can either use the laser to burn our way through quickly, or we do it the hard way with hammers and chisels, which will take much longer. We can't use the saws because the lead will gum up the blades and that would be very hazardous."

"I'd rather you didn't use the laser," blurted the Doctor before anyone else could say anything.

Braun and the General glared at him for a moment, and then the General turned back to the technician. "Use the laser. We need to get in there as quickly as possible."

"Yes, Sir," said the technician. He walked back to the chamber to convey the order to his men.

"And why don't you want to use the laser, Doc?" asked the General in a low voice when the technician was out of earshot.

"I'm afraid it will harm the body in some way and we won't be able to get accurate autopsy results. Remember what happened before when they used the acetylene torches," said the Doctor with a frown.

"The laser won't create heat and liquefy the lead like the torches did. Besides, there's no need for an autopsy since we already know Harry Latter died of a heart attack," said the General.

"A heart attack? I didn't say that! We can't know for sure until we do an autopsy," exclaimed the Doctor.

"No, Doctor. It's obvious. Harry Latter's heart stopped beating. He had a heart attack," said the General, enunciating each word slowly as if he were talking to a schoolboy.

The Doctor hung his head. He got the message. "Then if that's the case, his heart attack was brought on because you ran the downloading too long. His sedative wore off and he came to in an isolated black room strapped down to a cold hard table," he muttered.

Braun tapped him on the shoulder. "No, Doctor. The experiment ran the planned length of time. You simply didn't give him enough sedative."

The Doctor looked up angrily. "What! Of course I gave him the proper dose! You think I'd make a mistake like that?"

The General intervened. "Enough. The official record is that Harry Latter suffered a heart attack and died in his hospital bed. It's not uncommon with Alzheimer's patients. Got it?"

The Doctor nearly choked on the bile that had risen in his throat. "Yes, Sir, I've got it," he said.

"Good," said the General. "That's what you'll write in your report. I'll expect it on my desk tomorrow morning."

The Doctor could only nod. He watched the rest of the assault on the chamber through tear-blurred eyes, saying nothing—nothing, that is, until he saw the condition of Harry's body an hour later.

* * *

2 p.m.

Cyn opened the door to General Masters's suite of offices. A blonde-haired young man dressed in Air Force military uniform was sitting with his back to her at a desk in the far corner of the room next to the double doors to the General's office. Cyn glanced around. No one else was there. The young man was preoccupied with keying in something on his computer, and he did not look around.

Cyn cleared her throat as she started to walk toward him, not wanting to startle him. He looked around and saw her and quickly rose to his feet. He was tall—Cyn guessed 6"4".

"Yes, Ma'am, may I help you?" he asked in a distinct Texas drawl. Cyn guessed San Antonio or Houston.

"Yes. I'm here to see Captain Denton," said Cyn.

"Well, you've found him. I'm Captain Denton." He grinned and his pale blue eyes sparkled. "You must be Ms. Hoover."

"Yes, I'm Cynthia Hoover. General Masters told me to report to you at fourteen hundred hours."

"Good. I've been expecting y'all. I have everything ready for you if you'll be so kind as to accompany me to my private office." He stepped out from behind the desk and indicated a door just to the left of the desk area.

As Cyn approached, he held open the door for her and bowed slightly. "After you, Ma'am."

Cyn burst out laughing as she passed by him into the office. "Oh, please, Captain. Please don't call me Ma'am. It makes me feel ancient."

He blushed slightly and then grinned good-naturedly. "OK, Ma'am...er sorry...Ms. Hoover. No harm intended. You certainly don't *look* ancient."

Cyn looked around. The office was larger than she had expected.

Captain Denton followed her into the room and closed the door. He motioned towards a long table that took up most of one wall. "I have everything laid out over here," he said. "Please have a seat."

Cyn did as she was told, and he pulled up a chair next to her. He opened a steel box that looked like a safety deposit box. He withdrew a printed form from the box and placed it in front of her.

"OK, first order of business. You need to give me your driver's license, bankcards, identity cards and anything else that has your Cynthia Hoover identity on it. We'll itemize everything on this form and both sign it, and then they'll be kept here in our secure safe until you're ready to leave."

Cyn nodded and began withdrawing the items from her bag. She knew the routine.

"Your new name is Barbara Jones," said the Captain as he placed her credentials in the box. He shut it and set it aside. "Now, what we have here is an Oregon driver's license issued to Barbara Jones, a debit card for Barbara Jones's checking account with Bank of America, and a Platinum Capitol One Visa. The checking account has $10,000 in it, and the available credit on the Visa is $100,000. Also, here is $500 in cash."

Cyn looked closely at each item before placing it in her wallet. "They look good," she said. "The photos of me are better than the ones on my real driver's license and Visa."

"We aim to please," said Captain Denton. He picked up a thin black leather wallet. "And this is Barbara Jones's passport, just in case she needs it," he said handing it to her.

"You never know," said Cyn with a smile. She put the passport in a hidden compartment in her bag.

"Now, you're going to be driving the Grand Cherokee while you're here, and I've put registration papers for Barbara Jones in the glove compartment. You have reservations under the name of Barbara Jones at the Rancho Bonito Inn in Roca Grande. I got you a corner room on the top floor next to a stairwell that goes down to a back entrance. The inn has a coffee shop and bar. There's a general store nearby."

"Good job. You've thought of everything," said Cyn.

Captain Denton smiled. "When you work for General Masters, you have to think of everything. Now, one more thing before I get to the fun part. Here is your Level One Security Card for admittance to all areas in Apparition Mountain. You'll have to wear this around your neck while you're in here. It has your photo and your palm print on it. To gain access into the secure areas, you'll have to insert this into the scanner at the door and enter your security pass code—similar to what you do at an ATM. Your pass code is Eagle 511. Remember that, because we don't want it written down anywhere."

"Eagle 511. Got it," said Cyn as she accepted the identity card from him and placed it in another pocket in her bag.

"Good, Ms. Jones. Now for the fun part." He reached across the table and drew a small red and black plastic case towards them.

"And what have we here?" asked Cyn with an eyebrow raised.

Captain Denton smiled mysteriously as he opened the case. He held up a titanium-plated object the size of a credit card and only slightly thicker. "This, Ms. Jones, is the XJ14—the very latest in secure cell phone technology, compliments of the NSA. It's waterproof, shockproof and tamperproof. You can use it in the shower or underwater in a swimming pool. You can run over it with a semi. You can drop it onto concrete from a hundred feet, and still this little baby just keeps goin' like the Energizer™ Rabbit. In addition, you can send and receive messages from anywhere—even if you're five thousand feet underground or sealed up in a tomb."

"Wow What will they think of next?" said Cyn, grinning excitedly as she took the tiny phone from him.

"You can use it just as you would a regular cell phone, but you can't call out of Apparition Mountain without first going through the operator. Also, you can't call someone in the Mountain from outside without going through the operator. Now, this is important to remember: if you ever have an emergency, press *33 and help will arrive quickly. The phone is equipped with a locating device that is only activated by pressing *33, so even if you can't talk, all you have to do is press *33. Do not, under any circumstances, call 911 if there's an emergency, and do not let someone who does not have Level One Security clearance use it. Any questions?"

"What about long distance calls?" asked Cyn.

The Captain nodded. "You can call anywhere anytime, including all foreign countries. NSA's satellite network is the most secure in the world. When you call another secure number, your conversation is encrypted. However, if you call a non-secure number, it's just like any other cell phone, so you should be careful what you say in that case."

Cyn nodded. She ran a finger over the tiny phone that nestled in the palm of her hand.

"By the way, that little baby is also a digital camera and a camcorder. You can access the Internet from it, and it will give you voice directions to anywhere you want to go. If you press #SS, you can block out frequencies from any possible listening devices wherever you are. You name it, it does it."

"Wow!" said Cyn. She caressed the little phone reverently again and then slipped it into its case and deposited it in her bag.

"That's everything," said the Captain as he pushed back his chair and rose to his feet. "I'll walk you out to the Jeep. There are a couple of things I want to show you there, and while we're on the way, you can practice opening some doors just to make sure you've got it right."

"Good," said Cyn. "I'd better get going so I can get some overnight things and get checked into the inn."

"One other thing," said Captain Denton, looking down at her intently. "I'm your point man. If you have any problems or need any assistance while you're here, just let me know."

"Thanks, Captain. You've been a real help," said Cyn as she stood up and shouldered her bag. "I'll remember that."

"I hope you do. I'm looking forward to assisting such an attractive lady as yourself. Let's dispense with the Captain Denton stuff. You can just call me Charlie, and I'll come runnin'."

Cyn smiled up at him. "Well, I truly appreciate your concern, Charlie. It's always good to know you have a friend you can call on."

Charlie Denton beamed at her as he held the door open for her again. "And you can call me...Barbara," she said as she walked past him.

* * *

4 p.m.

Cyn entered the town of Roca Grande after driving back down the fifteen-mile stretch of gravel road, past the Air Force Base and onto Highway 554. Roca Grande was situated at the junction of Highway 554 and Highway 84 that ran north to Pagosa Springs, Colorado. She passed a sign that read "Welcome to Roca Grande. Population 235."

She drove past a few ramshackle houses into the heart of town. On her right was a weathered log cabin with a faded sign proclaiming it as "Dos Amigos Cantina." Next to that was the Hernandez Brothers Texaco. Across the street on her left squatted a long, low wooden structure with a boardwalk veranda and a sign that identified it as "Roca Grande Mercantile."

She drove on down the street, passing an empty dilapidated building that looked as if it might at one time have been a café. Then, after a dry rock and weed-choked vacant lot, she saw the Rancho Bonito Inn situated near the intersection of the two highways. Compared to the other buildings, the Inn looked relatively new and modern. It was four stories high, built of adobe in the Spanish mission style.

There was a tall marquis sign in front of the entrance that could be read by drivers zipping along Highway 84. Cyn smiled when she saw the message under the "Vacancy" notice. It said, "Appearing at 8 p.m. in the Adobe Walls Lounge, Friday and Saturday: Mac Gentry and Riders of the Purple Sage. Cover charge $2."

Cyn turned the Grand Cherokee around and headed back to the store. During her drive she had not seen one vehicle on the road, although she did see several semis and a couple of SUVs speeding up and down Highway 84. There was a dusty, dented red Ford pickup outside the cantina, and a couple of Chevy trucks and an ancient Dodge van parked outside the store. The Texaco across the street appeared deserted. There was a crude hand-lettered sign hanging on one of the pumps that read: "For service, call 466-2240."

Cyn pulled into a parking space in front of the Roca Grande Mercantile. As she got out of the Grand Cherokee she noticed three men staring at her out of swarthy, creased faces. They were dressed in Levi jeans and jackets and were nearly identical except for the different colors of their cowboy boots and hats. They were sitting on the verandah in wooden chairs tipped back against the wall next to a soft drink dispenser, thumbs hooked in their jeans pockets.

Cyn nodded and smiled at them but got no response other than one of them spitting a long stream of tobacco juice into a nearby brass spittoon. She shrugged and walked on into the store.

When her eyes adjusted to the darkened interior, she found herself in a virtual hodgepodge. Canned goods were stacked next to fishing gear. Work gloves and boots resided beside a rack of scented car deodorizers. Cases of beer were stacked high on the floor next to a melange of tractor and cowboy hats. In between a refrigerated unit filled with more beer, soft drinks, cartons of milk and orange juice, and a display of mostly Country and Western CDs was a rack of clothes. Cyn headed for that.

"Can I get you something, Hon?"

Cyn started at the sound of the cigarette-hardened feminine voice. She looked around. A hard-looking woman with leathery skin and dyed jet-black hair had materialized out of nowhere. She was wearing a red and black flannel shirt tucked into worn Levi's. Her feet sported flaming red cowboy boots.

"I'm going to be staying in the area for a few days and I need some overnight gear and some changes of clothes," explained Cyn.

The woman planted her hands on her hips and eyed Cyn's designer pants suit and expensive crocodile shoes and matching sling bag. "All we have in the way of women's clothes is Western wear," she said with a shake of her head.

"That will suit me just fine. I grew up on a ranch near El Paso," said Cyn with a smile.

"El Paso, eh? I got a brother living down there. Name's Harley James. He's in the cattle business. Wouldn't happen to know him would you?"

Cyn shook her head. "No. I've been away from El Paso for many years now."

"Well, that figures. Harley's only been there for about five years. He was in Las Cruces, but ended up getting a divorce and wanted to get away from his ex. I'm Shirl, by the way."

"I'm Barbara," said Cyn.

"Well, Barbara, what brings you to this dried-up spot? The only thing we got around here is the Air Force Base a few miles up the road."

"Yes, I know. That's why I'm here," said Cyn thinking fast. "I work for a government contracted company that supplies paint for military installations."

Shirl snorted. "Paint! Beats me why they can't buy it from me. I could sell it to 'em a helluva lot cheaper than what they're probably paying some hotsy-totsy company back east and save the taxpayers some money."

There was an awkward pause as she glared at Cyn and then her face softened slightly. "No offense intended," she murmured.

"No offense taken," said Cyn. "I know exactly how you feel, but this is special paint that only my company manufactures. It's a top-secret formula used for camouflaging planes."

"Shoot! There's nothing top-secret about camouflage paint. You mean that green and brown stuff?"

Cyn smiled mysteriously and looked around the store. She leaned in closer to Shirl and said in a hushed voice. "I'm really not supposed to be telling you this, but I'm sure you can keep a secret. It's paint that makes the planes invisible."

"You're kidding!" said Shirl.

Cyn shook her head. "No, I'm not kidding. Just remember, it's top secret, and I shouldn't have told you, so please don't tell anyone." She glanced around the store again.

Shirl looked around too and then leaned in close enough that Cyn could smell her breath that was redolent of cigarette smoke. "You can count on me. I won't say anything," she said in a voice just above a whisper. "You must be working for that secret place up to Apparition Mountain."

Cyn leaned back in mock surprise. "What secret place are you talking about? I don't know anything about that."

Shirl glanced around again. "The gov'ment has some sorta top secret operation going on at Apparition Mountain. They got the whole area blocked off—about fifty square miles. They's only one road in, and they got armed guards posted everywhere. If yuh ask me, I think they're up to more of that aliens from outer space stuff like they was in Roswell." She leaned back and crossed her arms over her chest as if to say, "So there!"

Cyn's eyes grew wide. "You really think so?"

Shirl nodded. "Damn straight."

The bell over the door tinkled and they heard heavy boot steps on the wooden floor. Shirl looked around. "Be with you in a sec, Marv," she said to the bearded man who had just entered.

"Just need a six-pack of Bud," he said as he headed for the beer cooler.

"Get whatcha need and I'll be right there," said Shirl. She turned back to Cyn. "OK, Barbara. The toothbrushes and that kinda' stuff are over there by the soup, and the women's clothes are over there. You want boots, we have a few. Nothin' smaller than eights, though," she said, glancing down at Cyn's feet.

"I can get by with eights," said Cyn. "I normally wear seven and a half, but I can wear eights with socks."

"Socks are over by the jeans," said Shirl.

"Go ahead and help your other customer. I'll find what I need," said Cyn.

Shirl nodded and strode off towards the checkout counter. Cyn couldn't help smiling to herself as she pawed through the racks and stacks. At last she emerged with two pairs of Levi's, three flannel shirts, two bulky woolen sweaters, a quilted down-filled vest, two pairs of boots, three pairs of Jockey-for-Women briefs, and an assortment of toiletries.

Marv was just leaving when she walked over to the counter and piled everything on it.

"Find everything you need?" asked Shirl as she began ringing the items up on the cash register.

Cyn nodded. "Enough to get by on for a couple of days. I can always come back if I think of anything else."

"You staying at the Inn?" asked Shirl.

"Yes," said Cyn. "How is it?"

"Pretty nice. It's the only decent place 'tween here and Santa Fe, and the *only* place 'tween here and Pagosa Springs. Jack and Rita Harper own it, and they do a good job. They give some o' the folks 'round here some work. During tourist season it's really hopping. They have bands in the lounge every night. This time o' year, it's pretty slow—mostly truckers stopping over for a few hours of shut-eye. The bar's closed during the week, but they still have bands in on weekends. It's the only entertainment 'round here; otherwise, you gotta drive clear to Santa Fe. Coffee shop's open twenty-four hours year-round, though."

Shirl finished ringing up Cyn's purchases and began to place them in brown paper bags. "That comes to $97.86 with tax," she announced.

Cyn was pulling some cash out of her bag when the bell tinkled again.

"Hey, Charlie," said Shirl.

"Shirl," said a familiar voice.

Cyn glanced around and saw a tall man in Levi's, sheepskin coat and Stetson hat walking toward the liquor case. He touched the brim of his hat as he passed her. "Ma'am," he said.

Cyn nodded at him and tried to keep the grin off her face. It was Charlie Denton. She wondered what he was doing here.

Shirl was counting out Cyn's change when Charlie returned to the counter with a quart of Jack Daniels.

"Looks like you're startin' the weekend celebration early," remarked Shirl as he plunked the bottle on the counter.

"Got to get some fortification. It's gonna be a cold one tonight. Temperature's already dropped ten degrees," he said, smiling at Shirl.

"I know whatcha mean. Looks like we could be in for some snow."

Shirl pushed Cyn's bags across the counter, and she began to collect them, juggling them around to try to hold them all.

"Here, let me help. Looks like you got your arms full. I'll carry them out to your car for you," said Charlie.

"Why, thanks. That's kind of you," said Cyn.

Shirl laughed. "Always the gentleman, eh Charlie? Specially when it's a purty gal needs help. And she's a tall one, too."

"Don't pay any attention to Shirl," said Charlie. "She's always ribbing me like that."

"Well, you watch him, Barbara. He's a smooth one," said Shirl winking at Cyn.

"I will, Shirl. Thanks for the advice," said Cyn winking back. She headed for the door, and Charlie followed carrying the bags.

Outside the three cowpokes were still there chewing their tobacco. They watched Cyn walk to the rear of the Grand Cherokee and open the back. "You can put them in here," she said to Charlie as she held the back door open.

As he leaned in to place the bags in the compartment behind the seats, Cyn said in a low voice without moving her lips, "What are you doing here?"

Charlie did not look at her as he arranged the bags. "Just checking to make sure you're all right," he muttered.

"Thanks, but I can take care of myself," Cyn hissed.

"I'm sure you can, but it never hurts to check," he said. Then he straightened up and looked at Cyn. "There you go, Ma'am," he said in a voice loud enough for the cowpokes to hear.

"Thank you very much," said Cyn as she closed the back door.

"No problem, Ma'am. Just pleased I could help." Charlie touched the brim of his hat again and strode back into the store leaving Cyn staring at him.

She quickly collected herself and got into the Jeep. The cowpokes were still staring and chewing. She ignored them, put on her seat belt, fired up the engine and drove off towards the Inn.

* * *

5 p.m.

The sun was low on the Western horizon when Cyn pulled up in front of the Rancho Bonito Inn. When she got out of the Jeep she pulled her jacket more tightly around her to ward off the icy breeze. Inside the large lobby was tiled with terra cotta and decorated in southwestern style with several leather couches and armchairs facing a huge fireplace. Burning wood in the fireplace filled the room with the pleasant odor of mesquite. Indian basketry, pots and weavings were abundant, and on one wall was a huge painting of Kit Carson done in the Art Nouveau style. Music was playing over hidden speakers, and Cyn smiled when she recognized the familiar flute songs of *El Halcon Subir Muy Alto*—The Soaring Hawk.

The massive reception desk, built in the Mexican colonial style, was deserted. As Cyn approached, a tall lean man dressed in Western gear emerged from a door behind the desk. He smiled at her and placed his hands on the desk. "Can I help you?" he asked in a deep bass voice.

"Yes, I have reservations," Cyn began.

"Ah-ha. You must be Barbara Jones," said the man as he whipped out a reservation form and placed it on the desk in front of Cyn.

"That's right," said Cyn. "But how did you know?"

"Oh, that's easy," said the man with a chuckle. "We only have one reservation for tonight. Slow time of year for us, but it picks up on weekends. I'm Jack Harper, by the way. My wife Rita and I own the place."

"So I heard," said Cyn. When Jack raised an eyebrow at that, she added, "From Shirl at the Mercantile."

Jack chuckled again. "That figures. If you stop at the Mercantile and talk to Shirl you'll know the entire history of the place in short order."

Cyn laughed. "I know what you mean. Well, I'm pleased to meet you, Jack. You have a nice place here."

"That we do. I think you'll enjoy your stay. You have our best room— the corner suite on the top floor. Now, all I need is for you to fill out this form and a credit card for room charges. You can charge restaurant and bar fees to your room while you're here."

"That sounds fine," said Cyn as she produced her Barbara Jones visa card. She filled out the form as Jack produced the card key for Room 405.

"This works to open the back door as well," said Jack as he handed her the key. "Do you need some help with luggage?"

"No, thanks," said Cyn. "I'll just drive around back and take my stuff up to the room from there. I don't have all that much."

"Oh, by the way, we don't have the new phone messaging system installed yet. If you want a wake-up call, you have to call us at the reception desk. Also, if anyone wants to leave a message for you when you're out, they have to leave it with us. We'll write it down and put it in your box or slip it under your door."

"OK. Thanks very much," said Cyn as she shouldered her bag and walked out the door.

The first thing Cyn did when she entered the room was to pull a small black handheld object from her purse. She pressed a button on it and a small screen lit up. Then she walked all around the room and into the bathroom, and even pulled open the closet doors, all the while staring intently at the screen. After a while, she pressed the button again and the screen went blank. She returned it to her bag and pulled out her own cell phone. She rapidly typed in a coded text message: "Room 405 at the Rancho Bonito Inn in Roca Grande under the name of Barbara Jones."
She pressed "Send," and waited. In just a few seconds a message flashed on the screen: "I'll be there at seven."

Cyn smiled and clicked off the cell phone. She took a few minutes to survey the accommodations. It was a large room with a king-sized bed. To the left of the bed was a sitting area with a couch, two armchairs, a coffee table and a small gas log fireplace. To the right of the bed was a Jacuzzi large enough to hold four people. There was also a curved, padded bar with four barstools, a small refrigerator, a coffee maker and a microwave. Along the wall across from the bed were a small writing desk and a large armoire. The lower half of the armoire contained three roomy drawers. When Cyn opened the cabinet doors in the upper half of the armoire she discovered a large television set that could be pulled out on its tracked base and swiveled for viewing anywhere in the room.

In the hallway that led to the door was a large closet with double doors. Next to that was an alcove with a dressing table and lighted mirrors. The next door led into a huge bathroom equipped with a steam shower and two sinks set into a long tiled counter with a wall-to-wall mirror above it.

Cyn deposited her bag in one of the built-in drawers in the closet, took her key with her and went down to collect the rest of the paper bags from the Jeep. After hauling these up to the room, she quickly unpacked and put everything away.

She glanced at her watch. It was 5:30. Time for a quick shower and a change of clothes. Thirty minutes later she emerged from the bathroom dressed in a new pair of jeans, a blue and green plaid western shirt, and her new chamois-colored cowboy boots. She collected her bag from the closet and pulled out the cell phone Charlie Denton had given her and pressed #SS to turn on the jamming device.

Then she pulled out her own cell phone, turned it on, and pressed two keys. After a bit, she said, "Barbara Jones reporting in. Everything is according to plan. I'm in Room 405 at the Rancho Bonito Inn in Roca Grande."

She listened for a moment and then said, "That's correct. I'm interviewing one tonight. I'll be back at the Mountain early tomorrow."

After another moment, she said, "Yes. I'll report back tomorrow around Midnight after I've made contact with the team."

After another pause, Cyn smiled. "Yes, I'll be sure to do that."

She clicked off the cell phone and put it back in her bag. She turned on the television and surfed to the CNN Headline News channel. Taking the TV remote with her, she sank down on the couch to wait for her visitor.

* * *

6:50 p.m.

Somewhere up in the San Juan Mountains of Colorado, a man sitting in front of a monitoring device yanked off his headphones in disgust. "Nada!" he said to someone standing nearby. "All I've got is garbage. She's got a jammer."

"That's not really a big surprise, is it? You might as well shut down that channel for tonight. She's not gonna make that kind of mistake."

"Yeah, I guess you're right. You'll have to get the info from her in another way."

"That's exactly what I plan to do. Shut down now and we'll go get some chow."

The man nodded. He turned a dial on the electronic scanner, rose from his chair and pulled a lever leaving them in total darkness.

* * *

7 p.m.

At exactly seven o'clock there was a discreet tap on the door. Cyn got up from the couch and walked quietly to the door. "Yes?" she asked.

"It's me," said the familiar voice in a low tone.

Cyn opened the door. Brent Jacobson stood there grinning at her with a large shopping bag under each arm. Cyn stood back to allow him to enter and then she closed the door and engaged the dead bolt.

When she turned back into the room, Jake had set the two bags down on the bar counter. "Nice digs," he commented. He pointed to his ear and raised his eyebrows.

Cyn nodded. "It's fine. We can talk in here. What's in the bags?"

Jake smiled. "Knowing you, I figured you'd be so busy taking care of business you'd forget about the essentials like food and wine. Am I right?" he asked, opening the small refrigerator and peering in.

Cyn laughed. "Yes, you're exactly right. I thought I'd go down to the coffee shop later."

"No need for that. We can talk better in here," said Jake as he pulled two bottles of wine from one of the bags. "You still like Aussie Sheraz?"

"Sure," said Cyn. "It's still my favorite, and I see you got Jacob's Creek, too. You remembered."

"I remember everything about you," said Jake as he opened a drawer and pulled out a corkscrew.

Cyn opened a cabinet above the bar and set two wineglasses on the counter. "And what's in the other bag? Something smells good," she said, sniffing the air.

"*Halcon's* famous blue corn Taos tacos, that's what," said Jake with a chuckle as he uncorked one of the bottles. "I'm sure you remember that."

"How could I forget! We only had them twice a week when we were at MIT," said Cyn.

"Yeah, in between Cyn's famous Cowpoke Briskets, as I recall."

Jake poured the deep burgundy-colored wine into the two glasses. He picked them up and held one up to the light admiring its color before handing it to Cyn.

Cyn smiled and touched her glass to his. "Here's to the hawk. Long may he soar," she said. They each took a sip of the wine and she looked at him in anticipation. "Well?" she said.

Jake looked puzzled. "Well, what?"

"Well, aren't you going to give me that traditional Taos Indian toast?"

He grinned. "Oh, that. OK. Here's mud in your eye!" He clinked his glass violently against hers and they both took another sip.

They stood there grinning at each other for a moment, remembering. Then Cyn suddenly looked down and turned away. Jake's smile faded. "What is it?"

Cyn shook her head, refused to look at him, refused to let him see the tears that had welled up in her eyes. "I was just remembering," she mumbled.

Instantly he was at her side, his arm around her, clasping her to his chest. "Don't, Cyn-Cyn," he whispered into her hair. "Don't remember the bad things. I was very stupid—off on a false vision quest. I know that now. I've known it for a long time—ever since I lost you. Can you forgive me? I miss you so much."

After a moment, Cyn took a deep breath and pushed him away. "I don't know, Jake. I can't think about it now. I have a job to do. Maybe we can talk about it when I'm finished."

Hearing no response, Cyn finally managed to look at Jake and saw that he looked crestfallen. She touched his arm. "I do miss you, too," she said softly.

Jake looked up and the light came back into his eyes. "As long as I know that, maybe there's hope," he said. "OK, Cyn. I won't talk about it again until you're ready, but once your job is over, don't think you're going to disappear from me again. My spirit will find you, you know."

"All right, Jake. I promise as soon as I am finished, we'll talk. That's all I can promise right now, OK?"

"All right. That's good enough for me." He raised his glass to her and then drained it.

"Now, Jake, I need to ask you some questions about the project at Apparition Mountain," said Cyn as Jake strode over to the bar to refill his glass.

"You mean what we insiders call *Project Cracking Heads?*" asked Jake, with a grin.

Cyn laughed. "Is that what you call it? I thought the code name was *Brainstorm.*"

"You're right," said Jake. "That's the official title. I'll tell you what I can, but I'm not at the top level, you understand. I'm just in charge of the technology." He opened the bag containing the food. "Let's eat while we talk," he said. "I'm starved."

"Me, too," said Cyn. "Let's eat over here in the sitting area. I'll turn the fireplace on."

While Cyn drew the drapes and turned on the gas logs in the fireplace, Jake found a couple of plates and some napkins in the bar cabinet. He filled the plates with the tacos and brought them over to the coffee table. Then he opened the second bottle of wine and brought it over. Cyn sat down on the couch, and Jake sat in the armchair at the head of the coffee table facing the fireplace. He picked up the bottle of wine and refilled Cyn's glass. She took a sip of wine and picked up one of the tacos.

"So what do you want to know?" asked Jake as he reached for a taco.

Cyn took a bite of the taco. "Mmmmm, good as always," she said. "You can start by telling me about Karl Braun. How did you get involved with him?"

"Three years ago NSA assigned me to work on *Project Nightingale* and Braun was the chief scientific advisor on that. He liked my work and so he put me in charge of the technology on this project," said Jake with a shrug of his shoulders.

"*Project Nightingale?* Wasn't that the NSA experiment with satellite tracking devices?" asked Cyn.

Jake nodded. "Yeah. We were working on that at the top-secret base down in Georgia. I was down there for a year. Then I had a break and went back to the rez for a little over six months. Put the old band together and made some CDs. We did a little touring—mostly Indian casinos."

Cyn grinned at him. "You're too modest. I saw the PBS show. It was fantastic."

Jake shook his head. "You know it is not the way of the Taos for one person to stand out over the others. I was becoming uncomfortable with the small amount of fame we were achieving, so I dropped out and concentrated on the horses for a while. Then I got the call that Braun wanted me to work with him on this project at Apparition Mountain. I've been here for fourteen months now."

"So tell me about Braun. What do you know about him?"

"Personally, I don't know much. He's very close-mouthed, mostly all business. He pretty much tells me what he wants and relies on me to come up with the technical solutions, which suits me just fine. I haven't had many social experiences with him, other than the fact that he likes to go gold prospecting in his free time, and I've led him on a couple of expeditions into the wilderness areas around here."

"What? Gold prospecting? He doesn't seem the type," said Cyn. "Where does he come from?"

Jake shrugged. "I don't have a clue. I've always assumed he came from the New England area because of his accent. He has a ranch just outside of Santa Fe now, but I think he just recently bought that— probably when he started work on this project at Apparition Mountain."

Cyn frowned. "The Senator said he was an MIT grad when he introduced us. I don't recall any mention of a Karl Braun at MIT, do you?"

"No, but then, he would have been before our time."

"It seemed odd to me that he didn't know about some of the basic stuff we learned—the Fibonacci sequence, for example. Makes me wonder if he really went to MIT," said Cyn.

Jake shrugged again. "I really don't know anything about his background, but you know some top scientists forget things that don't immediately have to do with what they're concentrating on. You know the zillions of stories about absent-minded professors. Besides, just because someone's a scientific advisor on the government's payroll doesn't necessarily mean he's knowledgeable. He relies on people like me to get the job done. If Braun takes the credit, it's all right by me. Maybe that's why he likes to work with me."

Cyn laughed. "Yeah, I know what you mean. So tell me about this project. You've tried the experiment before today?"

Jake nodded. "Today was the third time, and thanks to you, we were finally successful in being able to read the data."

"Who were the patients you used for the first two trials?

"I don't know. No names were given, but the rumor was they were quote, unquote *volunteers* from the Army military prison."

"What happened to them? Did they die during the experiment?"

"I'm not sure. There were a couple of incidents with the oxygen like today. As far as I was told, they were returned to the prison. In those two trials we didn't download as much as we did today. We were just trying to see if we could read the data before we used it to retrieve critical information. After the second one, we thought we had everything figured out, but as you know, we didn't."

"It seems that Braun prolonged the experiment too long, which may have caused Professor Latter's death," said Cyn.

Jake leaned forward. "I don't know about that, but I do know *why* he prolonged it."

"Why is that?" asked Cyn.

"Well, the scuttlebutt was that if today's experiment was not successful, the whole project would be shut down, even though we've already spent over a billion on it."

Cyn nodded. "Yes, that's true. That's why Senator Goodman was here today. He's the one who has to convince the Intelligence Appropriations Committee to fund the project. If he hadn't been convinced, there'd be no more money to continue."

Cyn took a sip of wine and thought for a moment. "So, what you're saying is that Braun ran the experiment as long as he possibly could to assure that we had enough of Harry Latter's memory to solve the problem with the E-Weapon?"

Jake affirmed with a nod of his head. "Yes, but I'm not so sure that's what caused Professor Latter's death."

"What do you mean?" asked Cyn.

Jake looked at her long and hard for a moment, then tilted his head back and closed his eyes. "I think Harry Latter's spirit chose to flee," he murmured.

* * *

FRIDAY

8 a.m.

A freezing wind was blowing when Cyn climbed out of the Grand Cherokee in the parking lot at Apparition Mountain the next morning. As she put her head down and raced for the entrance, she was grateful for the warm clothes she had bought at the Roca Grande Mercantile. She had no trouble gaining entrance, and she headed directly for General Masters's office.

The moment she entered the door to the General's suite, Charlie Denton jumped to his feet and stood beaming down at her from behind his desk.

"Hi, Charlie," said Cyn. "Is the General in?"

"Sure is, and waiting to see you," said Charlie. "How'd you get on last night? Everything OK?"

Cyn smiled. "Great, Charlie. The Inn is much more than I expected. Very comfortable."

"Well, I see you're dressed for the weather," he said, motioning toward her down-filled vest, flannel shirt, jeans and boots. "Damned cold wind blowin' out there. Did you find everything you need at the Mercantile?"

"Yes, thank you," said Cyn glancing at her watch. "I'd better check in with the General now. There's a lot to do."

"Sure thing," said Charlie. He came out from behind his desk, tapped on the General's door, and then opened it slightly. "Ms. Hoover is here, Sir," he said.

Cyn heard a muffled response from inside, and then Charlie opened the door wide and stood back to allow her to pass through. "You be sure to let me know if there's anything you need. Anything at all," he said as she walked past him.

"Thanks, Charlie. I will," said Cyn as she entered the room. Then she turned and closed the door.

"Good morning, Ms. Hoover." The General's voice was cheerful as he slammed down his phone. He rose to his feet from behind his desk and came forward to greet her.

"Good morning, General Masters." Cyn clasped his outstretched hand.

He motioned to some chairs grouped around a coffee table. "Help yourself. There's' coffee and donuts and some fruit."

As Cyn poured herself a cup of coffee, the General sat down in one of the chairs. "Now, then, you got anything you want to tell me before I get Braun in here?" he asked.

Cyn sat down with her cup of coffee and smiled at him. "Not yet, Jeff. All the accommodations are fine and everything is going to plan so far. Maybe I'll have something later today."

"Good. Just let me know if you need any help. Now, I'll get Braun in here so we can get on with the project." He plucked his cell phone out of his pocket and started to punch in a number.

"Oh, that reminds me. There is one thing," said Cyn raising her hand.

"Yes?" asked the General with his finger poised above the button.

"Somebody told me that Professor Braun likes to do some prospecting in his spare time. Think you could get me together with him for that? It would give me a chance to be alone with him on a more social level."

The General raised an eyebrow. "You're right. He does like to go prospecting every chance he gets. Let me think about it. Maybe there'll be an opportunity this weekend for me to suggest it. Have to make sure it doesn't appear contrived."

"Sure," said Cyn. "I'll leave it up to you."

The General nodded and pressed two buttons on the cell phone.

A few moments later there was a tap on the door and Charlie Denton stuck his head in. "Professor Braun's here, Sir."

"Come on in, Karl," said the General without bothering to get up from his chair.

Karl Braun strode briskly into the room looking exactly as he had looked the day before. He was dressed in a white lab coat and carried a clipboard. He walked over, sat down in one of the chairs and placed the clipboard on the coffee table. He nodded expressionlessly at Cyn. "Ms. Hoover," he said in his icy voice.

"Professor Braun," said Cyn in a tone that she hoped matched his.

The General glanced from one to the other and then slapped his knee. "All right, now that we're all here, let's get on with the task at hand," he said. "Karl, let's have your assessment of where we're at."

Braun leaned back in his chair, placed his elbows on the arm rests and steepled his fingers together in front of his chin. "I deem yesterday's experiment a great success. We've now demonstrated that it's possible to download both short- and long-term memories and play them back in visual form. The only thing we were not able to do because of having to shut down was to scan the full magnetic spectrum to determine if any of the brain's data is stored in other than the visual spectrum."

"You mean audio as well as visual?" asked the General.

Braun nodded. "Yes, it appears we can only see and hear what the patient saw and heard—not what he said or thought. Still, there's enough to find out what we need to know. It will just take longer to find it. However, I'm confident that with the next downloading, we'll be able to work that out, now that we have the key to reading the data."

"Thanks to Ms. Hoover, here," interjected the General.

Braun scowled slightly. "Yes. Thanks to Ms. Hoover," he said without looking at Cyn.

Cyn shrugged. "It was just a matter of having some technical knowhow and working it out with your guy Jake. He probably would have come up with it himself given a little more time."

Braun looked at her for the first time. There was just the slightest hint of a smile at the corners of his mouth. "Yes, you're right, Ms. Hoover. I have every confidence in Jake."

"So, what's next?" asked the General. "Are we able to proceed as planned?"

"Definitely," said Braun. "We can proceed with the next experiment just as soon as the chamber is repaired. In the meantime, Ms. Hoover, here, and Jake can continue to examine Professor Latter's memory to find the answer to what went wrong with the E5 test."

"What happened to the chamber?" asked Cyn.

"Remember, I told you when I shut the experiment down that they couldn't get the door open and had to cut through the walls. Now we have to restore the magnetic shielding and rebuild the door, and this time, they'll correct the problem we had with the door," said Braun.

"How long is that gonna take?" asked the General.

"I'm not sure," said Braun shaking his head. "They've been working on it all night. They should have it ready by this afternoon, I would think."

"All right. Let's you and me go see if we can speed things up. It's critical that we extract information from the next candidate as soon as possible. Ms. Hoover, you and Jake can proceed with researching Professor Latter's memory, and we'll check in with you in an hour or so. Meanwhile, you know how to reach me if you find anything?"

Cyn nodded. "Yes, General Masters. I have your cell phone paging number," she said as she picked up her bag.

"You remember how to get to Jake's office?" asked Braun.

"Yes," said Cyn. "No problem. I assume he's there?"

Braun nodded. "Yes, he's been there since six this morning, and we've already had our briefing."

Cyn smiled to herself remembering Jake's habit of rising early. She nodded absent-mindedly at Charlie, who beamed at her again as she walked past him on the way to the door.

* * *

9 a.m.

Cyn had just reached up to knock on the door to Jake's office when it flew open. Jake reached out and grabbed her arm. "I've been waiting for you, Ms. Hoover," he said. "I have something to show you."

He pulled her into the room and closed the door.

"And good morning to you, too," said Cyn with a wry smile.

Jake grinned at her. "Good morning, Cyn. Did you have a good night?"

"Yes, very good. I had a soak in the Jacuzzi before going to bed, and I slept like a baby."

"The Jacuzzi. Hmmmm, wish I could have been there with you. Remember how we used to...."

Cyn raised a hand. "Jake, you promised, remember? After this is over, we'll talk about it. I have to concentrate on other things right now."

Jake hung his head. "You're right. I slipped up. Forgive me?"

Cyn grinned at him. "You're forgiven, *Halcon*. Now, what was it you wanted to show me?"

Jake looked up with excitement printed in his eyes. "You won't believe this. I brought up the data from where we left off yesterday— you know, where there was an overhead view of Harry's body and then the flash?"

Cyn nodded.

"Well, I took a look at the signal that we converted into that picture, and it turns out it's in the high-energy particle range way beyond the Gamma band," said Jake.

Cyn"s eyes grew wide. "You must be mistaken, Jake. It wouldn't be possible for our sensors to pick that up. It would be like hearing a human heart beat from a million miles away."

"I know, but that's what the computer says. Come over here. I'll show you."

Cyn followed Jake over to the computer and sat down in the chair next to him.

He pulled up a data screen and then pressed the F1 function key. A chart of the Electromagnetic Spectrum appeared, and in the area beyond the Gamma band a small red dot blinked.

Cyn gasped. "I don't believe it! That wavelength is the size of a molecule with an energy level to match. Do you have any idea how our sensors are able to pick it up?"

"I haven't the foggiest," said Jake. "Let's go back to the visual interpretation and see if that tells us anything."

Cyn watched as Jake typed on the keyboard. The clock came up in the corner of the screen and sped backwards until it reached 1330 hours of the day before. Jake pressed another function key and the image came up of Harry Latter lying on the table. Again the image hovered and then scanned back and forth from ceiling height above the table. At 1331 hours there was a brilliant flash and the screen went blank just as before.

Jake leaned back, crossed his arms and stared at the blank screen. "I have no idea how the sensors could pick up that kind of signal," he said.

"Look, Jake!" cried Cyn suddenly. "The clock is still moving forward just like it was yesterday!"

"Yeah, I see that," said Jake frowning at the screen.

"Can you run a search forward to see if any more data came in after we quit yesterday?" asked Cyn.

Jake"s fingers were already poised over the keyboard. "Sure. I'll do an auto scan up until the current time. It shouldn't take long."

He pressed some keys and the clock gathered speed until the numerals became a blur. In a short time the clock stopped at 1914 hours and 16 seconds. Jake glanced at his wristwatch. "Dead on," he said. "Now, I'll pull up the data file to see if there's anything in it."

Cyn watched the screen intently as Jake tapped on the keyboard. A graphic came up. There were several vertical bars in different colors. At the far right was a purple bar that was half the height of the others. As they watched, the bar continued to grow in height.

Cyn and Jake looked at each other.

"You know what that means?" asked Jake after a second.

Cyn nodded. She could barely speak. "It means the data stream has been continuous since 1330 hours yesterday afternoon, and…it's still…coming in."

"That's what it means, all right," said Jake as he continued to stare at the purple bar that was now at three-quarters of the height of the others.

"I just don't understand how that could be," murmured Cyn. "Harry Latter has been dead for over eighteen hours."

"Let's go back to 1335 hours yesterday and see if we can pull up any visuals," said Jake. He began to tap keys on the keyboard again, and the clock zoomed backward to the appointed time. He pressed a function key and sat back in his chair.

At first the screen was dark. Then there was a flicker and suddenly they were viewing Harry's body again from above.

"Oh, my God!" exclaimed Cyn. "What happened to Harry's body? It looks like a mummy!"

"You're right. It's totally dehydrated, just like those mummies they took out of the Egyptian pyramids! But look at the helmet. It's still intact," said Jake. He froze the clock and zoomed in on the body.

"It's nothing but bones covered with a thin layer of leathery skin," said Cyn peering at the image on the screen. "Whatever would cause that to happen?"

"I don't have a clue," said Jake, shaking his head. "I'll start the clock again and see if there's anything that will tell us what happened."

As the clock clicked ahead in real time, they continued to view the mummified body from above for another minute or so. Then there was another flash of light and they saw a hole open up in the wall where the door was. A technician rushed into the room and stopped short when he saw Harry's body. He rushed out again and within seconds Dr. Graham entered the chamber with General Masters and Professor Braun close on his heels. As they gathered around the table looking down at Harry's body, suddenly the view began to shift. They seemed to be zooming upward and soon they were looking down on the mountaintop and the surrounding terrain. The image hovered in this position for an instant, and then it was moving upward again at great speed, with the mountain rapidly becoming smaller and smaller until the curvature of the earth came into view.

Cyn and Jake both jumped when the door opened and Karl Braun entered the room. "Just checking to see if you've found anything about the E-Weapon yet," he said as he came toward them.

"Not yet, I'm afraid," said Jake. He tapped a key and the computer screen went blank before he swiveled around in his seat to face Braun.

"We're trying to come up with a way to zero in on the information we want without having to go through days, months and even years of Professor Latter's memory in real time," said Cyn, trying to distract Braun's attention away from the computer screen.

"Yes, I see what you mean," said Braun. "It appears to me that the best place to start would be with the day of the fire and work backwards. It's critical that we retrieve the information as quickly as possible."

"Yes, Sir, I understand," said Jake. "We're trying everything we can think of."

"Good," said Braun with a nod. "Perhaps Ms. Hoover can continue on her own later this afternoon because I'm going to have to pull you away for the next download. The chamber has been repaired, and we're ready to proceed with the next candidate."

"But we sent all the technicians home for the weekend," said Jake, surprised.

"Yes, I'm aware of that," said Braun. "Only the General and I have clearance to see what's in this candidate's memory. You can proceed with the technical aspects of the download, and after we have enough, you can return to retrieval of the E5 information. The General and I will review the other candidate's memory, now that we know how to read the data. You can handle the download by yourself, can't you?"

Jake nodded. "Yes, Sir, I believe I can. If I run into a snag, do I have permission to confer with Ms. Hoover?"

Braun frowned and glanced at Cyn. "Yes, I suppose that will be all right, but I'll have to clear it with General Masters because she reports directly to him."

"I'm sure it will be all right with General Masters," said Cyn. "I'll call him right now and ask if you want."

"Yes, why don't you do that," said Braun.

Cyn pulled out her cell phone and pressed a couple of keys. "General Masters, it's Ms. Hoover," she said after a pause. "I'm with Professor Braun and Brent Jacobson. We're wondering if you will approve me as technical backup for Jake on this afternoon's download."

After a bit, she smiled and said, "Yes, I'll do that. Thank you, General."

She clicked off the phone and looked up at Braun. "The General says it's fine as long as Jake and I continue working on the E-Weapon retrieval. What time do you anticipate starting with the next download?"

Braun glanced at his clipboard. "I've instructed Dr. Graham to have the candidate prepared for two o'clock. We should be able to finish the download by four."

"Good," said Cyn. "That gives us almost four hours to continue our search of Professor Latter's memory."

"All right. I'll leave you to it then. I have a number of things to do now in preparation for this afternoon's procedure. Call if you find anything, Jake. Otherwise, I'll see you in the Control Room at 1:30."

"Yes, Sir," said Jake. He remained silent until Braun closed the door behind him.

"Whew! That was close," he said in a low voice. "Maybe I should have told him what we saw."

"No, I wouldn't say anything about that right now," said Cyn. "It doesn't have anything to do with the E5, and he'd probably think we were shirking our duties and poking our noses into matters that don't concern us."

"Yeah, you're probably right," said Jake. "We'd better get on with the search, but I'd sure like to see more of that incoming data and the view we'd end up with."

"You mean the satellite view?" asked Cyn.

Jake looked at her with a strange expression. "You can call it a satellite view if you want, but I know where it was coming from."

"And where was it coming from, Jake?" asked Cyn softly.

"From Harry Latter's spirit, of course," said Jake. "I've seen the same view many times when I transported my spirit into the soaring hawk, although not from so high up."

"And what do you think caused Harry's body to be in that shape?"

Jake shook his head sadly. "I think his spirit became distraught and had to escape. It must have felt like a trapped bird desperately beating its wings against the walls, looking for a way out. I think what we did violated Harry's spirit, and that, my dear, is a sin worse than murder."

* * *

10 a.m.

Cyn found Dr. Graham in his office scowling at a medical chart on his computer screen. He glanced up in irritation when he heard the tap on his door. "Yes?" he growled.

"It"s me, Dan," said Cyn as she poked her head in the door.

Immediately his face softened, and he turned around to face her. "Cyn, come on in," he said.

Cyn quickly entered and closed the door behind her. "Are you alone?" she asked in a low voice, glancing around.

Dr. Graham sat back in his chair and took off his reading glasses. "Oh, yes," he said with a modicum of disgust in the tone of his voice. "Betsy has the day off—orders from the General."

"Good," said Cyn as she drew a chair up in front of his desk. "I need to ask you a few things, and I only have a short time. I'm working with Brent Jacobson on reading Professor Latter's memory. We're taking a short break, and I have to get back."

"Ah, yes, Jake. He's a good man," said Dr. Graham. "We get together occasionally to explore the country around here. He knows it like the back of his hand. Amazing, the things he knows about survival and medicinal plants and animals. It"s inherent, I suppose. You know he's a Taos Indian?"

Cyn nodded. "Yes, I read his file. Pretty impressive."

"I like to go hunting occasionally, and he knows where to find the mountain goats and the *jabalino*—the wild boar." Dr. Graham began to polish his reading glasses with a faraway look in his eyes. "But that's not what you came to ask me about, is it?"

"No," said Cyn. "First, I wanted to ask you what happened to cause Professor Latter's death."

Dr. Graham's face became rigid and totally expressionless. "He died of heart failure, just like many Alzheimer's patients before him. That's the official report."

"Come on, Dan. What really happened? I'm sure you examined the body after they got into the chamber."

Dr. Graham stared at her for a moment. Then his face crumbled and tears came into his eyes. He wiped his forehead with the cloth he'd used to clean his glasses. "Oh, Cyn, it was the most horrible thing I've ever seen. Professor Latter's body was completely dehydrated as if he'd been mummified and dead for a thousand years."

"What!" cried Cyn feigning surprise. "What on earth would cause that?"

"I don't really know," said Dr. Graham. "There will not be an autopsy, not that there was much left to do an autopsy on."

"Surely you must have an idea about what happened, Dan," prodded Cyn in a soft voice.

Dr. Graham wiped his forehead again and stared at her. "I don't know, Cyn. I'm not sure we should be playing with the human mind in this way. I had a premonition about Harry's death when we put him in the chamber."

"But, Dan, you know what we're doing has the potential to save millions of lives in the long run," said Cyn. "You didn't have any trouble with what we were doing when we were on the interrogation team."

"I know, but dealing with terrorists is a far different cry than dealing with someone like Professor Latter. Oh, I know the reasoning—that he would have consented to the procedure if he had been able, and that the information he had locked inside was a matter of national security, but still I can't help thinking we're taking the Patriot Act too far…."

Cyn looked at him with a stern expression. "Come on, Dan. After all these years with the NSA? You know how the Patriot Act has helped us prevent terrorist attacks in this country. Perhaps you need some R and R. I can recommend it if you want."

"Maybe you're right. I'll see how I feel after this project is over."

"Good. You do that. I know how people get stressed out in our line of work," said Cyn in a more compassionate tone. "Now, what about our friend in the other room? Is he ready for the download this afternoon?"

Dr. Graham's face suddenly hardened. "Oh, yes. He's been doped up ever since we flew him in from Guantanamo. I'll give him the sedative at 1:30—enough to last until 4:30, which should be ample time for him to finally spill his guts, as it were."

Cyn nodded. "Yeah, he's a hard case—Tarique abu Jazar—if that's his real name. They haven't been able to crack him at Gitmo for the last two years, but now Mr. Jazar will have no choice. We'll soon know who's running the terrorist network here in the U.S."

Dr. Graham gave her an odd look. "Provided he doesn't die like Harry before we have enough of his memory downloaded," he said.

* * *

10:15 a.m.

Cyn and Jake were back at the computer in Jake's office after their break.

"Where do you want to start?" asked Jake.

"I've been trying to think how to speed things up," said Cyn. "Why don't we try putting in a keyword and doing a search of Harry's memory that way?"

"Good idea. What keyword do you want to use?"

"Try 'E-Weapon' and see what we get," said Cyn.

Jake typed in the word "E-Weapon" and clicked on "Search" with his mouse. An hourglass icon appeared on the screen indicating that the computer was searching. In a few seconds, a long list of E-Weapon references popped up.

"Damn! There are 62,052 references to E-Weapon in Harry's memory," said Jake. "Where do you want to start?"

"Let's start with the first one and see what we get," said Cyn, pointing at the first underlined "E-Weapon" reference.

Jake clicked on the word and an image came up. The clock on the screen read 15 April, 1972, 1300 hours. They were looking at shelves of vitamins. A hand reached out and picked up a bottle from the shelf.

"Oh, no! Look at that!" said Cyn with a laugh. "It's a bottle of Vitamin E— Brand name E-Weapon!"

Jake laughed. "Yeah, and he's going to buy it. That bottle contains a hundred capsules, which means every time he takes one there'll be a reference to 'E-Weapon' in his memory."

"Well, we don't have time to look at every one of these references," said Cyn. "I know. Go down about a thousand and look at that."

Jake nodded and scanned down the page. Then he clicked on another reference and brought up a new image. The clock read 15 October 1975, 1114 hours. The view was of a lecture hall with about fifty students sitting in armchair desks facing them. They could see Harry's hands resting on each side of a podium directly in front of them. As they watched, a skinny young man with shoulder length black hair and a raggedy beard raised his hand and stood up in the front row.

"Karl Braun, third year student, Professor Latter. The sequence is named after the man who first discovered it—Fibonacci. The sequence is achieved by adding the last number to the next: one plus one is two; two plus one is three; three plus two is five; five plus three is eight, and so forth."

Cyn and Jake looked at each other in surprise.

"Professor Braun?" asked Cyn.

"It must be," said Jake. "You'd never recognize him with all that long black hair, but I do recognize that lecture hall, don't you?"

Cyn nodded. "How could I forget? I spent many hours in that room at MIT!"

"I don't remember Harry Latter being a professor there, do you?" asked Jake.

"No, but then 1975 was way before our time. Look!" she exclaimed as they saw the view shift again.

Now they saw Harry's hand flip a page of newsprint over on an easel and point to some numbers that had been written in bold black marker.

"Looks like Professor Latter is lecturing on the Fibonacci Sequence and the Elliot Wave theory," said Jake, reading the writing on the newsprint.

As they watched, Harry flipped that page over and began to write a list of items under the heading "E.W."

"Aha!" said Jake. "I was wondering what any of this had to do with our keyword 'E-Weapon.' The search engine brought up 'E.W.' as well, even though, in this instant, it refers to 'Elliot Wave'."

"Yes, you're right," said Cyn. "It was fortunate that we did stumble over this reference, though, because of seeing Professor Braun. I find it rather odd that apparently he studied the Fibonnaci Sequence, but yesterday he seemed not to know anything about it. Can you figure that out?"

Jake shrugged his shoulders. "Must have just been placed on the back burner in his memory. I studied a lot of stuff at MIT that I've never used, and I'd probably not remember some of it either."

They continued to watch Harry's hand writing the list of items. When he wrote the fifth item, Cyn chuckled. "Predictability slot machines?" she read out loud.

"Wow!" said Jake. "Do you suppose he had a theory about how to beat slot machines?"

"Let's find out," said Cyn. "Go to keyword 'slot machines' and let's see what comes up."

Jake did the search and frowned when the results came up on the screen. "There are over 28,000 references to 'slot machine'."

"How can we narrow it down?" Cyn asked. "I know! Try keyword 'Jackpot' and see what happens."

Again, Jake did the search and a new set of results came up. "Well, that narrowed it down some. There are only 1,561 references this time."

"We don't have a lot of time to mess with this," said Cyn. "Just click on the first one and see what happens."

Jake did as she asked and an image came up. This time they were staring at the screen of a slot machine. Four red sevens were lined up across the centerline and a bell was ringing. The view shifted upwards to the payout chart above the slot machine's window. Four red sevens were labeled "Jackpot."

"Wow! Look at that! Harry just won $5,000!" exclaimed Cyn.

Jake glanced at the clock on the monitor. "Look. This is only one day after he was giving the lecture."

"Let's go to the next 'jackpot' reference," said Cyn, leaning forward in her chair.

Jake clicked the mouse and a new image came up. Now they were looking at a slot machine that again had four red sevens on the centerline.

"He's won $5,000 again!" exclaimed Jake.

"Yeah, and look at the clock. It's just a half hour later than the first one we saw," said Cyn. "Quick! Go on to the next reference."

"I don't believe this," groaned Jake when the next image appeared.

Again they were staring at a slot machine with four red sevens lined up on the centerline.

Cyn gasped. "Oh, my God! He's won it again! Another five thou!"

"Yeah, and this is only a half hour later again," said Jake pointing at the clock.

"I wonder where he's playing," said Cyn.

"Let's just hope he's in Atlantic City, not some poor Indian casino," said Jake with a grin.

"Well, you can rest easy. They didn't have Indian casinos back in 1975," said Cyn.

As they continued to watch, the view suddenly shifted as Harry backed away and swiveled to the right. Now they were looking at a cluttered desktop.

Jake burst out laughing. "He's not in a casino at all. He's in his office. He was playing his own slot machine!"

"I see that now," said Cyn. "He must have been testing out his theory on a slot machine that he bought for himself. I wonder if he ever actually used his formula in a real casino."

"What's he doing now?" asked Jake.

A hand had reached out and pulled a paper from a muddled stack on the desk. As it came closer, they saw that it was a newsletter from MIT. They were now focusing on a column with the heading "Honor Students 1975." As they scanned down through the column through Harry's eyes, they stopped at a subhead that read "Molecular Physics and Advanced Mathematics." The name of the top honor student under that heading was a familiar one: Karl G. Braun.

"Well, well, there's our Professor again," said Cyn.

"Yeah, top honors in Molecular Physics and Advanced Math. That's impressive," said Jake as he watched Harry's hand pick up a pen and underscore Karl Braun's name.

Cyn's cell phone rang and she quickly grabbed it and pressed the "receive" key. "This is Ms. Hoover," she said.

"Ms. Hoover, this is Captain Denton."

His voice was loud enough that Jake could hear. Cyn quickly put the phone closer to her ear and walked across the room. Jake looked at her curiously.

"Yes?" she responded in a hushed voice.

"I'm calling to let you know that the weather has changed for the worst. We've got heavy snow falling, and the National Weather Service has issued a warning for up to eighteen inches and blizzard conditions."

"Thanks for telling me," said Cyn. "I'm probably going to be staying here at the Mountain all night anyway."

"Well, if you would like me to drive you back to Roca Grande, I'd be pleased to do it. The roads will be treacherous."

"I'll keep it in mind, Captain, but I have lots of experience driving in snow storms. Thanks for the offer though."

"If you change your mind, or need any help, be sure to let me know." Charlie sounded disappointed.

"I will," said Cyn. "Thanks again for letting me know."

She quickly clicked off the phone and returned to her seat beside Jake.

Jake looked at her with a slight grin. "Charlie Denton, eh? It didn't take him long to zero in. You'd better watch him. He has a reputation of chasing every new woman who comes around."

Cyn slapped him on the shoulder. "Oh, it's nothing like that. General Masters had him make arrangements for me at the Inn is all. He was just calling to let me know we've got a blizzard outside and offered to drive me back to Roca Grande."

"Yeah, I'm sure he love to drive you back and just maybe get stranded in a snow drift for the night," said Jake.

Cyn frowned at him. "Well, he's not driving me anywhere. End of conversation."

She glanced at her watch. "We'd better get back to our E-Weapon search. Maybe after we've found what we're looking for, we'll have a chance to explore Harry's jackpots again and see if he ever put his theory to use in a real casino."

Jake went back to the E-Weapon search results. "Which one do you want to try next?" he asked.

Cyn thought for a moment. "Those references are date-marked, aren't they?"

Jake nodded.

"OK, let's go to the first reference in 1989—that would be seven years before the test."

Jake scanned down through the list and found the first reference in 1989. He clicked on it, and they sat back to watch as the clock spun to the appointed time. It stopped at 10 September 1989, 1340 hours.

The image formed, and they were looking at a hand holding a piece of chalk and writing on a blackboard. Scrawled across the top of the blackboard were the words "E5-Weapon."

"Now we're getting somewhere," murmured Cyn, as she watched the blackboard being filled up with calculus equations.

The hand stopped writing and underlined one of the equations.

"I don't recognize any of those," said Jake, squinting at the screen.

"I think they have to do with frequency modulation," said Cyn. "Maybe we've struck on Harry's concept meeting where he's explaining his theories."

As she spoke, Harry turned around and now they were looking at ten people sitting at a conference table. Two men were dressed in military uniform, while the rest wore civilian clothes. They were all sitting rigidly, staring forward in rapt concentration, apparently listening to what Harry was saying.

After a bit a man in a general's uniform put his hand in the air. "Do I understand you correctly, Professor Latter? You're saying that it is possible to select only one magnetic frequency at a time and cancel it out?"

After a moment as everyone at the table appeared to be listening to the answer, they turned to each other excitedly, and there was the sound of murmuring. The other man in military garb spoke up. "If your theory is correct, it will forever change the way we fight wars."

The view shifted back to the blackboard as Harry turned around. He erased the board in large sweeps, and then they saw his hand holding the chalk again. He drew a vertical line and bisected it with a horizontal line. He wrote the word "energy" against the vertical line and the word "wavelength" against the horizontal line.

"Looks like we're in for a lesson," said Jake.

"Shhhh," said Cyn, putting up a hand as she concentrated on what Harry was writing. He was now making lists of devices that ran off the different bands of the electromagnetic spectrum. Starting at the low end of the chart, he wrote "line telephones," then "submarines," then "AM radio," "short wave radio," "microwave," "radar," and "night vision devices." When he had finished this list, he rapidly drew crosshatch marks through all of them. The view shifted back to his audience.

The general jumped to his feet and began to applaud, and the rest quickly followed suit, clapping and cheering.

"I gather they liked what he had to say," said Jake with a grin.

"Hold on, Jake," said Cyn, pointing at the screen. The cheering had stopped and a short bald man in a pinstripe suit was speaking.

"On behalf of the committee, I can assure you that you have convinced us that the possibilities for the E5 are endless. You can be assured that we will recommend that the necessary funding be made available as soon as possible."

"Who's that?" asked Jake.

"That's Senator Bolton. He was chair of the Intelligence Appropriations Committee before Senator Goodman," said Cyn.

"Well, at least we're on the right track now," said Jake. "What do you think? Should we go on to the next E-Weapon reference?"

"Before we do that, turn the clock back to where we saw Harry's equations on the blackboard. Can you zoom in on that and print it out? Maybe those equations will tell us something, and we'll have something to show to the General and Professor Braun. Print out three copies."

"Sure thing," said Jake.

While Jake was printing out the information, Cyn got up and paced slowly around the room, stretching her back and thinking about what she had seen.

"Done," said Jake as he began to collect the papers from the printer. Suddenly, there was a strange sound and the computer monitor went blank. "What the hell?" murmured Jake. He pressed the power button on the monitor. Nothing happened.

"What is it, Jake?" asked Cyn coming back to look over his shoulder.

"I'm not sure. Might just be the monitor. The computer hasn't shut down. Here, let me try something," he said.

Cyn watched as Jake unhooked the monitor and plugged it into another computer on the other side of the room. He booted up that computer and waited for something to come on the screen. After a bit, the menu came up on a bright blue background. He shook his head. "Well, it's not the monitor. That leaves only one explanation—the video board in the mainframe has blown."

"What happens now?" asked Cyn.

"Nothing is what happens now," said Jake in a disgusted tone. "We don't have a backup. I tried to get Professor Braun to let me order one, but he said it was too expensive. Now, the only thing I can do is contact IBM and have them air freight us a new one. The earliest they can get it here, I'm afraid, is probably Monday morning. The Professor's not gonna be happy because we won't be able to do the other download this afternoon, but it's his own fault really for not letting me order a standby in the first place."

"I'm sorry, Jake. At least we were able to get those equations printed out, and that should give Professor Braun something to mull over while we're waiting. I'd better call the General and let him know. Do you want to call Professor Braun?"

Jake grimaced. "He's not going to be a happy camper."

* * *

2:30 p.m.

When Cyn pulled into the parking lot of the Rancho Bonito Inn in the driving snow, there were no spaces available. The front lot was filled with pickups, SUVs and a couple of motor homes and semis that took up several spaces.

She drove around to the back door closely followed by Charlie Denton, who had insisted on escorting her back from Apparition Mountain. It had taken over an hour to get to Roca Grande. They had crept along behind a snowplow clearing the road ahead of them, and they could barely see its flashing yellow lights in the swirling whiteout.

Cyn breathed a sigh of relief when she rounded the corner of the Inn and saw that her parking place beside the back door was empty. In fact, there were no other vehicles parked behind the Inn except for a huge bus parallel parked against the adobe wall across from the back door. Cyn smiled to herself when she saw the lettering on the bus printed over an image of a huge guitar: *Mac Gentry and Riders of the Purple Sage*.

She pulled into the parking space, put on the hand brake and cut the engine. Charlie Denton pulled up beside her, and before she could get out of the Jeep, he had jumped out of his Land Rover and was at her door. He opened the door for her. "Can I help you carry anything up to your room?" he asked.

Cyn smiled at him. "No thanks, Charlie. I just have my bag. Thanks for following me in."

"Do you need anything from the store? I could go get it and bring it back to you—beer, wine, sandwiches, anything?" he asked somewhat wistfully.

"No. No thanks," said Cyn firmly. "I have everything I need. I have some work to do. I'll be fine."

"Well, all right," said Charlie reluctantly as he stepped back to let her get out of the Jeep. "Remember, if you need anything or just want some company, be sure to call me."

"OK, Charlie, I will," said Cyn impatiently. "Hadn't you better be getting back to the Mountain now?"

"Yeah, I guess so. I'm not looking forward to spending the night there, but orders are orders. I'd like to come in and see that band tonight. I hear they're pretty good." He motioned toward the bus as Cyn climbed out of the Jeep.

"Well, you'll have company at the Mountain—General Masters, Professor Braun, Brent Jacobson and Dr. Graham. Pretty good company, I'd say."

"Yes, and I'm sure they'll keep me hopping. At least it's only for tonight. That band's gonna be here tomorrow night, too. Maybe you'd like to see them with me?" he asked, his eyes lighting up.

"I can't promise anything right now. I've got a lot to do. We'll have to see what tomorrow brings," said Cyn. "I really have to go now. Thanks again for everything."

"OK! We'll see what tomorrow brings—hopefully a little R and R," said Charlie. He touched his hat and turned to get back in his Land Rover.

Cyn sighed as she placed her card key in the slot in the back door. "He's becoming a real pest," she muttered through gritted teeth.

Charlie honked his horn in three rapid successions as he pulled out causing her to jump. She turned around angrily, but couldn't help smiling. He was waving at her as he drove away. She waved back and quickly went inside.

Her room was a welcome haven after the icy blizzard outside. She deposited her bag on the bar counter, went over to the sitting area and lit the gas logs in the fireplace. She sank down on the couch and stared at the fireplace for a few moments. Then she went to the bar and retrieved the

XJ14 cell phone from her purse, laid it on the counter and turned on the jamming device. She waited.

Before long there was a discreet tap at her door and a rustling sound. A white sealed envelope appeared on the floor. She waited for a second. Then she walked softly over and looked through the peephole and pressed her ear to the door before bending down to pick up the envelope. She took the envelope over to the fireplace, sat down on the sofa and opened it. Inside was a brief note written in the scrawled handwriting that she knew so well. "Downstairs in the bar at 1530 hours," was all it said.

Cyn smiled, shredded the note and the envelope into tiny bits and set them alight in a large glass ashtray on the coffee table. When they were reduced to ashes, she carefully washed the ashtray in the bar sink, making sure all the ashes had washed down the drain.

* * *

3:30 p.m.

At precisely 3:30 Cyn walked into the Adobe Walls Lounge on the lobby level of the Rancho Bonito Inn. It was very dim and cozy with a large horseshoe shaped bar along one wall. Cocktail tables were scattered around the rim of a large circular dance floor. Two men and a woman were on the stage in front of the dance floor. They were all dressed identically in black Levi's and black T-shirts with Riders of the Purple Sage silk-screened in purple on the front. The men were setting up amps and microphones while the woman went from microphone to microphone testing each one.

To the left of all this was a huge open pit fireplace with small sofas and armchairs grouped around cocktail tables. Flames from small oil lanterns flickered on each table.

Other than the group on the stage, the lounge appeared deserted except for two men sitting at the bar. They wore tractor hats, heavy vests and flannel shirts, and Cyn guessed they were probably truck drivers who belonged to the semis parked outside. They were drinking beer and appeared to be in deep conversation. A woman dressed in a red satin cowboy shirt was wiping the counter behind the bar.

As Cyn's eyes became accustomed to the dim lighting, she looked over at the fireplace area, and there, in a seat tucked back in a dark corner, sat a large man with a ten-gallon hat perched on flaming red hair that curled nearly to his shoulders. He had a thick red mustache and beard, and he was grinning right at her, the light glinting off a gold tooth. Cyn grinned and walked over. "Hello, Mac," she said.

"Well, if it ain't my little cousin Barb," he said in his Texas drawl. "Park yourself, and I'll get you a drink. Name your poison."

"An Irish coffee if they have it. It's a miserable cold day out there," said Cyn as she sat down in a comfortable armchair across the table from him.

"That it is. Colder than a well-digger's ass."

He raised a hand in the air and bellowed at the woman behind the bar. "Hey, Lorraine, bring us one of them Irish coffees and another Velvet and soda for me, would yuh, Hon?"

"Comin' right up," the woman yelled back.

"So, Mac, when did you get in?" asked Cyn. "I saw the bus parked out back."

"Oh, we made it in just before the storm got bad—a little before noon, I guess. The band's settin' up for tonight, and I'm just kickin' back. How about you? You got anything to tell me?"

Cyn leaned forward and started to speak, but Mac held up his hand when he saw the bartender in the red cowboy shirt approaching with their drinks on a tray.

"Here you go, Mac," said the woman as she set their drinks down on the table in front of them. "You want me to just put it on the tab?"

"Yeah, that'll be fine. Lorraine, this here's my cousin Barb Jones," said Mac, motioning toward Cyn.

"Pleased to meetcha," said Lorraine. "You here for the show tonight?"

Cyn nodded. "Yeah. I just happened to be staying here because of some work I'm doing at the Air Base. I catch Mac and the band whenever I can."

Lorraine nodded. "Should have a good crowd tonight. Lotta folks pulled in to wait out the storm. Inn's almost full up."

"Hey, Lorraine! We're dry over here!" yelled one of the truck drivers who was sitting at the bar.

"Be right there!" Lorraine yelled back. She winked at Mac. "Gotta go. Them truckers can sure slug down the brew."

"See yuh later, Lorraine," said Mac. "When my band finishes settin' up, they're gonna be thirsty, too. Just put everything on my tab, OK?"

"Sure thing, Mac."

Mac and Cyn sipped their drinks as they watched Lorraine walk back to the bar.

After she was out of earshot, Mac looked at Cyn. "You were sayin'?" he prompted.

Cyn leaned forward again and spoke in a low voice. "I've got some ideas. There are some people we need to check out."

Mac nodded. "Good. As soon as the band gets over here and I've got 'em settled down with some drinks, I'll give you a tour of the bus."

Cyn smiled and leaned back in her chair. "I'm looking forward to that." She raised her mug and took a long sip of the Irish coffee.

Mac nodded. "Me too."

He took a big gulp of his drink and pointed over Cyn's shoulder with the glass. "Here they come now," he said.

Cyn looked over her shoulder and saw the two men and the woman sauntering toward them.

"All set for tonight, Mac," said one of the men as they all drew up chairs on either side of Cyn.

"Good," said Mac. "Now y'all can kick back until show time. Have some drinks, get somethin' to eat. Just put it on my tab. It's already set up."

"Thanks, Mac," said the woman glancing curiously at Cyn.

Mac picked up the cue. "Gang, this is my cousin Barb Jones. Barb, this is Veronica Vail, singer and fiddle player; Skeeter Johnson, drummer; and Hound Dog Houston, bass guitar."

They each gave Cyn a smile or a nod when they were introduced.

"Are you staying here at the Inn?" asked Veronica. Her narrow face was dwarfed by a mass of long black hair. Cyn thought it was probably a wig.

"Yes," said Cyn. "Looks as if I'm lucky to have a room. The bartender said the place is nearly full because of the storm. Do you have rooms in the Inn?"

"Nah. We have all the comforts of home in the bus, and we don't have to pack our gear in and out," said Veronica.

"Yeah, sleeps six and has two johns," added Hound Dog. Cyn could see how he had earned his nickname. He had puffy circles under his eyes that made him look just like that cartoon character Droopy Dog.

"Wow! I'd like to see that!" said Cyn.

"Well, come on, then," said Mac. "I'll give you a tour."

He rose from his seat and hitched up his jeans. He was wearing a black tooled leather belt with an enormous silver belt buckle that had his name engraved on it.

"You guys go ahead and drink. I'll show Barb the bus and be back later." He looked over at the bar. "Hey, Lorraine!" he roared. "Well's dry over here!"

* * *

4 p.m.

Mac entered a code on a small black remote attached to his key ring as Cyn hugged herself against the howling wind. As if by magic the door to the bus slid open without a sound. Cyn followed Mac up the steps and looked around as he pressed another button on the remote and the door slid shut.

"Wow! This is impressive. Much better than the other bus," said Cyn.

"It sure is," said Mac. "Actually, there are only two others like it in the entire world, and they are solely for the use and protection of the President and Vice President. Of course, those don't have guitars and *Mac Gentry* painted on the side."

Cyn laughed. "No, I imagine they have nothing painted on the side."

"Not even a flag," said Mac. "Enough of this small talk. Follow me."

Cyn followed Mac to the back of the bus. He again entered a code on the remote and a door slid open revealing a sizeable room lined with computer banks and electronic gear. He motioned her to a seat and with the press of a button closed the door behind them.

After hanging his hat on a hook near the door, he plopped down in a chair facing her and leaned back with his thumbs hooked in his belt. "OK. What's the skinny?" he asked.

Cyn quickly brought him up to date on the state of things in Apparition Mountain, including the blown video board and the resulting postponement of retrieving the E-Weapon formula.

Mac looked at her sharply. "Do you think that was just an accident?"

Cyn shrugged. "It's hard to tell. I was in the room when it happened, but I wasn't sitting at the computer right at that moment. It's possible Jacobson could have done something to cause it to happen. On the other hand, he said the reason they didn't have a backup was because Professor Braun wouldn't let him order one."

"Seems odd they wouldn't have backup components for a project this important," said Mac with a frown.

"I thought that was strange, too," said Cyn. "In fact, there are several things I find rather odd about this Professor Braun."

"You think he could be our mole?"

"It's possible. He's the first one I want to check out. I know the background on the others that have top-security clearance—General Masters and Dr. Graham. The next level would be Brent Jacobson and possibly the General's Aide Captain Denton. But I want to start with Braun."

Mac reached over and turned on the computer. "Where do you want to start?"

Cyn paused for a second. "Well, he was a top honors student at MIT, but yesterday he didn't seem to comprehend some pretty basic math theories. We saw him in Professor Latter's memory in 1975 at MIT, but he looked totally different than what he looks like now. The first thing I want to find out is if he's really Karl Braun."

"OK. First thing we do is pull up his NSA file. Then we'll take a look at his photo in the MIT yearbook," said Mac as he began to type on the keyboard.

"So, what's the latest on Mario?" asked Cyn as they waited for the file to download.

"We're still picking up a lot of chatter, but nothing we can use to pin him down. We find out where he's been, rather than where he is. He's a slippery bastard. Meanwhile, terrorists are still escaping, and we don't have a clue where they've gone."

Cyn nodded. "The mastermind behind 'Damascus Road.' I wish we could figure out who he is."

"Yeah. The only thing we know about him is he's not an Arab from that DNA sample we got off an envelope a couple of years ago."

"That probably makes it easier for him to go undetected—especially going in and out of the U.S."

"That's right. We thought we had him the other night. Had a tip that he was flying from London to Cairo. We alerted the Egyptians, and they collected DNA from everyone who landed in Cairo from the London flights. Nothing matched up."

"How did they manage to get everyone's DNA?" asked Cyn.

"Fairly easy through a retina scan. It's the latest technology developed for us by a small company in California. Passengers just think they're having a retina scan for matching passport ID, but at the same time we get a scan of the blood vessels in the back of the retina, which gives us the DNA."

"Wow! That's cool," said Cyn. "I hadn't heard about that."

"Something new every day with the NSA," said Mac with a grin.

"Have you been picking up any communication about Apparition Mountain since I've been here?"

"Yeah. It's still going on. We're picking up two to three messages a day."

"That's good in one aspect. I assume it means our mole doesn't suspect me of being an agent, at least not yet."

"That's right," said Mac. "We've got to expose the bastard before you find out what went wrong with the E-Weapon. All we need is for Mario to get his hands on that. Can you imagine what would happen if terrorists all over the world had E-Weapon capability?"

Cyn shuddered. "I know. We can't let that happen."

"We won't, Cyn," said Mac in a reassuring tone. "I'm glad you're working for me on this mission. Between the two of us and the rest of my team, that mole doesn't stand a snowball's chance in hell."

Cyn smiled at him. "I'm glad to be assigned to you again, too, Mac."

* * *

Mac Gentry was head of the National Security Agency's Worldwide Mobile Intelligence operation. He had at his fingertips the latest, most sophisticated technology available for eavesdropping, surveillance, and tracking. He had various guises depending on the part of the world he was in at any particular time. In the United States he was a Country Western singer.

His real name was Melvin Morris, and he had grown up in abject poverty in a podunk town in West Texas. His father, Robert "Bobcat" Morris, was a biker who was head of a motorcycle gang called Satanic Vision. The SV's chief occupation was terrorizing small towns, taking over pool halls and robbing liquor stores. His mother Moonbeam—he never knew her real name—was a motorcycle mama who spent her life in a drug and alcohol haze and in and out of bed with every biker in the gang.

When Melvin was only six years old, Bobcat was killed in a shootout with another gang. Out of respect for their fallen leader, the rest of the gang members set Moonbeam up in a ramshackle house on the outskirts of Pumphandle, a tiny town near Langtry where Judge Roy Bean once administered frontier justice.

The gang made this their base, and when they weren't across the border in Mexico, they stayed there. By the time Melvin was ten, he had two younger brothers and a sister. Despite the fact that each of them had a different father, Moonbeam applied the Morris surname to all, even though it was never entirely clear that she and Bobcat Morris had actually been married.

Melvin and his half-siblings spent a miserable childhood being taunted at school and then coming home to utter chaos. Then the summer before Melvin entered his sophomore year in high school, Moonbeam died of a crack overdose. Social services took over. An elderly minister and his wife adopted the younger children, but no one was interested in adopting a boy of Melvin's age—especially one who had been brought up by a motorcycle gang.

After school Melvin had gotten into the habit of stopping at Harlan Davis's Texaco station and auto mechanics shop. He began to do odd jobs for Harlan and in the process learned about car engines and repair, but he especially had a knack for fixing CB radios.

Harlan had a back room in his shop and Melvin finally convinced him to let him stay there. He would pump gas and work in the shop in exchange for room and board while he finished high school.

In school Melvin was bright and made good grades, but he kept to himself. He had no time for extracurricular activities and hanging around with the other teens. He could not wait to graduate and get out of Pumphandle.

In his senior year an Army recruiter visited the school and provided the way out.

Melvin signed up and happily went off to boot camp before the ink on his diploma was barely dry.

In the Army, he studied and excelled in communications. After his four-year commitment, he re-upped. His talents were noticed and he was chosen to serve in the Special Forces. He commanded a team that went into Afghanistan ahead of the 2001 war to buy off warlords and gather intelligence on the whereabouts of Taliban leaders and Osama bin Laden.

While the world was focused on Afghanistan, he and his team were already in Iraq. After the routing of Saddam Hussein, Melvin returned to the U.S. to work in the Pentagon. It wasn't long before the NSA tapped him to run their Worldwide Mobile Intelligence operation, which he had been doing ever since.

4:15 p.m.

"Here's Braun's file," said Mac as the image came up on the screen. They were looking at the cover page of the file marked **Top Secret** in big bold letters. Professor Braun's name was printed in the center of the page, and the National Security Agency seal was stamped at the bottom.

Mac clicked on the next page. A photograph of the Professor appeared. "That him?" he asked glancing at Cyn.

"Yes. That's what he looks like now," she said recognizing the icy pale eyes and the short cropped white hair.

Mac clicked on the next page and quickly scanned the text. "He's been vetted every year for the past ten and cleared for Ultra Top Secret projects," he said.

"Yeah," said Cyn. "I know he worked on *Project Nightingale*. Seems NSA thinks he's OK, but I'm still leery of him."

"All right. I'll scan his picture over, and we'll take a look at the MIT yearbook. What year did you say?" asked Mac as he pressed a couple of keys and the scanner window came up.

"Well, I know he was a top honor student in Molecular Physics and Advanced Math in 1975," said Cyn.

Mac saved the scanned photo from the NSA file on a separate screen. Then he rapidly typed on the keyboard and an image of the 1975 MIT yearbook appeared. He entered the name Karl Braun in the search engine and a page number appeared.

"He's on page 142," said Mac. He quickly pulled up the page, and there at the top was the face Cyn had seen in Professor Latter's memory.

"That's the face I saw," said Cyn pointing at the photograph.

Mac zoomed in on Braun's photograph. "God! You're right. This looks nothing like the NSA picture," he exclaimed. "Look at all that wild black hair and beard. You can't even really see his face."

"I know," said Cyn. "The eyes seem to be a deeper color, too. Of course this was taken over thirty years ago, and people do change."

"I'll scan it over next to the NSA picture and apply the biometrics program to it and see what we come up with," said Mac.

Cyn watched as the biometrics scanner swept over the yearbook picture of Braun. A series of vertical and horizontal lines scanned back and forth and up and down for a few seconds. Then the picture disappeared and soon reappeared as an overlay on the NSA photo. The vertical and horizontal lines reappeared sweeping over both photos.

"Well, would you look at that," said Mac. "The biometrics says there's less than a 25 percent chance these photos are of the same person."

Cyn frowned and thought for a moment. "That doesn't tell us for sure that the NSA's picture isn't Karl Braun. Maybe he had plastic surgery or something. The only way to tell for sure would be through a DNA test."

"DNA could be a little dicey. We only have his DNA from the time he's worked for NSA. We don't have anything to match it to from back when he was at MIT."

"How about parents or brothers and sisters? Maybe we could get a sample from one of them and see if there's a match."

Mac shook his head. "Nope, sorry. According to his file, his parents are both dead, and he had no brothers or sisters." He paused for a second, frowning. "I'll tell you what, though. It's a slim chance, but just maybe MIT has something in their records that would give us a clue. I'll get Hound Dog working on it after we finish our gig tonight. That's his specialty. We should have something for you by tomorrow."

"Good," said Cyn. "Are we finished for today? I need to get something to eat and have an early night."

Mac nodded and shut down the computer. "Yeah, that's enough for right now. Come on. We'll go get something in the coffee shop."

He grabbed his hat from the hook, pressed a button and the door slid open. Cyn went out and he followed her, securing the door behind them. Then they exited the bus bracing themselves for the short dash through the howling wind and snow to the back door of the Inn.

As they entered the lobby, they could hear laughter from the bar raised over the honky tonk voice of Hank Williams singing "Jambalaya" on the jukebox. Mac chuckled. "Sounds like they're heatin' up pretty good in there. Should be a rowdy crowd for tonight."

When they passed the reception desk on the way to the coffee shop, Jack Harper called out, "Ms. Jones, there's a couple of messages for you."

Cyn glanced at Mac and walked over to the desk.

"These just came in about a half hour ago," said Jack handing her two white envelopes.

"Thanks," said Cyn glancing at the envelopes. "Looks like you're busy tonight."

"Yeah. Nothing like a snow storm to boost business around here. Hope you didn't have trouble driving."

"Not too bad. It was just slow going is all."

"Well, enjoy the band tonight."

"Thanks, I will."

Cyn walked over to where Mac was now standing in front of the roaring fireplace in the lobby sitting area.

"Wonder who these are from?" she said as they both sat down on a sofa facing the fire. She tore open the first envelope and retrieved a piece of notepaper with the Rancho Bonito logo printed across the top.

"Oh, bother!" she said as she read the message and disgustedly tore it up.

"What's that?" asked Mac.

"Oh, it's from Charlie Denton, the General's aide. He said he doesn't have to stay at the Mountain all night, and he's coming here to see the band. Wants to know if he can buy me a drink."

"Aha! Sounds like you have an admirer," said Mac with a chuckle.

"One I can do without," said Cyn shaking her head. "He's becoming a regular pest."

"Does he know who you are?" asked Mac.

"No. He knows my real name, but he just thinks I'm Senator Goodman's Aide. All he knows is that the General asked me to work for him on the technical aspects of the project. The General had him make arrangements for me at the Inn and get me set up with the Barbara Jones identity. You know the routine."

"Well, maybe you should have a drink with him. Try to arrange it for around 9:30 when we take our break. That'll give me a chance to scope him out."

"Oh, all right, but I really don't want to give him any encouragement," said Cyn.

"Leave it to me. I know a way to get him off your back," said Mac with a wicked grin.

"What are you going to do?"

"You'll find out," said Mac mysteriously. "Just have a drink with him in the lounge while we're on break."

Cyn looked at him questioningly, but he just shrugged and grinned.

"Hadn't you better find out who the other message is from?" he asked.

Cyn frowned at him as she tore open the other envelope. She looked down and quickly scanned the message.

"Well?" asked Mac.

Cyn handed the note to him and he read it. It said simply, "Barbara, please call Jeff at your earliest convenience."

"My, my, aren't you popular? Is that who I think it is?" asked Mac.

Cyn nodded and tore up the note. She deposited the shredded notes in a compartment in her bag.

"Sounds as if you've got some phone calls to make," said Mac. "You want to call from inside the bus?"

"No, I'll go to my room. I've made sure it's secure."

"All right. Do that and then meet me in the coffee shop in about half an hour." Mac rose to his feet and hitched up his jeans. "I'll be interested to hear about your two admirers."

"Right," said Cyn. She shouldered her bag and headed for the elevator.

* * *

5 p.m.

When Cyn got to her room, she quickly pulled out the XJ14 cell phone and pressed the numbers for Apparition Mountain. She nearly laughed out loud when she heard a male voice answer the call.

"Apparition Mountain Game Reserve. How can I help you?"

"Yes, I'm returning Jeff's call," said Cyn.

"May I say who's calling?"

"Yes. This is Barbara Jones."

"Would you repeat that, please, slowly? I'm a little hard of hearing."

"This is Barbara Jones," said Cyn, drawing out the syllables. She smiled to herself, realizing he was scanning for voice recognition.

"One moment, please. I'll see if I can locate him," said the voice after a pause.

Suddenly the General's voice boomed over the phone. "Cyn, you got my message?"

"Yes. What's up?"

"Just wanted you to know that there's a further delay in getting the replacement for the main frame video board. IBM can't get it here until late Monday afternoon, which means the next memory download will have to be postponed until Tuesday morning."

Cyn frowned. "That's not going to make our friend happy."

"I know," said the General. "I can't believe we didn't have a spare on hand. I ordered three from IBM just in case it blows again."

"That also means we won't be able to continue exploring Harry Latter's memory for the E5 info," said Cyn.

"Not until late Monday afternoon, I'm afraid," said the General. He cleared his throat and there was a pause. "Unless you can think of some other solution?" he asked.

"I'll think about it and let you know if I come up with something. What about Jacobson? Does he have any ideas?"

"We've got him working on it, but he hasn't come up with anything yet. By the way, Professor Braun was delighted with the formulas you managed to print out before the video board blew. He's studying them now for clues as to what went wrong."

"Good. At least we managed to get that much."

"Perhaps that will appease our friend and the Senator when you report in?"

"It will help a little—especially with the Senator who doesn't know about the second download." Cyn paused for a moment to think. "Meanwhile, Mac and the team are here and we're already working on the other situation. That should help to appease our friend a little, but it's still critical that we complete that second download as soon as possible."

"Believe me, I am well aware of that, and so is Professor Braun," said the General.

"That reminds me. I've been meaning to ask you how long you've known Professor Braun," said Cyn.

"Just since we've been working on this project, which is nearly two years now."

"How did you pick him to head up the project then?" asked Cyn.

"Actually I had little to say about it. The Scientific Advisory Department recommended him because of his splendid work on *Project Nightingale*. Why do you ask?"

"Just curious, that's all," said Cyn. "If there's nothing else, I'll report in to the Senator and our friend and try to think of a way to speed things up."

"No. That's all I have for the moment," said the General.

"In that case, can you transfer me to Captain Denton?" asked Cyn.

"Captain Denton? Is there a problem with any of your accommodations or equipment?"

"Oh, no, nothing like that. He just left me a message and I'm responding is all."

"I see. Nothing to do with business?"

"No, not really," said Cyn with a chuckle.

"Aha! Watch out for Charlie. He has a way with the ladies, you know," said the General.

"I'm fully aware of that," said Cyn. "It's nothing like that."

"OK. I'll transfer you over. Be sure to call if you think of a solution to our problem."

"I certainly will. I'll be back in touch tomorrow for sure," said Cyn.

After telling Charlie that she would meet him for a drink at 9:30, Cyn clicked off the XJ14 and plucked her other cell phone out of her bag. She made sure the jamming device on the XJ14 was still on before making calls to the Senator and to her other boss. Then she headed for the coffee shop to meet Mac.

* * *

SATURDAY

5:30 a.m.

Cyn awoke the next morning to the sound of her cell phone ringing. She reached out and grabbed it off the bedside table and squinted at the clock. It was only 5:30. Before pressing the receive button she noted the caller ID on the screen: "Harley One."

She sat up on the edge of the bed and pushed the receive button. "What's up, Mac?" she asked.

"I have a solution to your video problem," said Mac in his Texas drawl. "Wanna' hear it now?"

"Sure," said Cyn. She glanced at the XJ14 cell phone. The jamming device was still on.

"OK. All you have to do is upload the data and send it over the NSA satellite to Roswell. Then you can access it off the NSA computer just like you would on the Internet."

Cyn thought for a second. "That makes sense, Mac, as long as it's secure."

"That goes without saying. There's nothing on earth more secure."

"I'll run it by the General. He'll have to get clearance."

"Good. Now, there's other news. Come to the bus as soon as you can. We have a team briefing at 0600."

Without waiting for a response Mac clicked off. Cyn pressed the "end call" button and mulled the idea over for a moment. Then she picked up the XJ14 cell phone and called the General at Apparition Mountain.

* * *

6 a.m.

Cyn threw on some clothes, washed her face and swiped a comb through her hair. She grabbed her bag and rushed down the back stairs and out the door. The snow had stopped, but there was still a cold wind. As she approached the bus, the door magically slid open. She walked up the steps into the bus and the door whispered shut behind her.

"Good morning, Agent Jones. You're just in time for the briefing," said Mac. He was seated in a comfortable swivel chair beside a table. The other members of the team were seated on a couch and a couple of chairs across from him. He motioned to the chair on the other side of the table. "Have a seat. There's fresh coffee in the pot."

Cyn smiled and nodded at the others as she sat down. She poured coffee in the cup that had been set out on the table for her.

"Now, here's the skinny," said Mac. "The Brits picked up more chatter last night about Apparition Mountain. The message was coming from somewhere in Mexico and going to somewhere in Saudi Arabia. The nature of the message almost certainly confirms our suspicion that there's a leak inside the Mountain, and because there was only a handful of people at the Mountain last night, that narrows the playing field."

"What time was the message sent?" asked Cyn.

Mac consulted a piece of paper in front of him. "At 8:32 p.m. local time," he said, glancing up at Cyn.

Cyn frowned. "Well, the only people who were at the Mountain at that time were General Masters, Professor Braun, Dr. Graham, Charlie Denton and Brent Jacobson, as far as I know. Of course, there was also Jazar, but he's under heavy sedation."

"What about the switchboard operator?" asked Mac.

Cyn shook her head. "The switchboard is actually at the Air Base."

"Jazar's code name was mentioned in the chatter as well as the fact that the procedure has been delayed because of a technical failure," said Mac.

Cyn's eyes widened. "But the only people who know about that, outside of the present company, are the ones who were at the Mountain last night, with the possible exception of Charlie Denton. As the General's aide, he's not in the top-secret clearance level, although I'm sure it's possible he could have the means to find out."

Mac nodded. "We can't afford to rule anyone out. I've assigned each team member to check out a suspect, and we'll see what we come up with by the end of the day. Hound Dog here is already checking with MIT to see if we can come up with anything to find out if Braun is really Braun."

"How are you doing that?" asked Cyn.

"Oh, I"m checking to see if they have any dental records, blood type, or fingerprints on file—that kinda' thing," said Hound Dog.

"And I'm checking out Charlie Denton," said Veronica with a sly smile.

Cyn laughed. "Thanks, Veronica, for getting him off my back last night. He was becoming a real pest."

"No problem," said Veronica. "I have a date with him tonight after we finish playing."

Mac chuckled. "I told you I had a way of taking care of him. OK, I've got Skeeter on the good doctor, and that leaves the General and Brent Jacobson."

"I'll take Jacobson," said Cyn quickly.

"Makes sense since you're working with him on the technology," said Mac. "That leaves me with General Masters. By the way, is he OK with my suggestion?"

Cyn nodded. "Yes. He is anxious to get started. I told him I'd be at the Mountain at 0700."

Mac glanced at the clock. "You'd better get going then."

"One other question before I go," said Cyn. "How long would it take to get clearance to check someone's financial records?"

"Almost immediately so long as it's in the interest of national security. We just have to get a secret court order from a federal judge to cover our behinds. Why? You got someone in mind?"

"Yeah," said Cyn. "Right now it's just a hunch, but I'd like to check Harry Latter's records. I don't know if it has anything to do with anything at the moment, but we should probably get on it before they release his death notice and his accounts are frozen."

"Consider it done," said Mac. He rose from his seat and hitched up his jeans. "OK, gang. Chop! Chop! We got work to do."

* * *

12:30 p.m.

Cyn parked the Grand Cherokee in her usual spot behind the Rancho Bonito Inn. She grabbed her bag, jumped out and headed toward the bus.

The bus door slid open when she reached the bottom step. Mac was waiting for her. "Well?" he asked as soon as the door slid shut behind her.

She glanced around. "Where are the others?"

"Inside at the coffee shop. I told 'em to get somethin' to eat. You hungry?"

Cyn deposited her bag on the table and sat down. "No. I had a sandwich at the Mountain. I could use some of that coffee, though, if you still have some."

"Sure thing," said Mac. "Coffee's always on here."

He strode over to the small kitchenette and poured her a cup of strong black coffee. He brought it over and set it on the table in front of her. Then he flopped down in the swivel chair across from her.

"I repeat my question," he said. "Let's have it."

"The General called a conference with Braun and Jacobson as soon as I got there. Turns out Braun and Jake had been working on a scheme to download Harry Latter's memory onto DVDs so we could continue our search for what went wrong with the E-Weapon," said Cyn.

Mac frowned and leaned forward in his chair. "So they don't want to do the upload to Roswell?"

"They didn't until I pointed out to them that it would be much faster than trying to download to DVDs—even with the speed they've got."

Mac leaned back in his chair again. "So?"

"So, the General called his director who has to call the director at Roswell for clearance and so on. You know how it goes," said Cyn with a wave of her hand.

"Yeah, I do know how it goes," said Mac shaking his head. "So where do we stand now?"

"They're hoping to get clearance so they can begin the upload this afternoon. The General said he'd call me when we can resume the memory search—possibly by this evening or maybe tomorrow. Meanwhile, Braun is studying the formula we managed to print out before the board blew. He thinks it's possible that he might be able to figure out what went wrong."

"Do you think he'll figure it out?"

Cyn grimaced. "I highly doubt it. He just doesn't seem that competent to me."

"Well, I've got a bit of news," said Mac. He opened a file folder that was lying on the table. "Hound Dog managed to find out that MIT has blood type and fingerprints on file for Karl Braun, but, of course, we gotta get a court order to get 'em, and it's the weekend. We can track down a judge, but by the time MIT gets the order and transfers the info, chances are we won't have anything until Monday morning at the earliest."

"Meanwhile Braun has his hands on the E-Weapon formula, and somebody—possibly him—is leaking info to the Middle East," said Cyn.

Mac leaned back, hooked his thumbs in his Levi pockets and thought for a moment. "Tell you what. Let's you and me take a little jaunt to Braun's place this afternoon and scope it out. I take it the same cast of characters is spending the night again at the Mountain and Braun won't be home?"

Cyn nodded. "All except Charlie Denton and he'll be there until around eight tonight."

"And we know what he's doin' after that," said Mac with a grin. "He'll be here for the show and after that Veronica will be keepin' an eye on him and findin' out if he knows anything."

"Good," said Cyn. "It sure helps to have him off my back so I can concentrate on the others."

"Oh, I almost forgot. There's another bit of news regarding your request about Harry Latter's financial records," said Mac reaching for another file folder. "So far we've found money stashed in six different banks plus three brokerage accounts to the tune of about seven million in cash and twice that in stock portfolios."

"You're kidding!" said Cyn.

"Nope. It's all here in black and white. Not bad for a professor, eh?"

"Do you have records of deposits?"

Mac flipped a page and peered down at it. "Looks to be mostly in the form of checks from—of all things—casinos. A bunch from different casinos in Vegas, a couple from Reno, and some from the Bahamas."

Cyn laughed and clapped her hands. "He really did it!"

Mac looked up from the file with a frown. "Did what? Appears our professor was quite the gambler."

"Oh, Mac, he was more than a gambler! He figured out some kind of formula for beating the slot machines!"

"Hot damn! I'd like to get my hands on that," said Mac. "But how do you know about it?"

"Jacobson and I stumbled across it when we were looking at Harry's memory," said Cyn. "The part we saw was where he was practicing it on a slot machine in his office at MIT. We didn't have time to look further and see if he ever put it to use in an actual casino. Apparently, he did!"

"And how!" exclaimed Mac with a snort.

Suddenly Cyn became serious again. "Mac, when did he make the last deposit?"

Mac peered down at the file and flipped another page. "Looks like just over ten years ago. No more deposits, just withdrawals. Let's see— monthly automatic bill payments for the usual stuff—cable TV, utilities and so forth... Hello, hold the phone! Here's a big one! $100,000 a month to a Bank of America account! Wonder what that's for?"

"Can you find out who the account belongs to?" asked Cyn.

"Yeah, but it'll take a little more time. Probably have to get another court order," said Mac. "I'll put it on Skeeter's to-do list."

He scribbled a note and paper clipped it to the front of the file. He got up and grabbed his hat and sheepskin coat from a nearby wall rack. "You ready to boogie, Agent Jones?" he asked as he planted the hat on his head.

Cyn didn't answer. She was already at the door.

* * *

2 p.m.

When they arrived at the outskirts of Santa Fe it was a typical Saturday afternoon. The parking lots around the strip malls were full.

"I'll pull over here," said Cyn. She nodded at an open parking place beside the driveway into a Best Western motel. "Then we can see where we want to go."

Mac reached into his coat pocket and pulled out a folded piece of paper and consulted it. "The address is 16150 Southeast Sunrise Road," he said. "I looked on the GPS, but it doesn't show up, so we'll have to try to figure it out on the map."

Cyn stopped the Grand Cherokee and put it into park, leaving the engine running. She reached into a pocket on the door and drew out a map of Santa Fe. Mac took it from her and spread it open. After a few moments, he drew a line on the map as Cyn watched.

"Follow this road, Highway 84, until you come to the Old Taos Highway. Turn left on that and follow it through downtown until you come to the Old Santa Fe Trail. Turn south on that and follow it for two to three miles. Southeast Sunrise Road should be on your left just after you pass Zia Road, which hooks into Old Santa Fe Trail on your right."

Cyn put the Jeep in drive and pulled back onto the highway. About ten minutes later, she spotted Southeast Sunrise Road and turned onto it. After about a quarter of a mile, she saw a mailbox with 16150 on it. She pulled over just past the mailbox.

"What do you think?" asked Cyn. "That surely can't be it." She pointed to a small crumbling adobe house next to the mailbox that appeared to be abandoned.

Mac craned around and squinted through the window at the rundown house. "No, that's not it. The number on the house is 16140. You can just barely read it there by the door. Paint's peeling," he said. "Drive by again."

Cyn made a U-turn on the deserted road and slowly drove back by the mailbox.

"There! Stop!" said Mac suddenly.

Cyn stopped and looked to where he was pointing. Just at the side of the abandoned house almost hidden by overgrown mesquite was a narrow dirt road.

"That must be the road to his place," said Mac. "Maybe I'd better drive. You get in the back and keep your head down just in case we run into someone who might recognize you."

Cyn quickly jumped out of the driver's seat and got into the back seat of the Jeep. Mac shoved over into the driver's seat and made a left-hand turn onto the dirt road. After bouncing along the rutted road for about half a mile through rugged desert terrain, they rounded a curve and without warning they were driving on smooth asphalt wide enough for two vehicles to pass.

"If this is Braun's driveway, it must have cost a fortune," said Mac. "See how it cuts through the side of the mountain?"

"Yeah," said Cyn who was peering over Mac's shoulder from the back seat.

They were silent as they continued up the road that wound its way upward through the rock-strewn mountainous landscape. Ten minutes later they crested a hill and then they saw it spread out below them at the foot of a mountain.

"My God! Would yuh look at that!" exclaimed Mac.

Cyn caught her breath at the sight of the huge sprawling adobe house and outbuildings laid out below them.

"That's some hacienda," said Cyn. "How on earth can a professor afford these digs?"

"Let's see what we can find out," said Mac. He picked up his cell phone and pressed a couple of buttons as he continued driving slowly down the hill toward the house. Cyn hunkered down on the floor behind the driver's seat.

"Yeah, Skeeter. Need you to check property records for Santa Fe and see what you come up with for 16150 Southeast Sunrise Road. Yeah, that's right. Call me back."

Mac pressed the "end call" button and clipped the cell phone to the windshield visor. Then about five hundred yards from the house, he pulled to the side of the road and stopped.

"What's up?" whispered Cyn from the back seat.

"I'm gonna walk up to the gate," said Mac quietly through gritted teeth. "There's a security camera up there, so I don't want to drive all the way up. You stay put and keep your head down. I'll find out if anyone's there."

"OK," mumbled Cyn.

She heard Mac unbuckling the seat belt and getting out of the Jeep. He clicked the door shut softly behind him. Then she heard his boots clocking away from her on the pavement. The sound grew fainter and fainter until there was only silence. All she heard was the wind blowing grit against the side of the Jeep. She fidgeted and shifted her position slightly to alleviate a cramp in her hip. She was dying to take a peek out the window, but she overcame her curiosity and stayed put.

After what seemed an eternity, she heard the boot steps on the pavement again. The door clicked open, and the Jeep bounced slightly as Mac lifted his bulk into the driver's seat. The door slammed shut. She heard the snap of the seat belt buckle and then the engine roared to life. She said nothing. As Mac turned the Jeep around, Cyn risked a quick peek out of the back window and saw something she hadn't noticed before. There, to the back of the house, where the mountain rose, was the boarded up shaft of an old abandoned mine. She ducked her head back down.

After Mac had driven some distance back up the road, he said, "OK, Cyn, we can talk now, but stay down."

"Good. What happened?"

"Turns out there was someone there," said Mac.

"Oh, yeah?"

"Yeah. Braun has a live-in housekeeper. I talked to her on the two-way monitor at the gate, and I have a date with her tomorrow."

"What!" Cyn cried and then remembered to keep her voice down. "How on earth did you get a date with the housekeeper?"

"Oh, I made up a cock and bull story that I was an old classmate of Braun's from MIT and that I was in Santa Fe to see the sights and thought I'd look him up. She said Braun was away for several days. I said that was a shame 'cause I was only here through tomorrow and sure wished I had someone who knew the area to show me around. She said she had the day off tomorrow and would be happy to show me around. Said she grew up here. Name's Serena Flores. Good lookin' gal, too, I might add, from what I could see on the monitor. Told her I'd meet her tomorrow at 12:30 in the La Fonda hotel bar and we'd go from there."

"Oh, Mac, I can't believe it," said Cyn with a laugh. "Next thing you know, she'll invite you in to Braun's place."

"Just what I had in mind. How'd you guess?" said Mac.

The cell phone on the visor rang. Mac plucked it off the visor, pushed the receive button, and held it to his ear. "Yeah?"

Cyn waited patiently as Mac listened to his caller. After a while he said, "Good job, Skeeter. Next thing is to find out who the officers are and check out their backgrounds."

Mac clicked off the cell phone and clipped it back on the visor.

"Well, well. The plot thickens," he said.

"What?" asked Cyn.

"That property Braun lives on is owned by a gold mining company incorporated in Utah—name of Valhalla Exploration, Inc."

"Gold mining?" repeated Cyn. "You know, Mac, that might make sense, because Jacobson told me that Braun likes to go gold-prospecting during his leisure time."

"Well, I'm havin' Skeeter check out the company—find out who the officers are, when it was incorporated, and all that," said Mac. "Skeeter had some other news, too. You know your question about Harry Latter's finances and where that monthly $100,000 was going?"

"Yes?" said Cyn.

"Well, guess what. The money is being paid into a checking account owned by, of all people, Karl G. Braun."

"Harry Latter was paying $100,000 a month to Braun?"

"That's right. Now, Skeeter's tryin' to see if he can find out what Braun's doin' with the money."

"Well, Mac," said Cyn trying to digest all this latest information. "As you say, the plot certainly thickens."

* * *

4:30 p.m.

As they turned into the parking lot of the Rancho Bonito Inn, Cyn felt her cell phone vibrating in her pocket. She did not answer it. When she pulled into her parking space, she turned to Mac. He already had his seat belt unbuckled and his hand on the door handle.

"I've got to check in with the General and find out if they got the data uploaded to Roswell," said Cyn.

"Well, I gotta check with the team and see if there's anything new. Then we gotta get ready for the show tonight. Let me know if you have to go to the Mountain tonight," said Mac as he climbed out of the vehicle.

"I'll do that," said Cyn.

She grabbed her bag, climbed out and locked the Grand Cherokee. She paused at the back entry door. Mac had already entered the bus and the door was sliding shut behind him.

Cyn rushed up to her room, closed the door and turned on the jamming device on the XJ14. Then she clicked on her cell phone and saw that she had a coded text message from Jake.

"Hey, Babe. Just finished uploading the data to Roswell. General Masters wants us to take a look at Harry's memory again as soon as you can get here. I'm looking forward to having you by my side again. I miss you."

Cyn smiled and sent a simple return message: "I'm on my way." Then she erased Jake's message and picked up the room phone on the bar.

"Any messages for Barbara Jones?" she asked when Jack answered at the front desk.

There was one message to "call Jeff as soon as you can." The message had come in just fifteen minutes ago.

Cyn picked up the XJ14 and called the General at Apparition Mountain. He came on the line quickly. "Cyn, we need you in here. The upload to Roswell is complete, and you and Jake can continue searching for what went wrong with the E5."

"Good, Jeff. I just have one phone call to make and I'm on my way," said Cyn glancing at her watch.

"There's some more good news," said the General. "I leaned on IBM, and we're sending an Air Force plane to pick up the video boards tomorrow. We'll have 'em here tomorrow afternoon, so we can move the memory download up to Monday morning."

"That *is* good news," said Cyn.

"Yeah. Well, I hope you pass that on to your boss."

"That goes without saying. The boss will be pleased."

"I thought that might make your day. See you soon," said the General, ending the call.

Cyn put the XJ14 cell phone on the bar and picked up her own cell phone. She quickly made two calls—one to her boss and one to the Senator. Then she put the cell phones back in her bag, paused in front of the mirror to apply fresh lipstick, and dashed out the door.

* * *

5:30 p.m.

When Cyn reached the first security gate on the way to Apparition Mountain, she was pleased to see the number of private security guards who surrounded her vehicle. She rolled down her window and handed her ID card to the stone-faced guard who stood beside her door. He said nothing as he checked the card against a data bank on a small hand-held computer. Then he merely handed her card back to her and nodded. The barrier lifted and the other guards stepped aside to allow her to pass.

At the second gate, the guard checked her ID and then asked her to step out of the Jeep and go into the guardhouse. Cyn turned off the ignition and stepped out. Inside the guardhouse a huge beefy man dressed in street clothes met her.

"What's this all about?" asked Cyn. "They already checked me out at the first gate."

"Standard procedure. High alert," said the man. He looked closely at her ID and then motioned to her. "Please stand in front of the screen."

Cyn complied. She stood where she was told and looked directly at the scanner target in the middle of the screen. The man pushed a button, and she heard the faint whirring sound as the scanner went to work. In a couple of seconds, there was a flash and a robotic voice announced, "Identification Validated."

The man handed her the ID card and opened the guardhouse door. "You're cleared to proceed, Ms. Jones."

"Thank you," said Cyn with a smile as she walked past him. He simply nodded without returning the smile.

Cyn drove on up the gravel road to Apparition Mountain. At the main entrance, she parked the Grand Cherokee in her designated space and got out. More guards and agents surrounded her before she had taken two steps toward the entrance. They scanned her with hand-held metal detectors and checked her ID again. At last she was free to go to the entrance and enter her code. The door swung open. Charlie Denton was waiting just inside.

He beamed down at her. "Welcome back to Apparition Mountain, Barbara."

"Hi, Charlie. What are you doing down here? I know my way around by now," said Cyn.

"Just wanted to make sure you didn't have any trouble getting through the beefed up security. General's waitin' for you," he said.

"What's the reason for the extra security?" asked Cyn as she followed Charlie to the General's office.

"Oh, somebody in Washington got hyper again. Seems there's been some chatter over the airwaves and they think there's a possibility of a terrorist attack. Homeland Security issued a Code Red for all government installations."

"I see," said Cyn. "Well, let's just hope it's another false alarm."

"Yeah," said Charlie as he opened the door to the General's suite. "They keep cryin' wolf like this, one of these days there'll be a real attack and nobody will take the warning seriously."

General Masters was standing in the open door of his office. "Ah, here you are at last," he said. "Come on in. There's work to be done."

"Yes, Sir," said Cyn. She walked into the General's office.

"Captain Denton, get on the horn and double check with IBM again. I want to make sure there are no snags in getting that equipment here tomorrow," said the General.

"Yes, Sir," said Charlie as the General closed his office door.

"Well, Cyn, you've been busy," remarked the General as he strode over to her and sat on the edge of his desk. "Thanks for the extra security."

"Compliments of my boss," said Cyn. "We want to make sure nothing goes wrong with the project."

"I just hope there are no more snafus," said the General. He ran a hand through his hair and frowned, staring off into space. Cyn noted the puffiness around his eyes and deeper lines in his forehead than she had seen before.

"How much sleep have you had in the last forty-eight?" she asked softly.

The General looked at her sharply. "A cat-nap here and there. Why?"

"No reason. I just thought you might be a little fatigued," said Cyn.

The General waved a hand impatiently. "No sleep in forty-eight hours is nothing compared to being in the field," he said. "Ever wonder why they call military field uniforms 'fatigues'? Now you know."

Cyn laughed, and a slow grin crept over the General's face. "Well, maybe you can take one of your cat-naps while I find out what went wrong with the E5," said Cyn.

"Yeah. How long do you think it'll take you to find it?"

"Actually, it shouldn't take long. Jake and I were on the verge of discovering it when the video board blew. I know just where to start looking."

"Good. Jake's got everything set up. The upload to Roswell seems to have gone off without a hitch. If you want to get started, I think I will take one of my cat-naps, but I want to know the minute you find anything."

"Sure thing," said Cyn as she headed for the door.

* * *

6:50 p.m.

Professor Braun and Brent Jacobson were deep in conversation when Cyn used her code to enter Jake's office. They looked up when the door swung open.

"Ms. Hoover, we've been waiting for you," said Braun. He rose from the chair where he had been seated next to Jake in front of a computer monitor.

"I came as quickly as I could," said Cyn. "I trust the upload to Roswell went smoothly?"

"Yes. We were able to start around two this afternoon after the General finally got clearance. They had to track down the director of the Roswell operation on a golf course in Las Cruces," said Braun. "At any rate, we're ready to proceed."

Cyn looked at Jake. "Any technical glitches?"

He shook his head. "No. The upload went smoothly. I'm linked to Roswell, and we can view the data on this monitor."

"I'll leave the two of you to it. We need to find that problem with the E-Weapon. I've gone over the formula that you printed out, and I can't see anything wrong with it. I'm going to check in with Dr. Graham and go over procedures for the next memory download. Thanks to General Masters, we'll be getting the video boards tomorrow afternoon and will be able to do the procedure Monday morning," said Braun as he walked to the door. "I hope the Senator is satisfied?" he asked looking at Cyn with his hand poised on the door handle.

"Yes, for the moment. I've been keeping him posted," said Cyn.

"Good. Call me the moment you find anything."

Cyn and Jake said nothing until the door was firmly closed behind the Professor.

Jake patted the chair beside him, smiling at her. "Come sit down, Cyn Cyn. I need you beside me in more ways than one."

Cyn smiled at him and sat down. He reached over and squeezed her thigh. She put her hand over his and squeezed it slightly before firmly removing it. She shook her finger under his nose.

He grinned. "I know, I know. All business," he muttered, and turned his attention to the monitor in front of them. "OK, Ms. Hoover. Where do you want to start?" he asked.

"Let's start with the day before the fire at, say, 0600."

"Done," said Jake as he tapped commands onto the keyboard. A picture came up on the screen, accompanied by a loud buzzing sound.

They were looking at a digital clock on a bedside table as Harry's hand reached out and pushed a button to turn off the alarm. The clock read 6:02 a.m. The screen went black for a moment as Harry presumably closed his eyes. Suddenly, there was a loud ringing sound that made them jump.

"Can you turn down the volume a little?" asked Cyn.

Jake pressed the down arrow on the volume control on the keyboard as a picture came back up on the screen. They saw Harry's hand groping for a phone that rested in its cradle on the bedside table. Then the view bounced and shifted from the bottom of the bed to a wall across the room as Harry apparently sat up in bed and answered the phone.

Then they heard a male voice with a distinct Germanic accent coming from the phone. "Sorry to call you so early, but I have an urgent question for you regarding the money transfers, and I didn't want to call you at work, if you know what I mean."

The view shifted from the wall to a window with heavy blue velvet drapes drawn across it, then to the bottom of the bed where they could see the outline of Harry's legs and feet under a pale blue sheet.

The voice continued. "The bank that does the transfers has elected an American as Chief Executive Officer, and he is under pressure to disclose the names of American clients to the United States Internal Revenue Service. I wanted to make you aware of this and see if you want your identity to be disclosed."

The picture shifted rapidly from side to side as Harry shook his head. There was a long pause and then the voice continued.

"Yes, we could do that. There are other financial institutions that could take the account over, but it would mean you would have to become a Confidential Naturalized Swiss Citizen, or CNSC, as we like to call it."

The picture shifted around the room again and then came back to rest on the view of Harry's legs and feet under the crumpled sheet.

"Yes, it's just a procedural matter. I can take care of everything. I will withdraw five thousand franks from the account to pay the judge. By day's end you will have naturalized status, and the account will be transferred to the Bank of Switzerland. Then your monthly transfers will continue without risk of disclosure."

There was another pause as they continued to stare at Harry's feet.

"Good. It will be done. I hope you can manage to come over for a visit this year. It has been several years since I've seen you."

After another short pause, they saw Harry's hand holding the phone as he placed it back in its cradle on the bedside table. The clock now said 6:20 a.m.

"Well, well," said Jake "Harry had a Swiss bank account and became a Swiss citizen just like that. Wonder how he managed to get money out of the country to Switzerland in the first place."

"Much as we'd like to know, it's really none of our business," said Cyn. "I remind you our only real interest in Harry's memory is to find out what went wrong with the E-Weapon."

"Yeah, I know. Still I'd sure like to see if he ever did anything with his formula for beating slot machines," said Jake.

They were now viewing Harry's arm reaching out to turn on the shower.

"Run it forward. Let's not waste time with another shower scene," said Cyn impatiently.

"Right," said Jake. He fast-forwarded until the clock showed 0800 hours.

Now they were looking through a car windshield at a sign over a security gate that read "Los Alamos Research Center." Then the view shifted to the left as Harry turned his head. The driver's side window rolled down and a man with bushy red eyebrows smiled at them. He was clad in a security guard's uniform.

"Good morning, Professor Latter," he said as Harry's hand reached out to him. "Looks like it's going to be another beautiful day."

The guard took the ID card from Harry's hand and scanned it with a hand-held device. Then he handed the card back to Harry and stepped back from the vehicle.

Now they were looking out the windshield again. A security gate lifted in front of them and the car moved forward. They saw a sprawling single-story concrete structure ahead of them. The car pulled into a parking space near the entrance. As Harry looked into the rearview mirror, they saw another car approaching. It pulled into the parking space next to Harry.

Harry got out of the car and paused at the entrance to the building. The driver of the other car got out and came toward him. He had dark hair and a beard and was wearing sunglasses.

"Good morning, Professor. It's going to be another splendid day," said the new arrival in a voice that seemed familiar to Cyn.

The view shifted to the entryway and Harry's hand placing a card key in the door lock.

"Just a second," said Cyn. "Go back and freeze-frame that guy's face. He seems familiar."

Jake did as she asked, and they were looking at the dark hair and the beard and Harry's face reflected in the sunglasses.

"Does he seem familiar to you?" asked Cyn.

Jake peered closely at the monitor. "Well, I can't really tell with those sunglasses and that beard, but he kinda' reminds me of Dr. Graham."

"That's what I thought, too, when I heard his voice," said Cyn. "I wonder what he was doing at Los Alamos. Surely, he wouldn't have had any involvement with the E-Weapon project."

"I don't know," said Jake. "Maybe he was just there for a meeting or something."

"Yeah, maybe," said Cyn with a frown. "Well, let's get on with it. Maybe he'll appear again."

Jake fast-forwarded until they saw a cluttered desk and a computer monitor. Harry's fingers were rapidly tapping on the keyboard in front of them.

The screen lit up and they could see Harry's right hand maneuvering a mouse. A cursor on the screen pointed to a magnetic frequency number and highlighted it. Then a mathematical formula came up.

"Better make a copy of that," said Cyn. "Maybe this is what we have been looking for."

"It's all Greek to me," said Jake clicking the print button. "Look. There is more," he added, pointing to the bottom of the page. "There are fifty pages total."

Cyn was studying the formula on the existing page. "It has something to do with emitting a chosen frequency to counterbalance an existing one, I think," she muttered. "Unfortunately, we can only print out what Harry is looking at—not the entire fifty pages."

As they sat watching, Harry clicked to page two, and Jake quickly printed it. "This looks just like the first page to me," he commented.

"It is very similar to the first page except this applies to a different magnetic frequency. It has something to do with power levels," said Cyn slowly.

Jake nodded. "Oh, yeah, I see it now. I just hope Harry looks at all the pages so we can get a complete printout."

"Speed it up a bit and we'll see," said Cyn.

Again Jake fast-forwarded and after ten minutes he had printed out forty-nine pages. Harry was now looking at page fifty and seemed to be perusing it far longer than the other pages.

"It looks like Harry is trying to work something out. See that column to the right? It's blank," said Cyn.

Jake nodded. "I see that. There appears to be one constant and five variables. Now, if we just knew what those variables are."

"There should be a listing somewhere to say what they are. We'll just have to be patient and see if Harry leads us to it," said Cyn.

The view shifted as Harry leaned back and looked around his office.

Then they were looking down at his desk again. Harry's hand reached out and picked up a pencil. He jotted down the formula on the screen on a writing pad. Then he drew five vertical columns for each of the five variables.

"Now we're getting somewhere," said Jake as he printed out page fifty.

They watched as Harry entered the formula and a series of numbers to represent the variables into a calculator. He wrote the answer down in another column and did another calculation using the next set of variables. After Harry had completed all of the calculations, Jake hit the print button.

"Hold on, Jake! I think the last calculation Harry did was incorrect. Go back," said Cyn jumping up from her chair in excitement.

Jake did as he was told while Cyn stared at the monitor. Suddenly she said, "Stop there! Look at the numbers at the bottom of the column and watch Harry enter them in the calculator. Fifty-seven, OK. Sixteen, OK. One hundred five, OK. Square root of sixty-four is eight, OK. Square of seventeen is four thousand nine hundred thirteen. That's the mistake! Do you see it?"

"Yeah!" said Jake. "Harry cubed seventeen instead of squaring it. His answer is seventeen times too high!"

"Harry seems to be unaware of his mistake," said Cyn as they watched him writing the number down in the column.

"That's right," said Jake. "Maybe someone will double check his numbers."

"Maybe…." Cyn began. She was interrupted when the telephone on Harry's desk rang.

They saw Harry pick up the phone. Now the view was of the wall across the room as they heard a deep masculine voice coming over the phone.

"Good morning, Professor Latter. Brown here. Just wanted you to know I'm ready to set up the trial run for tomorrow. Do you have the magnetic modulation numbers for me?"

Harry picked up the notepad with his left hand and brought it up closer to read. For a few moments the notepad filled the screen, then he put it down on the desk again and they were staring at the computer monitor on Harry's desk.

"Just to be sure, Professor, I'll read the numbers back to you, OK?" said Brown.

Harry lifted the pad up again, and they heard Brown recite the numbers back to him. They could see that they were exactly what Harry had written on the pad. There was a pause, and then they heard Brown say, "Yes, Sir. I will install the modulators.

I…uh…I hope you don't mind my saying so, but…uh…that last number seems pretty high."

They focused on the last column through Harry's eyes. After a bit, Brown said, "No, Sir. I didn't mean to question you. It was just an off-the-cuff observation."

There was another pause and Brown said, "Yes, Sir. I will make sure everything is ready for the trial to begin at eleven tomorrow morning."

Harry put the telephone down and turned back to view his computer monitor. After looking at the formula display on page fifty for a while, he typed in the results of his computations from the notepad. When Harry entered the last number, Brent printed the page, and none too soon because Harry quickly encrypted the formula and closed the program.

Jake looked over at Cyn. "Well, what do you think?"

"I think that wraps it up," she said. "We have the complete formula, and I'm almost positive we have the miscalculation that caused the fire."

"I think you're right. The last number he calculated was seventeen times too high. It must have overloaded the circuitry and caused the fire. We already know the fire began right at the beginning of the test the next day."

"What is Harry doing now?" asked Cyn. Harry was writing something down in another notebook.

"Another formula by the looks of it," said Jake squinting at the screen. "I wonder what this is for."

Harry wrote for several minutes, and then moved his hand away showing the title at the top of the page.

Cyn read it out loud. "Predicting Random Events."

She and Jake looked at each other with raised eyebrows.

"You thinkin' what I'm thinkin'?" asked Jake with a slow grin spreading across his face.

"Yes! This must be Harry's magic formula for winning jackpots on slot machines.

Look. He's jotted down the number of reels and the number of the different types of symbols on each reel."

"This I want to know!" said Jake leaning forward in his chair. "Then maybe you'll go to Vegas with me when we're finished here."

"Hold on, Jake. We don't know if Harry actually came up with anything or not. All we saw was Harry playing on his own slot machine, and I'm sure there'd be ways to manipulate that."

"Nevertheless, I'm printing this page for sure," said Jake. "I'd love to look back further in Harry's memory to see if he actually used it in real casinos."

"So would I, but it doesn't really have anything to do with our job here. Don't print that out right now. We're going to have to keep this slot machine thing to ourselves. Maybe we can come back to it later. Right now, I've got to let the General know that we've found what we were supposed to be looking for."

"Sure. Mum's the word. General Masters and the Professor will be thrilled that we've discovered what went wrong at Los Alamos," said Jake. "Maybe this means I'll be able to get out of here until tomorrow afternoon. If so, do you want to have dinner with me tonight at the Inn? It's only seven-thirty now."

"Let's see what happens. I've got things to do when I get back," said Cyn as she pulled out her cell phone. Seeing Jake's crestfallen look, she quickly added, "Maybe we could have a drink in the bar later."

"Sure. That works," said Jake, the smile returning to his face.

"Remember. I said 'maybe'," said Cyn.
"Maybe is good enough for right now."

Cyn pressed a couple of buttons on the cell phone as she continued to return Jake's intense gaze.

* * *

7:40 p.m.

General Masters and Professor Braun burst into Jake's office. "You found it?" asked Braun with more animation in his voice than Cyn had heard before.

"Yes. We think so, Sir," said Jake holding up the fifty pages they had printed from Harry's memory.

"Good job," said the General. "Let's have a look."

They all drew up chairs around Jake's small conference table, and Jake placed the document in the center of the table. Braun grabbed it and began leafing through it. "Looks as if this is the complete formula. Where did you find it?" he asked.

"The morning before the trial run," said Jake. "Professor Latter went through the entire formula and did the final modulation calculations. He gave them to a technician named Brown to set everything up for the test the next morning."

"So what caused the fire?" asked the General.

Jake looked at Cyn and she nodded at him to continue. "Professor Latter made a mistake when he calculated the last frequency modulation. It's the last number on page fifty."

Braun looked up from the document. "What? Surely Harry Latter wouldn't make a simple math error and not catch it," he said in a sharp tone.

Jake looked at Cyn again and she responded. "Unfortunately, that's exactly what happened. Look at the last number," she said.

The Professor quickly flipped to the last page and traced a finger down over the numbers Harry had entered. "I see the last number is four thousand nine hundred thirteen. How do you know that's a mistake?"

"Because we saw Harry actually doing the calculations. On this last number he intended to square seventeen, but he cubed it instead. The last number is seventeen times too high, and we think that's what caused the fire," explained Cyn.

"I don't believe it. I want to see that," said Braun. "Can you run that part for me, Jake?"

"Sure thing," said Jake pushing his chair back. He went over to the monitor he had been using to view Harry's memory. The Professor and the General walked over and stood looking over Jake's shoulder at the computer screen.

Jake tapped on the keyboard. Nothing happened. He frowned and tapped on the keyboard again. The screen remained blank. "That's odd," he muttered.

"What's wrong?" asked Cyn from across the room.

"I don't know for sure. I don't seem to be getting any data flow from Roswell."

Cyn got up and walked over as Jake again tapped in commands with no result. "Try it again," she said as she leaned over his shoulder and watched him enter the commands. This time there was a blip of light and several static-like lines and then the screen went blank again.

"Maybe the computer at Roswell is down," suggested the General.

Cyn shook her head. "No, I don't think the NSA computer would go down. There seems to be some interference. Jake, why don't you shut down and then try establishing the link again."

"OK," said Jake. He shut the computer down and rebooted it. After it had finished loading he tapped on the keyboard again. "Voila!" he said as the screen came to life. "That did the trick."

Jake quickly pulled up the scene where Harry was performing the computations. Professor Braun read through the process aloud as Cyn had done earlier. "Fifty-seven, that's correct. Sixteen, correct. One hundred five, correct. Square root of sixty-four is eight, that's correct. Square of seventeen is four thousand nine hundred thirteen. My God! He did make a mistake! You're sure he didn't catch it before they performed the test?"

"No, he didn't," said Jake. "The technician even commented that the last number seemed quite high, but Professor Latter didn't correct it."

"Well, that's it then. That's what caused the fire. Just a simple math error," said Braun shaking his head.

"How would that cause a fire?" asked the General. "I'm going to have to explain this, so give it to me in terms a lay person would understand."

"That's your forte, I believe, Ms. Hoover," said Braun.

Cyn smiled. "Yes. Well, let's see. What's a good analogy? I know." She turned to the General. "You know when you fire an Uzi very rapidly for a sustained period of time how the barrel gets really hot?"

He nodded. "Sure. That I understand."

"But if you fire it in short bursts the barrel remains relatively cool?" The General nodded again.

"Well, that's what happened to the E5. Because of that miscalculation, Harry was firing that gun way too fast and it overloaded the electric circuits and sparked the fire."

The General looked at Braun. "That makes sense to me. Is that how you would characterize it?"

"I would characterize it in much greater detail, but that's a simple enough explanation," said Braun.

"Good!" said the General rubbing his hands together. "I'd say half of this mission is complete then. I'm going to get a little shut-eye and then work up the reports for the powers-that-be. There's no reason for the rest of you to stay. You might as well get a little R and R before we get those video boards in here tomorrow afternoon. Other than that, we're all set for the next download on Monday morning, aren't we?"

Braun nodded. "Yes. Everything's ready in the chamber, and Dr. Graham is all set. It should go quite well after what we've learned with the last experiment."

"All right. Speaking of Dr. Graham, I'm going to relieve him until Monday morning. He's been pretty stressed since the last experiment, and some time off ought to help. Jake, you get outa" here and relax. We'll need you back in here late tomorrow afternoon to install the new video board.

You've done a great job. Get out and get some fresh air. It's supposed to be a good clear day tomorrow."

"Thanks, Sir. I will," said Jake with a grin. He glanced at Cyn, but she was looking at the General.

Braun cleared his throat and touched Cyn's shoulder. "Er, uh…Ms. Hoover, the General tells me you have an interest in gold prospecting."

Cyn turned to him with a slight smile. "That's right, Professor Braun. I've been into that since I was a little kid."

Braun's face colored slightly. "Well, it's a hobby of mine and I have some interesting sites you might want to explore. Since we have a free day tomorrow, I could pick you up at the Inn and show you. That is, if you don't already have other plans?"

Cyn's smile broadened. "No, no other plans. I'd love to do a little prospecting. Thanks for asking."

"Good," said Braun looking down at his feet. "What time shall I pick you up?"

"The earlier the better," said Cyn enthusiastically. "How about nine? Is that too early for you?"

"No. That suits me fine," said Braun. "I'll see you then."

Cyn could feel Jake's eyes boring into her back as she followed the General and the Professor out of his office. She did not turn around.

* * *

8:55 p.m.

The Adobe Walls Lounge was jam-packed and jumping when Cyn walked in just before nine o'clock. The band was playing "Give Me That Old-Time Rock and Roll," and the dance floor was crammed with gyrating bodies.

Cyn stood just at the edge of the bar, tapping her fingers in time to the music, and looking directly at Mac up on the stage. She reached into her pocket and pressed a key on her cell phone. Mac scanned the room as he continued to sing and strum on his guitar. He spotted her and grinned. His gold tooth glinted in the spotlight.

"What's your pleasure, Hon?" yelled a voice in Cyn's ear causing her to jump. She turned and saw Loretta, the bartender, grinning at her.

"Nothing right now," Cyn shouted back at her. "I'll come back later!"

"Right!" shouted Loretta. She moved on down the bar to another customer.

As Cyn left the lounge, the band finished the song, and there was a long drum roll. Then she heard Mac announce, "Break time, folks. We'll be back in thirty. Wet your whistles for the next set."

Cyn hurried to the back door, went outside and stood by her Jeep. In a few minutes, Mac burst through the back door and motioned to her to follow him. The bus door slid open and Cyn followed him inside.

"So, what's new, Ms. Jones?" asked Mac as he sank down in his usual chair, tilted his hat back and mopped his brow with a bandana.

"We found the information we were looking for in Professor Latter's memory," said Cyn taking the seat across the table from him.

"You mean what went wrong with the E-Weapon?" asked Mac.

Cyn nodded.

"It was a simple math error, right?"

Cyn stared at him. "That's right, but how did you know?"

"We picked up more chatter. That mountain's leaking like a sieve. It's also out that the next memory download has been moved back up to Monday morning."

"Good grief!" cried Cyn. "When did this come out?"

"Just a little after eight o'clock. Right before we started playing." Cyn frowned. "Then it happened just after I left."

"So, who was still there?"

Cyn thought for a moment. "As far as I know, the General, Professor Braun, Jacobson, Dr. Graham and Captain Denton. The General is letting everyone off until late tomorrow afternoon, but I don't think any of them had gone before I did."

Mac shook his head. "So, it's still the same cast of suspects."

"Afraid so," said Cyn. "What I'm worried about is if someone out there now has the formula for the E5. Did the chatter indicate anything like that?"

"Nope. Just that the fire was caused by a math error. No specifics. I wouldn't worry about that yet. They'd have to have the entire formula."

Cyn nodded and breathed a little easier. "Yes, I guess you're right," she said.

"One more piece of info," said Mac. "The Brits tracked an e-mail message sent earlier today. It was a message written in Arabic originating in Riyadh, Saudi Arabia. It was relayed around the globe and ended up in Boston. The sender was Prince Ali Yuseph Farad, and the receiver was Ibrahim Abdul Farad. Turns out Ibrahim is the Prince's grandson who is attending MIT."

"What did the message say?" asked Cyn.

" 'Have you remembered your grandfather's birthday tomorrow? Praise be to Allah'."

"And?" asked Cyn. "Why is that suspicious?"

"Because shortly after Ibrahim received that e-mail, he turned around and made a phone call to a cell phone in this area, either at the Air Base or possibly even inside Apparition Mountain," said Mac.

"And what did he say?" asked Cyn.

Mac shook his head. "No one can figure it out. There was a short conversation in a language none of us have ever heard before. Sounds like a bunch of mumbo jumbo. Maybe it was scrambled or encoded."

"That does sound suspicious," said Cyn. "Were you able to track down the owner of the cell phone at this end?"

"No. It's apparently one of those pay-as-you-go mobiles. No telling who it's registered to. I've got the conversation on tape. Maybe you can make some sense of it." Mac reached over and turned on a small portable tape recorder.

He watched Cyn's face intently as they listened to the recording. "Ring any bells?" he asked as he turned the recorder off.

Cyn paused for a moment, frowning. "No," she lied. She knew exactly what it was, but she didn't want to tell Mac—at least not yet. The conversation she had just heard was in Tiwa, the ancient language of the Taos Indians.

Mac glanced at his watch. "I gotta get back on stage in a few minutes. Meanwhile, there's another bit of information on Braun. We checked further into that gold mining corporation, and, guess what? It has assets of fifty million dollars, and the only producing mine and refining facility is located on that property in Santa Fe that we visited today."

"What? I sure didn't see any sign of that, did you?" asked Cyn.

Mac shook his head. "Nope, but maybe it's back in the mountains behind the house. Another curious thing: Skeeter tried to find the name of the CEO and the directors, but he was denied access. The company's not on the stock exchange, and there's no news about it either, other than the property ownership records."

"Could be a scam," surmised Cyn.

"Maybe...." said Mac. "I'll see what I can find out when I meet the housekeeper tomorrow."

"I'd almost forgotten about that," said Cyn with a laugh. "Actually, I"m going you one better. I have a date with the Professor himself."

"You're kidding! How'd you arrange that?"

"He found out I like to go gold prospecting, and since we all have the day off tomorrow, he offered to show me some of his favorite sites."

"Well, I'll be damned! Think h"'ll show you the mine?"

"I haven't a clue," said Cyn, "but I'll sure try every which way I know to find out about it."

"Good. Oh, by the way, I'm gonna have to borrow your Jeep for my date tomorrow. Can't hardly take the bus and the band with me, and there ain't too many car rental agencies here in Roca Grande."

Cyn frowned, hesitating. "Well, it would be fine with me, but I'm sure they've got tracking devices on the Jeep and the keys. What happens if they discover someone else is driving it?"

Mac gave her a disgruntled look. "Use your head, Cyn. What business do you think I'm in anyway? They're using the standard NSA tracking stuff, and I know how to take care of that. As for the keys, hand 'em over and I'll fix that right now."

Cyn fished the keys out of her bag and handed them to him with a sheepish look.

"Ok, Mac, just as long as you don't leave before Braun picks me up. I don't want to be stranded."

"What time's he pickin' you up?" asked Mac as he took the keys and stood up.

"Nine o'clock."

"Oh, that gives me plenty of time, no problem," said Mac. "Stay put. I'll be right back."

Cyn watched him stride off toward the back room. He entered the room and the door slid shut behind him. Cyn sat there frowning and fidgeting for a few moments as she reviewed the day's events in her head.

Suddenly Mac emerged from the back room and walked quickly to the table. He tossed her keys down on the table. "Here's your keys back," he announced.

Cyn looked at him in surprise as she reached for the keys. "What did you do?" she asked.

"Made myself a new set of keys without the tracking chip," he said with a grin. He held up his left hand where a set of keys dangled from a ring around his pinkie finger. "Now, if they're trackin' you by the keys, they'll know you're where you're supposed to be—with Braun. As for the Jeep, it'll just show up in its usual parking space here at the Inn."

"Remember, if you're stopped for any reason that Jeep is registered to Barbara Jones," said Cyn.

Mac rolled his eyes. "You're such a worry wart, Agent Hoover! After all, Barbara Jones is my little ol" cousin from Texas, and she just loaned me her Jeep for a Sunday afternoon ride," said Mac with a chuckle. He nodded toward the door. "You ready to go?"

Cyn nodded, still frowning. As she rose from her seat, Mac patted her shoulder. "Relax, Agent Hoover," he said. "What could possibly go wrong?"

Cyn just shook her head. "I've heard that before," she muttered.

* * *

9:20 p.m.

Mac and Cyn walked back into the lounge together.

"Time enough for a short one before we start playin' again," said Mac. "The rest of the band's over at the back table. Come on. I'll buy you a drink before we start."

"OK," said Cyn. She followed Mac as he wended his way through the crowded room. She could not see beyond his bulk in the dim smoke-filled room.

As they approached the table, Mac stood aside slightly and said out of the corner of his mouth. "Looks like we got company."

Cyn glanced at the table and saw six people sitting around it. "Oh, no," she murmured.

"It'll be OK. Just follow my lead," said Mac in a low voice. He barged ahead and grabbed two empty chairs from an adjacent table.

"Looks like you got a party goin' on here," he said in a loud voice as he held out one of the chairs for Cyn.

"Hey, Mac!" said Skeeter. "You're just in time for a quick Velvet and soda. I'll go get it for you. What're you drinkin', Barbara?" he asked as he stood up.

"Oh, I'll just have a glass of red wine," said Cyn.

Skeeter walked off towards the bar.

"So, who's our friends here?" inquired Mac.

"Well, you remember Charlie Denton from last night," said Veronica.

Charlie was grinning at them from his seat next to Veronica. He had one arm draped around her shoulder and a pint glass of beer in the other hand. He raised his glass. "Good to see yuh, Mac…Ms. Jones," he said in a slightly slurred voice. "Brought two of my buddies along tonight. Jake and Dan, meet the leader of this fine band, Mack Gentry. I think you guys already know Ms. Barbara Jones."

Mac reached across the table and shook hands first with Dan Graham and then with Brent Jacobson. "Say," he said looking at Jake. "I've seen you before. You go by the name of *Halcon*, don't you? Play all those different kinds o' flutes? I admire your work, man."

Jake smiled. "That's me, all right. Glad you like my music. I hear you're pretty good yourself."

Mac grinned and shook his head. "Well, you can be the judge of that after the next set. We do OK, but we ain't exactly the artistes like yourself."

Skeeter arrived back at the table and handed Cyn and Mac their drinks. Mac took a gulp of his drink and pointed a finger at Jake. "What brings you here? You doin' a gig around here? Maybe you'd like to sit in during our last set?"

Jake raised a hand. "Thanks, but no. I'm taking some time away from the music business. I'm doing some work at the Air Base, and we have some time off, so Charlie invited Dan and me to come along."

"Yeah. Dan here's a doctor at the Base," announced Hound Dog, clapping Dr. Graham on the back.

"Is that so?" asked Mac raising his glass to Dan. "Well, we might need a doctor in here tonight as heated up as some o' these folks get when we play."

Dr. Graham shook his head. "Nope. Doctor's off-duty tonight. I've had a pretty stressful week, and I need the R and R."

"That's right," said Charlie. "The Doc and Veronica and I are gonna get outdoors tomorrow. Maybe take a jaunt up to Taos."

"Oh, yeah?" asked Hound Dog. "What you gonna do there?"

"Oh, we don't know. Whatever pops up, I guess. The Doc here's always wanted to see Kit Carson's house and maybe visit the Pueblo," said Charlie. "Veronica and I wanta visit some of those cantinas."

"What about you, Jake? You gonna give these guys a tour of the Pueblo?" asked Skeeter.

"No. I have to stick close. There's a chance I might be called back to the Base in the afternoon," said Jake. Suddenly he focused intently on Cyn. "And you, Ms. Jones? Got any plans for your time off?"

Cyn choked slightly on the sip of wine she had just taken. She glared back at him. "I'm going gold prospecting with a friend," she said.

"Oh, really. That sounds interesting," said Jake casually. "By the way, how do you know our friend Mac here?"

"Oh, Barb is Mac's cousin from Texas," said Veronica before Cyn had a chance to respond.

"Cousin? Well, well. It's a small world. Here you both happen to be in Roca Grande at the same time. What a coincidence," said Jake.

Mac chuckled. "Yeah, can you beat that? We haven't seen each other in a coon's age, and here we end up in the same place at the same time."

"Yeah, I was really surprised when I checked in and saw Mac's name on the billboard," said Cyn following Mac's lead.

Mac chugged down the rest of his drink and slammed the glass down on the table. "Well, girls and boys, time for us to get to work."

He stood up, hitched up his jeans and adjusted his hat. Veronica, Hound Dog and Skeeter pushed back their chairs and walked past him on their way to the bandstand. "See y'all after this set if you're still here," said Mac with a wave as he turned to follow them.

"Actually, I think I'm going to turn in. It's been a long day," said Cyn. "I'll see all of you later. Have a good day tomorrow."

"You, too," said Charlie. "Hope you find a gold mine so we can all retire."

Cyn laughed. "Me, too."

"Good luck," said Dr. Graham.

"Thanks," said Cyn. She smiled at him and nodded at Jake as she turned to leave. Jake did not return her smile.

* * *

SUNDAY

10:30 a.m.

Cyn could not believe it. She was in the passenger seat of Karl Braun's battered old Ford pickup, and they were bouncing over a road that was little more than a deer trail. Directly ahead of them was the boarded up mine shaft she had glimpsed the day before when she and Mac had scouted out Braun's property.

She glanced over at the driver. This was a Karl Braun who was entirely unfamiliar to her. He had arrived promptly at nine o'clock, and, although she was waiting from him in the lobby, she did not recognize the man who came in through the main entrance and walked over to her. He looked like someone right out of "Crocodile Dundee" with his broad brimmed hat strapped up on one side in the Australian style. He wore khakis, a sheepskin lined leather vest, and heavy hiking boots.

She did not realize it was Karl Braun until he took off his dark glasses and said, "Good morning, Ms. Jones. Are you ready to go?"

Even then she had a hard time believing it was Karl Braun. Those icy gray eyes had somehow taken on a richer hue and even appeared to be twinkling. The pale skin now seemed to glow with a healthy tan. Even the cold tones of his voice had warmed.

"Professor Braun?" asked Cyn looking at him closely.

"Yes, it's me," he said with a low chuckle. "I suppose you didn't recognize me without the lab coat. Please, no 'Professor' today. It makes me feel ancient. Just call me Karl."

"All right…Karl," said Cyn still amazed.

"Good," he said. "Shall we go? I left the pickup running out front. It's a glorious day, and I've got a lot to show you."

"Lead the way, Karl," said Cyn with a smile as she picked up her bag and coat.

He held open the door and gave a mock bow and flourish with his right arm. "After you, Madame," he announced.

"Why, thank you, kind Sir," said Cyn with a chuckle as she swept past him. "Phew!" she muttered to herself. "The 'Professor' Who Came in From the Cold'!"

All the way to Santa Fe, they had engaged in small talk about the countryside, the weather, where Cyn had grown up, and past prospecting adventures. Not once did Braun allude to the work at Apparition Mountain and Cyn followed suit. When they turned onto the almost hidden trail that led to Braun's estate, Cyn asked, "Where are we going?"

"You'll see," said Karl mysteriously.

Cyn said little as they drove on up the same road she and Mac had traveled yesterday. She didn't want to give any indication that she had been here before.

When they came over the rise and the huge estate came into view, she blurted, "Oh, would you look at that! What a huge place out in the middle of nowhere! I wonder who owns that. Probably a movie star or someone."

Karl glanced over at her with a sly grin. "No, not a movie star. Just a humble professor."

Cyn stared at him in surprise. "You mean?"

He nodded. "That's right. It's all mine."

"But how could you…."

"Afford all that?" he finished for her.

She nodded, looking at him with a raised brow.

He shrugged good-naturedly as he concentrated on the road ahead of them. "It's a long story," he said. "If you're good, maybe I'll tell you sometime."

Cyn glanced at him, but he didn't seem inclined to say more. She contented herself with studying the surroundings as he approached the massive gates in front of the property. Magically, the gates opened before them, and he drove straight through without slowing. She saw the gates closing behind them in the rearview mirror.

"Do the gates just automatically open when a vehicle approaches?" she asked.

"Only for me. They know who I am," he said cryptically.

Again he did not seem inclined to say more so Cyn didn't pursue it. She concentrated on the surroundings. They were driving along a wide avenue lined with a mixed variety of high desert plants. At the end of the avenue spread out before them was a huge hacienda-style mansion. Cyn was looking forward to seeing the inside of the mansion, but when they were about a hundred yards away Karl took a left-hand turn onto a dirt road. The road skirted the outbuildings of the estate and wound its way up through the foothills of the mountain in the distance. The road soon became a mere trail, and now here they were pulling up in a swirl of dust at the old mine shaft.

"Here we are," announced Karl. "This is what I wanted to show you."

He jammed the gears into neutral, cut the engine, and stomped on the foot brake. He whipped off his dark glasses and looked over at Cyn with a grin.

"You mean that old abandoned mine?" asked Cyn.

"Yeah, but it's an operating mine, it's a gold mine, and it's all mine," he quipped. His eyes were positively shining.

* * *

10:45 a.m.

"The reason I bought this property was because of this mine. It was abandoned years ago when it became too costly to dig out the ore and refine it," Karl explained as he and Cyn stood in front of the boarded-up shaft.

There was a padlock attached to a heavy rusted chain that crisscrossed wooden boards secured to a heavy iron gate. Cyn anticipated that Karl would produce a key and unlock the padlock. Instead he walked to the side of the entrance and placed his right palm on a rock that jutted out from the earth. There was a heavy grinding sound and the entire entrance—gate, boards and padlock—slid to the left like a patio door.

As the entrance slid aside, Karl studied Cyn's face for her reaction. "Wow!" was all she could say.

"Pretty cool, huh?" he said with a grin.

"I'll say," said Cyn. "Who came up with that idea?"

"Yours truly," said Karl. "I invented and built it myself, along with all the other things you're about to see. You'll soon find out this is not your ordinary gold mine."

"But what if someone else accidentally or on purpose put his hand on that rock?" asked Cyn.

"The door wouldn't open," said Karl. "It will only open for those I tell it to. It has to do with palm print recognition. Come on inside. I don't like to leave the door open too long."

He stepped inside the entrance and tripped a switch. The black hole was instantly bathed in incandescent light and Cyn quickly walked in to join him. Again Karl pressed his palm on a rock, and the iron gate slid shut.

Cyn looked around. They were in what had appeared to be an old mine shaft when viewed through the iron gate from the outside. In reality it was a small cave with chiseled rock walls and a gravel floor. The only object in the cave was a metal shop cabinet. Karl went over to the cabinet and opened it. He took off his sunglasses and hat and placed them inside the cabinet. Then he produced two miner's hardhats.

"Here. You'd better put one of these on, just in case," he said handing one of the hats to Cyn.

"In case of what?" asked Cyn as she donned the hat.

"The light on the hat will come on automatically if there's a power failure," said Karl as he put on his own hardhat. "But not to worry. There's little chance of that because I did all the wiring myself."

"Now you *really* have me worried," said Cyn with a grin.

Karl laughed. "I know you think I'm inept, but you'll soon find out different. Come on. Let's go into the mine."

Motioning for her to follow him, Karl walked to the back of the cave and stopped at what appeared to be a solid rock wall.

"This is the premier security barrier," said Karl pointing at the wall. "It is the ultimate in technology. It can take a direct atomic blast and you can't cut through it with anything. I designed and built it myself."

"It just looks like a wall. How do you open it?" asked Cyn squinting at the wall trying to detect a door.

"This black panel here," said Karl walking up to the wall. "All that is necessary is to put my hand in the center like so."

Cyn watched him press his outstretched hand on what looked like a smooth rock about chest-high on the wall.

"Now, I hold still for a second or two while the computer analyzes my heart rhythm, which, as you know, is unique for every individual," Karl continued.

Cyn heard a click.

"Now, Cyn, you do the same, so I can enroll you into the system. To get out of the mine, you will have to do the same thing coming out. I've already told the system there's someone with me that I want to admit."

"How did you do that?"

"I simply pressed my small finger a little harder on the panel than the rest of my hand."

"What if I'd had a gun at your back, and I was someone you didn't want to get in?" asked Cyn.

"In that case, I would have pressed harder with my index finger and a nerve agent would be dispensed that would do away with you."

"But wouldn't it do away with you, too?"

Karl shook his head. "No. I've been vaccinated. Come on. Let's get you enrolled. Just press your palm lightly on the panel."

When she had complied, Karl returned to the panel and pressed his hand on it again. A few seconds later part of the wall began to lift, and when it was high enough, they both walked through.

"Watch out!" said Karl as he pulled Cyn out of the doorway. The ground shook as the door slammed down. "It's slow rising but quick coming down."

"Whew! I'll say it is!" exclaimed Cyn, her heart racing. "You've got to be quick getting through there. It's like a guillotine!"

They were now in a large tunnel. Karl motioned for Cyn to follow him. They walked for what Cyn estimated to be at least a hundred yards before the tunnel opened into a large cavern that was filled with machinery and mining equipment.

"Welcome to my one-man gold mining operation," said Karl. He pointed at a huge piece of machinery. "There is where it begins, with the crusher. I just blast out the rocks and put them in the crusher, and it's all automatic after that, from raw ore to gold ingots."

"You mean you actually refine the gold right here by yourself?" asked Cyn in surprise.

"Yes," Karl said. "I invented a way to do it. Come on. I'll show you how to make a little gold."

Cyn followed him over to the crusher.

"First we put some rocks in the crusher," said Karl.

He turned a switch on what looked like an enormous garbage

dumpster. The dumpster hummed and creaked as it began to rise. When it was at the right height above the crusher chute, it tipped, and there was a deafening noise as the dumpster's load of rocks fell into the crusher. After the last rock had fallen, the dumpster hummed again and returned to its resting position. Then it automatically switched itself off.

Now the crusher came to life, and again the cavern was filled with a deafening noise as the machine hammered the rocks into gravel. At the same time a flame sparked to life in a huge furnace some distance away that was connected to the crusher by a conveyor belt.

"Now for the fun part," said Karl as the conveyor belt began transporting the finely crushed rock toward the furnace.

"What happens now?" asked Cyn, watching the first of the crushed ore enter the furnace.

"The temperature is high enough in that furnace to turn the rock particles to gas. Then the gold gas is filtered out by a gas centrifuge," said Karl.

"You're kidding! A gas centrifuge?" asked Cyn in amazement.

Karl smiled, pride registering in his eyes. "Yes. I invented the process myself. I understand your surprise, because as I assume you know, a gas centrifuge is normally associated with uranium refining. This is the first time it has ever been used to refine gold."

Suddenly, the cavern was filled with a high-pitched whining sound that seemed to gather momentum until it became a shriek.

Cyn looked at Karl with a raised eyebrow, hands covering her ears.

"That's the centrifuge spinning out the gold gas," yelled Karl over the noise.

Finally, the noise subsided, and Karl led her to the other side of the furnace. He pointed to a spout at the end of a pipe with a series of metal molds rotating beneath it. "After the gold gas is spun out into that pipe, it cools to liquid form. Then it will pour out of the spout into the molds, where it will harden into gold ingots and be cast out of the molds over there."

"That's absolutely ingenious," declared Cyn. "Now we know how Rumpelstiltskin spins his gold!"

"Well, it takes hundreds of tons of rock to extract even an ounce of gold, and it's a bit of a slow process, but even at that, I can spin more in a night than Rumpeltstiltskin could," said Karl with a laugh. "We should be getting some liquid gold in a little bit. We'll wait for that so you can see the end result."

"This is truly ingenious, Karl. You deserve a Nobel Prize," said Cyn.

Karl shook his head with a grimace. "That will never happen. This is all ultra top-secret. In fact, there are only five of us, and now you, who know about this operation and one of them is your boss."

"My boss?" asked Cyn in amazement. "You mean Senator Goodman? What's his role in this?"

"No, not Senator Goodman," said Karl with a sly grin. "I mean your *real* boss, the one who directed me to bring you here. You see, your boss is my boss, too."

Cyn was speechless. She could only stare at him with wide eyes. A thousand questions raced through her mind.

Karl waved a hand at her. "I know you have tons of questions, and I'll answer them in good time."

He glanced over at the machinery. "Look! We've got gold!" He pointed at the spout where liquid gold was pouring in a thin stream into the mold beneath the spout.

They watched as the stream increased. The first mold filled, and the next mold rotated into its slot under the spout.

"This round should give us about three full molds," Karl commented as they watched the process.

"How much gold have you produced?" asked Cyn.

"Come on, I'll show you," said Karl. He turned and walked toward another tunnel at the other side of the cavern.

"Where are we going?" asked Cyn, rushing to keep up with him as he entered the tunnel.

"To the vault," said Karl. "It is well back in the mountain, and we have to pass through three more security gates to get there. Here's the first one. This is the entrance gate. Now, pay attention."

He paused by a cavity in the wall where there was a blinking red diode. As Cyn watched, he pulled out a keypad that had ten digits printed over letters of the alphabet exactly the same as on a phone. He slowly punched in a series of numbers and looked at Cyn. "Did you get that?" he asked with a grin.

"Yes, I think so," said Cyn.

"Repeat it back to me."

"Well, let's see," said Cyn closing her eyes and trying to visualize the numbers in her mind. "It was 6-7-3-6 and uh, 7-3-7-2-6-3."

She opened her eyes. "Was I right?"

Karl nodded, still grinning. "And?"

"And...." Cyn looked at him with a puzzled expression for a moment, and then she grinned. "Oh, I know. 'Open Sesame.' That's what it spells, right?"

"Right!" said Karl with a laugh. "That's the code that will gain entrance into Aladdin's Cave."

"Gee! How original. I thought you'd have come up with something better than that," said Cyn.

"Sometimes the expected is the best cover," said Karl with a shrug. "Besides, I reprogram the code from time to time, and, don't forget this is only the entrance gate. You have to get through two more barriers before you gain access to the vault."

He pressed the "Enter" key on the keypad, and the blinking red diode changed to green. A heavy steel door began grinding its way upward a few paces in front of them.

Karl put the keypad back in its cavity and motioned to Cyn. They walked through the opening. As soon as they had passed through, the door crashed down behind them.

Cyn squinted to see in the dim light. All she could make out was what appeared to be a solid rock wall on all sides. Again Karl motioned to her to follow him, and he walked forward right up to the wall.

She peered over his shoulder and saw a small dark screen recessed into the rock. Karl pressed a button and a crosshair target appeared on the screen. He looked directly at it for a few seconds, and then a green light came on. He stepped aside and motioned for Cyn to come forward.

"Now, raise both hands in the air and look directly at the center of the target. That way the system will know that you are approved for entrance."

Cyn did as she was told. Soon another green light came on, and the wall in front of them began to rise.

"One more to go," said Karl as they walked through the opening.

They proceeded on through the tunnel as the second barrier closed behind them. After about twenty yards, the tunnel took a sharp curve to the right and appeared to dead-end at another rock wall. Again Karl went up to the wall and stood quietly. Soon a green light came on in a small crevice that was about waist-height up from the floor. Cyn heard a soft buzzing sound emanating from the crevice.

Karl stepped aside. "All right, Cyn. I want you to step up here and put your right index finger in this crevice. The system will verify that you are the same person who went through the second barrier."

Cyn complied. She felt a slight tingling sensation in her finger for a few seconds, and then it stopped. The buzzing also stopped.

"You can withdraw your finger now," said Karl. "That was a laser scan of your fingerprint. Congratulations. You have become a member of a very select group of people who have come through all the barriers."

"More people have made it into Fort Knox than here," said Cyn. "Do the others know the codes to gain entrance?"

Karl shook his head. "No. Only two others have the codes. The others have been here once as guests, the one who directed that I bring you here, and the President of the United States."

"The one who directed you to bring me here...you mean my...*our* boss?" asked Cyn.

"That's correct," said Karl. He abruptly turned and faced the wall again and the rock wall began to rise revealing a massive gleaming metal door. "This is the vault door. It's made of solid titanium, and as you can see, the rock wall is merely a façade."

"How does it open?" asked Cyn. She could not detect a button or handle or keypad anywhere on or near the door.

"We have to complete another test and then it will open," said Karl. "This is a DNA scan. The system has been programmed to recognize my DNA and that of the others who have the access codes. Now I will program it to recognize yours as well."

"You mean as a guest?"

"No. Our boss wants you to have the access codes."

"But why?" asked Cyn becoming exasperated with his cryptic remarks.

"All in good time," said Karl raising a hand. "After we're in the vault I'll explain. Now, I'll go through the DNA recognition scan, and then you'll do the same."

"But how is it going to recognize my DNA? I've never been here before," said Cyn.

"Don't worry. I've already programmed your DNA into the system," said Karl.

"But how...?" Cyn raised an eyebrow in concern.

Karl smiled. "It was really quite simple. How many cups of coffee do you think you've had since you've been at Apparition Mountain? It only took one cup to get a swab of your saliva."

Cyn glared at him. "I'm beginning to feel very uncomfortable with all this. Why would you have to sneak around and get my DNA sample that way? If you're telling the truth about why I'm here, you could have got it from my NSA records."

Karl raised a hand in defense. "No, that was not possible. For security reasons, we didn't want anyone in the NSA or anywhere else getting an inkling that we're looking into your records. Besides, it was faster this way."

Cyn continued to glare at him.

He shrugged. "I understand your suspicions, but you're just going to have to trust me until we get inside the vault. I'll explain everything then."

"I'm not so sure I should be going into that vault with you. In fact, I'm not even sure you are Karl Braun," said Cyn backing away a little.

"Oh, you mean that picture you saw of me in Professor Latter's memory, back at MIT," Karl said with a snort. "People change a lot over the years, you know. That was back in my hippie days."

"How did you know about that?" asked Cyn backing away even further.

He chuckled. "I was looking at the memory playback at the same time you and Jake were. It was part of my test to see if you could figure out what went wrong with the E-Weapon. I had to make sure for myself that you were as bright as my source said you were. In fact, I've been testing you ever since you appeared with Senator Goodman, and I'm pleased to say you passed all the tests with flying colors. Otherwise, you wouldn't be standing here with me at this moment."

"What other tests?"

"Well, the first one was to determine if you had the smarts to figure out how to translate the memory download into visual form. Do you really think I could invent all this without knowing how to do a simple thing like that?" he asked with a sweep of his hand.

"I did find it rather peculiar that you didn't seem to know anything about the Fibonnaci Sequence…something as basic as that," said Cyn slowly. "And then when I saw you explaining it in Professor Latter's class at MIT…."

"You naturally assumed I might be an imposter," Karl said. "I certainly understand your suspicions, but you must trust me. When we get in the vault I'll prove to you that I am indeed Karl Braun and the same person you saw in Harry Latter's memory. If it makes you feel any better, I would never have let you in on the secrets of getting past all the security barriers up to this point if I were up to no good. In fact, I want you to repeat them to me to make sure you know them in case something would happen to me and you have to get out. Remember, I told you that you have to go through the same process going out as coming in."

Cyn studied his face long and hard for a few moments. He did not flinch. He returned her gaze with a sincere look. Finally, she relaxed slightly. "All right. I've decided to trust you. I can't wait to hear what this is all about. Let's go through the DNA scan."

"Not before you recite your lessons, young lady. I want to hear step by step what you have to do in order to get out of the mine." Karl crossed his arms and waited.

"Oh, all right," said Cyn. She closed her eyes and retraced the steps visually in her mind. Then she began to recite. When she was finished, she opened her eyes and saw that Karl was nodding at her in approval.

"Perfect," he said. "I had been told you had a photographic memory, and now I'm convinced. Let's get on with it. I'll go through the scan first and then you."

He turned around and faced the vault door. He glanced down at his feet and readjusted his position slightly. Then he pressed an index finger on the door. Immediately he was engulfed in a web of laser beams coming from somewhere above. The process took only about fifteen seconds. The beams disappeared, and Karl stepped back from the door.

"Now it's your turn. Walk up to the door and stand with your feet on either side of the line on the floor. Then press your index finger on the door," he said.

Cyn followed suit, and when the beams had finished, Karl said, "Now press the palm of your hand on the door."

Cyn did as he asked and the door began to move. She watched as it slid aside disappearing into a pocket in the rock wall without making a sound.

"Amazing," she said as Karl walked past her through the door.

A few steps inside the door, Karl turned and gave her another low sweeping bow. "Welcome to Aladdin's Cave, Madame."

* * *

11:45 a.m.

She walked into the vault and stopped short. Her mouth fell open and her eyes popped at the sight in front of her. The vault was an enormous domed cavern, even larger than the one with the gold refining machinery. The walls were lined with what appeared to be polished marble tiles, and stretched across the back, stacked higher than her head, were thousands upon thousands of gleaming gold ingots in varying sizes.

"Oh, my God!" was all she could manage to say.

Karl grinned. "I thought you'd be impressed."

He walked over to the stacks with Cyn hot on his trail. He picked up a gold bar from one of the lower stacks and handed it to her. It was about the size of a pack of cards. She was not prepared for the weight of it and nearly dropped it.

"Wow!" she said, holding the bar in both hands.

"Turn it over," he said. "See the assayer's mark? This is 100 percent pure gold, the purest in the world. That's the benefit of the gas refining process. In fact, it is so pure that it could be classified as a strategic material for use as electrical contacts in satellites and E-Weapons."

"Amazing," said Cyn, turning the bar over and over in her hands. "You have certainly been a busy gold spinner. How much do you have here?"

Karl shrugged. "After two hundred tons I quit counting, and I haven't bothered to produce much more after that. You saw how easy it is to produce with my refining system. Each of these little babies is ten troy ounces. These are the smallest ones. The others range in weight from twenty to five hundred ounces."

"Wow!" said Cyn.

She started to place the gold bar back on the stack, but Karl grabbed her hand. "No. Don't put it back. It's yours, a little gift from me," he said.

Cyn looked at him in surprise. "A gift? But that's a very expensive gift. I haven't done anything to earn that."

"Don't worry. You will. Tuck it into your bag. You'll find that it may come in handy in the future."

Cyn frowned as she placed the gold bar in her bag. She looked around the vault. "Something is bothering me," she said. "I haven't noticed any tailings. What do you do with them?"

"I was waiting for you to ask that," said Karl with a grin. "As you know, the outside of the mine just looks like an ancient abandoned shaft. Any tailings would give it away that there's mining going on in here. I took all that into consideration when I invented the refining process. The tailings are on the walls here in the vault," he said, pointing at the tiles that covered the dome-shaped cavern.

"What? You're kidding, of course," said Cyn. She walked over to a wall and ran her hand over the smooth polished surface of one of the tiles.

"Nope. I use all the materials in the raw ore so there's no waste. After the gas centrifuge has spun out all the gold, what remains is cooled to liquid form and poured into tile molds."

"Truly amazing," said Cyn again as she admired the tiles on the wall. "They look like marble with all different colors of veins."

Karl nodded. "Beautiful, aren't they? If I were an architect, I could go wild with all the possibilities."

"What about the vault itself? How is it constructed?" asked Cyn as she gazed up at the ceiling.

"The walls are ten feet thick made of poured concrete with a ten-inch coating of armor plating. It is located in the center of the mountain, and the peak is three thousand feet above us. The mountainsides are about a half-mile in every direction. This vault is better protected than the nuclear missiles at Strategic Command."

"All of that just to protect this gold? What are you doing? Just storing it here?" asked Cyn.

"Storing it for times when my client needs it. Then it is shipped out."

"But how do you get it out? I haven't seen any outlets or tracks or anything, and the road we came in on certainly shows no evidence of anything like that," said Cyn.

"The road we came in on is not the way. There is another tunnel on the other side of the vault. It comes out on the other side of the mountain where there is an old dilapidated mountain man's cabin. That's in a wilderness area that is on restricted government property," explained Karl. "There are security barriers at that end, just as there are at the entrance. The access codes are the same, and again, only three of us know them. You are about to become the fourth."

Cyn shot him an aggravated look. "We're in the vault now. You said you'd explain what's going on. I think it's high time you did that."

"Yes, you're quite right. Let's go to my office."

Cyn followed him across the vault. He walked up to the wall and motioned for Cyn to step up beside him. He pressed a tile on the wall and it slid aside revealing a hidden camera. "This one is for physical and voice recognition," he said.

He looked directly at the camera screen and pressed a button at its base. "This is Karl Braun and I am here with Cynthia Hoover," he said.

He looked at Cyn. "Now you."

Cyn followed his example. Looking directly at the screen, she pressed the button and said, "This is Cynthia Hoover, and I am here with Karl Braun."

The tile slid back into place in front of the camera. The tiled wall next to it rose revealing another titanium door identical to the one they had passed through into the vault. Karl pressed his palm on the door and it slid aside.

Now they were in a large tiled room filled with banks of electronic equipment. Karl led her over to a control panel that covered the entire side of one wall. He pulled out two office chairs and they sat down.

Karl flipped some switches and the huge panel display came to life in front of them. They were looking at the entire globe spread out before them. Numerous gold lights the size of pinpoints twinkled in various places throughout the display.

"Welcome to *Project Nightingale*," he said.

"*Project Nightingale!*" exclaimed Cyn. "That was the NSA experiment that you headed up a few years ago involving satellite tracking devices. I thought that was *passe*."

"It is," said Karl. "At least that phase of it. The current NSA tracking systems evolved from it, and as far as everyone knows, *Project Nightingale* was shut down. Only four people know about Phase 2 of the Project, and that's what this is."

"I don't understand," said Cyn. "What does the gold mine have to do with it?"

Karl leaned back in his chair and swiveled to face her. "You know the old adage about tracking down a criminal—'follow the money'?"

Cyn nodded. "Oh, sure. The FBI has been doing that for years—uncovering criminals and terrorists by tracing their finances."

"Exactly, but in this case we've put a different spin on it. We distribute the money and then follow it," said Karl with a grin.

"But how...?"

"There's something very special about the gold I produce here, other than the method I invented to refine it. Take a look," he said.

He turned back to the control panel. "You see those pinpoints of light on the global display?"

Cyn looked up at the huge display. "Yes," she affirmed.

"Now, watch," he said as he tapped on a keyboard.

As Cyn watched the monitor, the view zoomed in on North America and then on the United States.

"Now what do you see? Any lights?" asked Karl.

"Only one," said Cyn looking closely at the display.

"And where is it?"

"Looks like it's in...New Mexico."

"And where in New Mexico?" asked Karl as he zoomed in closer.

"It's near Santa Fe...toward the mountains east of Santa Fe."

"And?" asked Karl as he continued zooming in. The boarded up mine shaft came into view and then the top of the mountain.

"It's the mine," said Cyn.

"Correct," said Karl. "Now watch this."

He zoomed in until a gold bar nearly filled the screen. It was resting on a dark leathery-looking surface. Cyn grabbed her bag, and the image on the screen shook. She reached in and felt the gold bar at the bottom of her bag. An enlarged image of her hand touching the bar appeared on the screen. She gasped and pulled her hand out. "It's the gold bar you gave me!" she cried.

"Correct again," said Karl, chuckling at her astonishment. He zoomed back out to the view of the mountaintop and swiveled his chair around to face her again.

"The gold bars have tracking sensors built into them?" she asked.

Karl nodded. "That's right. Each bar has a serial number matched to its own individual sensor, so I know precisely where each bar is at any given time."

"But you have thousands of gold bars in the vault. Why aren't there thousands of lights showing up at this location?" asked Cyn.

"I activate the sensors only when the gold is given out," explained Karl.

"You said only five people know about this operation. Who is the recipient of the gold when it is shipped out?" asked Cyn.

"There is only one person who can order the gold, and that is our boss who determines the necessary amounts needed by the CIA and Special Forces units operating throughout the world. The gold is taken to a top secret warehouse at CIA Headquarters at Langley where it is meted out to the various agents who use it to buy information. No one at the CIA knows where the gold comes from."

"I see," said Cyn. "So with the sensors you know exactly where these agents are and then where the gold is after they have given it out."

"That's correct," said Karl. "I'll show you where it all is on the global map, but before I do that, it's time to answer some of your other questions. I believe you wanted proof that I am really Professor Karl Braun and not an imposter?"

"Yes, please."

"Well, there's my picture taken with Professor Latter when I was at

MIT," said Karl pointing to a desk on the other side of the room. "I also have the picture taken for the MIT yearbook, and the photo that's in the NSA file."

He went over to the desk and rummaged in a drawer. He returned with the framed photo that was on the desk and two others he had pulled out of the drawer. He handed them to Cyn.

She examined them closely and then handed them back to him. "That's all very well and good, but how am I to know that the ones taken at MIT are of the same person in the NSA file? There is no resemblance that I can see."

"That's easy," said Karl as he turned to another computer residing on the control panel. He booted it up and glanced at her as it was loading. "I'll run the two pictures through NSA"s biometrics program. That should satisfy you."

Cyn watched as he scanned the two pictures into the computer. She wondered what explanation he would have when the program told them there was no match, as it had when Mac had compared them.

She watched closely as the pictures were overlaid and the biometrics scanner went to work. After a few moments, Karl pointed at the screen. "There, you see?"

Cyn stared at the screen in disbelief. The program had concluded there was more than a 98 percent probability that the pictures were of the same person.

"Satisfied?" asked Karl.

"Not totally," said Cyn with a frown. "That program is not always consistent."

"Well, then, I think you'd better call the boss. We can make the call on the secure videophone over there. The boss will verify my identity and confirm my orders to bring you here."

"Why *am* I here anyway?" asked Cyn.

"Because of my last physical," said Karl. "The doc discovered a bubble on my aorta that could potentially become an aneurysm, thus leading to a heart attack. It's necessary to enroll another person to take my place in case something happens to me, or I'm forced to retire. Remember, I told you that only two others have the codes? From the outset of this project, the policy has been to have three people who have access. Now, with one of us in potential jeopardy, we need to have a backup."

Cyn nodded. "Sorry to hear about your health problem. How serious is it?"

"They're monitoring it. If the bubble becomes larger, I may have to have surgery. In the meantime, any undue anxiety or stress could cause it to burst."

He patted his left breast pocket. "Just so you know I carry my little vial of pills here in my shirt pocket at all times in case of an attack. This is why it's imperative that we enroll you as soon as possible."

"Why didn't the boss tell me about this?"

"Because I'm the head of this project and I had to be satisfied you were the right person. The boss has every confidence in you, but someone else recommended you to me. I had no idea you were working for the same person until I called to get clearance to check you out."

"Well, if the boss didn't recommend me, that leaves only two others, excluding the President, who know about the project. Am I right?" asked Cyn.

"Correct again," said Karl with a smile. "You were recommended by one of my partners."

"Who is?" prompted Cyn.

Karl shook his head. "Sorry. Can"t tell you that yet for security reasons. When the time comes he'll make himself known to you. Shall we make that phone call now?"

* * *

12:15 p.m.

The well-known face of Jocelyn Langdon Drake filled the screen of the videophone. As Director of National Security she was the most powerful person in the United States next to the President. She was without a doubt the most powerful woman in the world.

"Cyn and Karl together at last," she said in her deep contralto voice. "What do you think of *Project Nightingale*, Cyn?"

"It's truly amazing," said Cyn.

"I assume you want some verification?"

Cyn glanced at Karl and nodded.

"Karl Braun has reported to me for years, ever since the inception of Phase 2 of *Project Nightingale*. I am sure Karl explained to you that there are only five people who know about Phase Two—myself, The President, Karl and his two partners?"

Cyn nodded again.

"We have been concerned that only Karl and two others know the access codes in case something happened to one of them. Now with Karl's health problem it has become imperative that we enroll another person. I told Karl to come up with a candidate, and when he called me with your name I couldn't have been more delighted. I would have approved you right away, but it was necessary that Karl himself was comfortable with your skills and trustworthiness. That's the primary reason I wanted you assigned to Apparition Mountain."

"I see," said Cyn. "What about the other work I'm doing at Apparition Mountain?"

"You are to continue with that work. Just like Karl, you have dual responsibilities. Because of the location of the gold mine that Karl discovered, I made sure the Scientific Advisory Council appointed him to the Apparition Mountain Project. That way he can live there without suspicion. After the project at Apparition Mountain is finished, we've decided it will be time for Karl to quote-unquote retire at his ranch near Santa Fe."

"What about me?" asked Cyn. "Won't I have to live in the area too?"

Jocelyn smiled and waved a hand. "First things first, Cyn. I want you to finish your job at Apparition Mountain. Then you will have to help Senator Goodman secure the financing for that project. You may be commuting for a while. We'll see how it plays out."

"Yes, Ma'am," said Cyn returning her smile.

"Good. Everything's settled to your satisfaction, Karl?"

Karl nodded. "Yes. The arrangement will work fine."

"All right, then. Carry on, and I'll expect you each to report in on the usual schedule," said Jocelyn.

The videophone went blank. Cyn stared at it for a second before turning to face Karl.

He wore a big grin as he extended his hand to her. "Shake, partner," he said. "Welcome aboard."

* * *

12:30 p.m.

Cyn and Karl were back at the monitor looking at a map of Western Europe and the Middle East. Dozens of gold lights twinkled throughout the map.

"These lights pinpoint where the gold is at the moment," explained Karl as he zoomed in on Saudi Arabia. "I'll use this example to show you how the tracking works."

He zoomed in further and clicked on one twinkling light in the city of Riyadh. A dialogue box came up that announced, "Five hundred gold bars in the vault of Royal Bank of Saudi Arabia. Owner is Prince Ali Yusef Farad for valuable information given to CIA agents during the Gulf War. Farad originally owned seven hundred-fifty bars. The other two hundred-fifty are now in the Bank of Switzerland, under different ownership."

"Prince Farad," said Cyn. "That name sounds familiar, but I can't think why."

"Could be from the news," said Karl. "Prince Farad was one of the Saudis living in the U.S. at the time of the attack on the World Trade Center. He and his family were transported out of the country by the Administration the day after the attack. That came out in the news much later."

"That must be it," said Cyn. Then she remembered where she had actually heard of Farad. She remembered the messages Mac had tracked from Farad to his grandson and a subsequent message from the grandson to someone inside Apparition Mountain. She decided to say nothing of this to Karl. Instead she pointed at the map. "What about the two hundred-fifty gold bars in the Bank of Switzerland that are under different ownership?" she asked.

Karl zoomed in to the gold light twinkling in the city of Geneva, Switzerland. He clicked on it and a dialogue box came up. "Two hundred fifty gold bars in Bank of Switzerland. Owner undisclosed due to Swiss banking regulations. Original owner Prince Ali Yusef Farad. Transferred to Harry Latter in June 1991 in Freeport, Bahamas. Gold deposited in First European Bank in Zurich in June 1991. Transferred to Bank of Switzerland in Geneva in August 2002."

"Harry Latter!" exclaimed Cyn. "Is that *our* Harry Latter?"

Karl was grinning at her. "Yes, indeed it is," he said. "Can't you guess why from your review of his memory?"

Cyn frowned, remembering the telephone conversation she and Jake had listened to in Harry's memory. "I know he received a call from a banker and apparently agreed to transfer some money to another bank to avoid disclosure in the U.S....." she said slowly. "I have no clue as to how he would have come into possession of two hundred-fifty of Prince Farad's gold bars."

"Let me give you a hint," said Karl, his eyes glittering. "Prince Farad owns the Crown Princess Casino in Freeport."

The light dawned in Cyn's eyes. "Do you mean Harry won that money?"

"Precisely," said Karl. "You know that Professor Latter invented a system for winning at slot machines because you observed that in his memory."

"That's right," said Cyn. "He must have won millions, but why was he squirreling it away in Switzerland? Why all the secrecy?"

And why was he sending $100,000 a month to you? she wondered, but didn't ask.

"Oh, come on, Cyn. The same reason a lot of people open Swiss bank accounts—to avoid disclosure to the IRS, of course. Harry wanted to set up a benevolent foundation, and he didn't want the government taking half of it in taxes."

"What kind of foundation?" asked Cyn.

"I'm not at liberty to tell you that, but you can rest assured that it's all for a very good cause and there's nothing crooked about it."

"I see," said Cyn looking at him closely. "And now that Harry's deceased? What happens to the gold and the foundation?"

"Harry made provisions long ago. The foundation will go on funded by the interest earned on the assets in the account. That's really all you need to know. The fact that Harry ended up with some of my gold was merely a coincidence and is of no concern to our project here. Now, I want to show you something that is of concern…something that may soon lead us to the identity of the elusive Mario."

"So you're working on uncovering him, too?"

Karl shrugged as he turned back to the monitor. "Aren't we all? I guess you could say catching Mario is the number one priority of our entire national intelligence program. Now, I want you to take a look at the history of this little gold star in Syria."

He began to zoom in on Syria. Suddenly a siren began to shriek. "What the hell!" He jumped up and raced to another bank of monitors on the opposite side of the room.

Cyn ran after him. "What is it?" she asked.

Karl was already seated in front of the monitors furiously tapping on a keyboard.

"Looks like we have company," he said.

* * *

12:45 p.m.

Cyn watched in horror as the image came up on the monitor in front of Karl. Two figures dressed in black, Ninja-style, were approaching the entrance of the mine. Karl zoomed in on the hooded faces. Nothing was visible but the eyes.

"My God! Who can that be?" exclaimed Karl.

Cyn studied the eyes. One set appeared familiar to her, but she couldn't be sure.

"I haven't a clue," she said. "What are they doing?"

"They're going to try to break in to the mine!" yelled Karl.

"Oh, my God!" exclaimed Cyn as she watched one of the figures withdraw something from a black kit bag. "That's a plastic explosive. They're going to try to blast their way in."

"Not to worry," said Karl grimly. "The outer barrier is made of spent uranium and it will reflect the explosion. It will be directed right back at them. Meanwhile the alarm system has already alerted the private security firm I hired to patrol this property."

They could only watch as the perpetrators placed the explosive at the entrance of the mine. Then they backed off down the mountainside.

"Damn!" muttered Karl. "That explosion is bound to destroy my pickup. I should have come in the back way. That's probably how they know we're in here."

"They must have been tailing us," said Cyn with a frown. She was now fairly certain that she recognized one of the invaders.

Karl and Cyn stared at the monitor as the two black-clad figures hunched down beside a large boulder. As one of them held up a wireless detonating device, Cyn held her breath anticipating the explosion. Suddenly, the one with the detonator fell back against the boulder clutching his arm. A red stain began to ooze through his gloved fingers. The other figure was on his feet and reaching into the kit bag slung across his shoulder. Puffs of dirt sprayed into the air around his feet. An automatic weapon materialized in his hand and he began peppering the air with bullets as he reached down and pulled his partner to his feet. In an instant the two black-clad figures had snaked behind the boulder and disappeared from view.

"Did you see that? One of them got shot! But who's firing? Has security arrived?" yelled Cyn.

There was no answer. She looked at Karl. He was slumped over in his chair, his head dropped down on his chest.

"Karl! Oh my God, Karl!" she shouted. "What's wrong?"

She leaned down and raised his head. His eyes were closed, and his skin had taken on a bluish cast, but she saw that he was breathing in shallow gasps. She felt for a pulse. It was very weak. She reached into his shirt pocket and pulled out the vial of pills. She took one out, pried open his mouth and placed one beneath his tongue. She waited. In a few seconds his breathing seemed to become more regular. She felt for the pulse again. Now it was slightly stronger.

"I've got to get you out of here... Now!" exclaimed Cyn. "But how?"

Karl was slumped in a desk chair that fortunately had wheels on it. Cyn frantically looked around for something to strap him to the chair. That's when a movement on the monitor caught her eye.

She froze as she saw a man holding a rifle stooping down to examine the wireless detonator left behind by the two invaders. She had absolutely no trouble recognizing this new visitor.

"What are you doing here?" she said aloud, but of course he could not hear her.

* * *

1 p.m.

Cyn raced as fast as she could back through all the security doors in the mine. She was pushing the office chair ahead of her. She had strapped Karl into the chair with some duct tape she had found in the vault. So far she had remembered all the codes and procedures to get through the barriers and now she was moving through the tunnel that led from the cavern with the gold refining equipment to the first major security door inside the mine.

She pushed Karl up to the barrier, which even on this side, looked just like a rock wall. She paused and searched her memory. What was the procedure for this barrier? Then she remembered. This was the door that dispensed the deadly nerve agent. She had one chance to get it right. Otherwise, she would be a goner because she had not as yet been vaccinated against the agent. She remembered this was the door where Karl had enrolled her into the system.

She searched the wall in front of her and finally located the smooth rock about chest height. She placed her palm on it remembering to stand still while it analyzed her heart rhythm as Karl had instructed her. Nothing happened. She stood perfectly still afraid to remove her palm from the panel in case it would activate the nerve gas. What else was she supposed to do? She went back through the process in her memory. Then she remembered asking Karl what would happen if someone was holding a gun on him. He had told her he applied more pressure with one of his fingers. More pressure with the index finger told the system one thing, and more pressure with the little finger told the system another thing. One finger would set off the nerve agent, and the other would open the door. Which finger was it?

Cyn wracked her brain. She glanced at Karl. He was still unconscious. She had to get him out of here and fast. She took a deep breath, gritted her teeth, and applied slightly more pressure on the panel with her little finger.

There was a slight hissing sound and Cyn jumped back. Then the wall began to rise. She stood there stunned for an instant, then breathed a sigh of relief, and quickly wheeled Karl through the opening before the door crashed down behind them.

Now, at last, they were in the small cavern just inside the entrance. All she had to do now was press the panel up by the shop cabinet and they'd be out of here. Cyn started wheeling Karl up to the entrance, and then she stopped short. She had to protect the secret of the mine. If she came out of here with Karl in a desk chair, whoever might be outside would know this was not just an abandoned mine.

She removed Karl's hard hat and her own and placed them back in the shop cabinet. Then she slung her bag around her neck and peeled off the duct tape that was holding Karl in the chair. She got his arm around her neck and grabbed him around the waist raising him from the chair. She grimaced. He was like a dead weight, but fortunately, he was not a big man. She managed to drag him up to the wall. She braced his body against her hip as she placed her right hand on the panel. Thankfully the boarded-up iron gate began to slide open. When there was just enough room Cyn quickly dragged Karl through the opening and collapsed with him on the ground as the gate slid shut behind them.

The sunlight was glaring after being in the mine. Cyn was trying to think where her sunglasses were when a shadow loomed over her.

"Cyn, what's going on here?" asked a voice she knew all too well.

Cyn shaded her eyes with her right hand and found herself staring up into Jake's lapis blue eyes.

* * *

213

1:30 p.m.

Cyn and Jake stood at gunpoint with their hands in the air as they watched two paramedics carefully lift Karl Braun onto a stretcher and load him into a waiting helicopter. They could see one of the paramedics hovering over him with a syringe in one hand just before the door closed.

The helicopter rose and rapidly banked off to the northwest.

Cyn glanced at Jake. She still didn't know what he was doing here. She had barely had a chance to tell him that Karl had had a heart attack when the helicopter arrived, stirring up a fierce wind and a cloud of gritty dust. It was impossible to talk over the noise. Then two armed men had jumped out and rushed toward them. They wore black combat boots, dark green khaki uniforms and matching aviator-style sunglasses. Their identical dark green peaked caps had the words "Eagle Force" embroidered in beige above the bill.

Cyn had been attempting to scramble to her feet but immediately sat down hard on the ground when one of the guards yelled "Freeze!" The guards had stopped a short distance away, assuming a shooting stance, guns held with both hands straight ahead of them. Cyn slowly raised her arms in the air.

One of the guards motioned with his gun at Jake. "Put down your weapon!" he demanded in a gruff voice.

Jake slowly lowered his rifle to the ground never taking his eyes off the guard. Then he slowly stood back up and raised both hands in the air.

The guards approached with caution and one of them picked up Jake"s rifle.

"Who are you and what happened here?" asked one of the guards looking at Karl lying on the ground and then at Cyn.

"I am Barbara Jones. Professor Braun brought me here to show me this old mine. While we were inside he had a heart attack and I managed to drag him out. I gave him one of the pills he carries in his shirt pocket, but he needs immediate medical attention," said Cyn in as calm a voice as she could muster.

The guard had pulled a walkie-talkie from his belt and talked rapidly into it. Two paramedics suddenly appeared in the open door of the helicopter carrying a stretcher. They rushed forward while the guards kept their guns trained on Cyn and Jake.

As soon as the roar of the helicopter blades had abated, the first guard waved his gun at Cyn. "Now we need to see some ID," he said.

With one hand still in the air, Cyn slowly reached into her bag and pulled out her Barbara Jones driver's license. She handed it to the guard. He looked at it carefully and studied her face. "It's all right, Ms. Jones. You can put your hands down now. Professor Braun gave you clearance to be on the property."

"Phew! Thank God for that," thought Cyn as she took the driver's license back and returned it to her bag.

"And you?" asked the guard turning to Jake.

"I am Brent Jacobson, and I work with Professor Braun at the Air Base," said Jake.

"ID?" asked the guard.

Jake kept one hand in the air as he reached with the other into his hip pocket and pulled out a tooled black leather wallet. He flipped it open and held it out to the guard.

The guard studied the driver's license in the wallet for a moment. "All right, Mr. Jacobson. You can relax. You have clearance to be here also."

Jake dropped his other arm and put his wallet back in his hip pocket.

The first guard nodded to the other, and they both holstered their guns. "Now," said the first. "Tell us what happened here to set off the alarm."

"All I know is what I told you before," said Cyn. "Professor Braun brought me here to show me this old mine. While we were inside he suffered a heart attack, and I managed to get him out. When I got out, Mr. Jacobson appeared. That's all I know."

"And why were you here, Mr. Jacobson?"

Jake glanced at Cyn for a second. "I was up on the mountain hunting when I saw two men dressed in black getting ready to set off an explosive at the entrance to the mine. I thought Professor Braun might be in there and in danger because his pickup was outside. I started firing hoping to scare them off, and I think I winged one of them. Unfortunately, they escaped before I could get any closer. The detonator and the charge are still over there. I was taking a look at that when Ms. Jones came out of the mine carrying Professor Braun. I was just asking her what happened when you showed up."

"Did you know anything about the attempted break-in?" asked the guard turning to Cyn.

"No," said Cyn with a straight face. "This is the first I've heard of it. Why would anyone be trying to break into an old mine?"

The guard looked back at Jake.

Jake shrugged. "I don't understand it either. All I know is what I saw. There were two of them dressed in black with masks, and they had guns and explosives. I thought they were trying to harm the Professor, so I fired at them. Come over here and I'll show you the detonator. I didn't touch it."

As they walked over to examine the detonator, Cyn touched one of the guards on the arm. "Could you tell me where you've taken Professor Braun?" she asked.

"To the hospital at the Roca Grande Air Base," he said.

"Why not to a closer hospital in Santa Fe?" asked Cyn.

"We're following Professor Braun's instructions. In the event of a medical emergency, he wanted to be taken to the Air Base facility," said the guard. "He's under the care of a doctor there."

"Would that be Dr. Graham?" asked Cyn.

"That's right. Dr. Daniel Graham."

"Well, I happen to know that Dr. Graham is off-duty today, and I believe he was going to Taos," said Cyn. "I have his cell phone number. Perhaps I'd better page him."

The guard shook his head. "We've already taken care of that. He's on his way back to the Air Base."

The other guard was bending over the detonating device. "Standard blasting equipment, nothing out of the ordinary about it. You say you didn't touch it?" he asked Jake as he straightened up.

Jake shook his head. "No."

"Well, we'll bag everything and take it back to run through some forensics tests. Maybe we'll find some prints."

"I doubt it," said Jake. "They were wearing gloves."

"You're probably right, but it never hurts to check. They might have gotten careless at some point. Now, show me where they went."

"They went behind this rock, and by the time I got down here they had disappeared," said Jake.

The guard turned to his partner. "OK, Bob, I'll have a look at where they went. Meanwhile, you collect the evidence. Mr. Jacobson, you come with me."

Jake and the guard disappeared behind the rock.

Cyn observed as the other guard put on some latex gloves and produced a large plastic bag from a pouch attached to his belt. He carefully picked up the detonator and placed it in the bag. Then he walked to the mine entrance façade where the explosive had been placed.

Cyn followed and watched as he carefully removed the explosive and placed it in another plastic bag. "They knew what they were doing," he muttered.

Jake and the other guard appeared from behind the rock. "Not a sign," said the guard. "No footprints, nothing. They surely must have had a vehicle hidden somewhere. Did you hear an engine or anything?"

Again Jake shook his head. "No, but then it wasn't that long before you arrived in the helicopter. If they had a truck or something, they could have got away under the noise of the copter."

"On the other hand, there's only one little trail from the ranch leading up here. We didn't see anything from the air as we were coming in. Even if they weren't using the road, a vehicle would have kicked up some dust.

Chances are they're still out there somewhere hiding out until we're gone. I'm gonna get a couple of copters over here, and we'll take a look."

The guard pulled a cell phone off his belt and started to press a number. Then he paused and looked curiously at Jake. "By the way, speaking of vehicles, how'd you get up here?"

"I've been wondering the same thing," said Cyn watching Jake intently.

Jake grinned slightly and looked down at his feet. He was wearing his high-top moccasins—the ones his mother had made for him. "The old-fashioned way," he said.

"You mean you walked?" asked the guard raising an eyebrow.

Jake shook his head. "No, I rode."

"Rode? Rode what?"

"Just a minute. I'll show you," said Jake. He put two fingers in his mouth and gave a shrill whistle. From a distance up on the mountain came an answering whinny. Before long a dappled white stallion trotted up to them from around some boulders at the north side of the mine entrance. The horse wore no harness, bridle or saddle. It came up to Jake and nudged him.

"And who might this be?" asked Cyn, her face softening at the sight of the beautiful animal.

"This is White Cloud, great grandson of Black Thunder. You remember Black Thunder?" Jake asked looking at her intently.

Cyn smiled at the memory, and for a moment there was only she and Jake and the horse. The security guards were forgotten.

"Say hello to the nice lady, White Cloud. She knew your ancestors," said Jake quietly, not taking his eyes off Cyn.

Cyn stretched out her palm and the stallion stepped forward and nuzzled it. "Oh, aren't you a beautiful fellow," murmured Cyn as she stroked White Cloud's neck with her other hand.

One of the guards stepped forward and White Cloud's head immediately came up. He backed away slightly, rolling his eyes and snorting. Jake reached out a hand. "It's all right," he said quietly and immediately the horse calmed and stood silently looking on.

"Still doesn't answer my question," said the guard. "I'm sure you didn't ride this horse clear from Roca Grande."

"No, of course not," said Jake. "I rode him up from the ranch. Professor Braun lets me board him in the stable down there. I drove down from Roca Grande in my Durango. It's parked in the stable, which is why you didn't see it."

"So, you're able to get into the ranch?" asked Cyn.

Jake nodded. "The Professor gave me my own access code so I can come and see White Cloud whenever I want, plus I have permission to ride and hunt on the property."

Cyn glanced at her watch with a frown. "I really need to get back. I want to check on Professor Braun."

"All right. We know where to find you if we have any more questions. Can you drive Professor Braun's pickup back down to the ranch, and then maybe Mr. Jacobson here can give you a ride back to Roca Grande. I gotta get those copters here and see if we can spot those intruders," said the guard.

Jake looked at Cyn with the hint of a smile in his eyes. "I'd be happy to take Ms. Jones back," he said.

Cyn glared at him and rolled her eyes.

"Better saddle up then," said the guard as he put the cell phone to his ear.

"No need for that," said Jake.

With lightning speed he swung himself up on White Cloud's bare back and reached down to take his rifle from the guard. Then he pressed his knees into the horse's withers.

By the time Cyn climbed into Karl's old pickup, Jake and White Cloud were halfway to the ranch.

* * *

2:30 p.m.

"We need to talk," said Cyn sternly. She was in the passenger seat of Jake's Durango, and he had just driven out of the gate of Karl Braun's ranch.

"Yes, I'm sure we do," agreed Jake. He did not look at her.

There was a long pause as he continued to drive and Cyn continued to glare at him. "Well?" she prompted.

"Well, what?" he asked, still not looking at her.

Cyn threw up her hand. "You know very well what," she said in a frustrated tone. "I want to know what you were doing up on that mountain."

He shrugged. "Just what I said. I took White Cloud out for a ride."

"And you just happened to have a gun with you, and you just happened to be there when those characters tried to blast into the mine," said Cyn sarcastically.

"That's right," he replied calmly.

"All right, then. Answer another question. I want to know what you were doing talking on a cell phone in Tiwa with an Arab in Boston yesterday afternoon."

This brought more of a response, much to Cyn's satisfaction. Jake looked over at her with a cocked eyebrow. "So you know about that?" he asked.

"That's right, and I also know the name of the person you were talking to—Ibraham Abdul Farad, grandson of Prince Farad of Saudi Arabia," said Cyn.

Jake suddenly swerved off the road and pulled to an abrupt stop beside a clump of sagebrush. He cut the engine and turned to her with a grim expression. Cyn started to reach into her bag, but he grabbed her wrist and held it in a tight vise. She winced and he loosened his grip slightly.

"Now I have a question," he said gruffly.

Cyn stared at him in surprise. She had never known Jake to be violent.

"I need to know if anyone else knows the language we were speaking in." His eyes were boring into her.

"No," she said quickly. "I recognized it, but I didn't let on that I knew what it was."

"That's good," he said, relief registering in his voice. He let go of her wrist and turned back to face the steering wheel. "Did you understand what we were saying?" he asked in a quiet tone.

Cyn was rubbing her wrist, not taking her eyes off him. "No," she said studying his profile. "I only caught a couple of words. You know I don't speak Tiwa."

There was another silence as Jake digested this information. Then he turned to her again. "That's the point," he said. "Only a few people in the entire world know that language. You must never tell anyone that you recognized what it was, Cyn. Do you understand?"

"No, I don't understand!" she said. "And another thing I don't understand is why an Arab would know that language."

Jake considered this outburst for a second and then a slow smile crept over his face. "That's because he's not an Arab," he said.

"Not an Arab? With a name like Ibrahim Abdul Farad?" asked Cyn in bewilderment.

"Nope. He's my cousin from the Pueblo. His name is Allen Fleetdeer."

"So he's not Prince Farad's grandson?"

"He's his adopted grandson, and that's all I can tell you right now, so don't ask any more," said Jake.

Cyn stared at him open-mouthed. Amused, Jake reached over and gently closed her mouth. "Now, Cyn-Cyn, I have a question for you," he said.

She continued to stare at him in stunned silence, the wheels spinning in her brain. She watched as Jake took out his cell phone and leaned over towards her.

"Are you paying attention?" he asked. Without turning the phone on, he proceeded to press a series of numbers on the keypad. "What does that spell?"

Cyn looked up from the keypad into his amused blue eyes. She gulped.

"Well?" he asked.

"Open Sesame…" she said haltingly.

"Very good," he said. "Open Sesame—the key to Aladdin's Cave, right?"

"Right," she said, and that was all she could possibly find to say as Jake started the engine and drove on down the road toward Santa Fe.

* * *

5:30 p.m.

Cyn was exhausted but too wired up to sleep. She was lying on the bed in her room at the Inn, a thousand thoughts clamoring for attention in her brain. She had thought she would take a nap before going down to the coffee shop for something to eat, but the events of the day kept replaying in her mind like summer reruns on TV.

First there had been the whole surprising business with Karl Braun and the gold mine and her boss. Then the attempted break-in and Karl's heart attack and Jake showing up unexpectedly. And finally the biggest surprise of all—Jake's revelations on the way back to Roca Grande.

Now she was fighting to suppress her emotions in the better interest of taking care of business, but they refused to be put on the back burner. A simmering anger was threatening to come to a rolling boil as she replayed the events of the day. She felt used and abused by everyone from her boss Jocelyn down to Karl Braun and Jake—most of all Jake.

"One of my partners recommended you," Karl had said, but had refused to reveal who he was. "He'll make himself known to you when the time comes."

She wondered how much longer she would have been kept in the dark if it hadn't been for Karl's heart attack.

"Damn you, Jake!" she said aloud.

He had said he wanted her back, and she had told him she would think about it after her business was completed. Now they were partners again, and she'd had no choice in the decision. Tears welled up in her eyes as she recalled the scene that was forever seared into her memory—how she had come into their apartment and found Jake with his arms around that blonde debutant, the one whose parents sponsored Native American artists.... Each time this reel played in her mind she felt the sting of betrayal and injured pride. She had fled...moved in with a friend who kept her whereabouts a secret. After graduation a few weeks later she disappeared into the anonymity of a career with the NSA and tried to forget. Now, here she was again, hurting and wallowing in self-pity.

Unaccustomed to being in this state, Cyn jumped up from the bed and paced around the room. Then another thought occurred to her. Just because she and Jake were partners in the secret of the gold mine didn't mean they were partners in any other way—not unless *she* wanted it to be more. Cyn smiled to herself and brushed away the tears. "It's still *my* choice after all, and we'll just have to see about that," she said to herself.

Right now she had to concentrate on the business at hand. She went over to the couch, flopped down, and began to take inventory. On the way back from Santa Fe she had called Jocelyn to let her know about Karl's heart attack. Then she had called General Masters. He already knew about Karl because Charlie Denton had driven Dr. Graham back from Taos and had called in. Karl was in ICU at the Base hospital, still in a coma, and they were preparing him for surgery. Meanwhile, the video boards had arrived and General Masters wanted Jake there ASAP to set up for the memory download even though he was postponing the procedure again because of Karl. "That way we'll be ready in case Karl is able to function in a day or so," he said.

Jake had dropped her off at the front entrance to the Inn. "I'll send you a text message as soon as I get the computer set up. I'll probably be at the Mountain all night," he said. She was barely out of the Durango before he roared off.

She had checked at the desk but there were no messages. She had walked outside the back entrance before going up to her room. Her Grand Cherokee was nowhere in sight. The bus was still there, but when she knocked on the door there was no response. No Mac, no team members. "Where the hell is everyone?" she groused to herself.

When she got to her room there was no message lying on the floor. She double-checked her cell phone, but there were no messages, text or otherwise. She had called Mac's secure number, but there was no answer. She left a brief message on his voice mail: "Mac, call your cousin Barb as soon as possible."

Cyn got up from the couch and paced back and forth again. Then she remembered the gold bar nestled in the bottom of her bag. She took it out and held it under the light admiring its rich golden glow. She turned it over and over examining every square inch. She could not detect the sensor. She shook her head and marveled again at Karl"'s ingenuity.

She stood there for a moment thinking and absent-mindedly stroking the smooth surface with her fingers. Then a smile crept over her face and she abruptly placed the bar back in her bag and left the room.

A few minutes later she walked back into the room and plunked her bag on the bar counter. Her Grand Cherokee was still not back.

She noticed the half-empty bottle of wine she'd left on the bar and decided it was time for a drink. Just as she pulled the cork from the bottle her cell phone rang, startling her. She grabbed it and saw Mac's code name on the screen.

"Mac! Where are you?" she practically shouted into the phone the moment she pressed the receive button.

"Hey, sorry to be late. I'm just leaving Santa Fe. Had to go to the Emergency Room," came the familiar Texas drawl.

"The Emergency Room? What happened?" asked Cyn.

"Had to have Hound Dog patched up. He had a small accident."

"What do you mean? What kind of accident?"

Mac chuckled. "Damn fool got shot in the arm. I'll tell you all about it soon's I get back."

With that he hung up. Cyn stared at the cell phone for a second and then headed for the wine bottle.

* * *

6:45 p.m.

"Hell, yuh didn't think we were gonna let you go off with the prime suspect without us keepin' tabs on yuh, did yuh?" Mac asked.

Cyn was glaring at him across the table in the bus. Mac was leaning back in his swivel chair casually picking his teeth with a gold toothpick. Hound Dog and Skeeter were sitting on the couch opposite the table.

"So, how did you manage to track me?" asked Cyn.

"Easy," said Skeeter. "When Braun was picking you up in the lobby, I planted a global positioning device in the tire well of his pickup."

He grinned at her and Cyn rolled her eyes and looked back at Mac. "So you all followed me in my Jeep?" she asked. "I thought you had a date with Braun's housekeeper."

Mac smirked and took his time putting his toothpick back in its case and into his shirt pocket before answering. "Oh, I met Miss Flores all right at the La Fonda. Didn't find out a damned thing about Braun. She either doesn't know anything or is very close-mouthed. So I made excuses and parted company after a couple o' drinks."

"But how did you get up to the old mine on Professor Braun's property?" asked Cyn.

"Oh, I didn't go up there," said Mac. "Skeeter and Hound Dog rented a four-wheeler in Santa Fe."

Cyn glanced back at the two seated on the couch. Hound Dog's right arm was in a sling, and his Droopy Dog eyes were even droopier. Those were the eyes that Cyn had recognized behind the black mask when she and Karl were viewing the intruders on the video screen inside the mine. Of course, she could not let on that she had seen them from inside the mine.

" 'Scuse me. I gotta go lay down," mumbled Hound Dog. "Doc shot me full of pain killers." He rose unsteadily to his feet and stood there swaying.

Mac quickly got up and grabbed his good arm to keep him from falling. "Sure thing," he said. "Skeeter can fill Cyn in on what happened. Here. I'll take you back to your bunk."

Cyn watched as Mac half-carried Hound Dog down the hallway. He supported him on his left hip as he reached out and opened a door. Then they both disappeared inside. Cyn looked back at Skeeter. "Well?" she asked.

"Yeah, well, we found a way to go across some hills to the north of the ranch. When we came to a fence, we left the four-wheeler under some sagebrush and hiked up to about a hundred yards from the mine. We could see Braun's pickup and no sign of you, so we sat down behind some rocks to wait. We figured you were in that old mine with him."

Skeeter paused for a second and took a sip out of his Budweiser beer can. Then he continued. "Well, you were in there for a long time, and we started to get nervous. We were on the cell with Mac and he made the call for us to go get you out. We all thought Braun might be up to no good," said Skeeter. "We tried to cut the padlock on the boarded-up door and discovered it was a fake entrance. We couldn't figure out how to get in, so we decided we'd have to blast it open. We were just about to do that when someone started shooting at us from up on the mountain. That's how Hound Dog got shot. I dragged him back down the mountain a way and called Mac. He told us to get out of there pronto."

"That's right," said Mac, joining in the conversation as he walked back down the hall and sat down in his swivel chair. "Didn't want anyone catchin' the boys and blowin' our cover. What the hell were you doing in there for so long anyway, Cyn?"

"Professor Braun was showing me a vein he had discovered in there. We were chipping out some samples. He wanted to know if I thought it would be worthwhile to try to mine it," said Cyn, "Then he had a heart attack, and I tried CPR and then I had to figure out how to get him out of the mine and get help."

Mac frowned. "Braun had a heart attack? Where is he now?"

"He's at the hospital at the Air Base. Apparently, he was wearing some sort of life alert device, and the minute I got him out of the mine some security guys and paramedics showed up in a helicopter and whisked him off. I spoke to General Masters about an hour ago, and he told me the Professor was still in a coma and they were preparing for surgery," said Cyn.

Mac looked closely at Cyn for an instant and then asked the question Cyn had anticipated. "So how did you get back here?"

"One of the security guys," she said. "I drove Professor Braun's pickup back down to the ranch, and he picked me up and drove me back here. I got back around five."

"These security guys…." said Mac slowly. "Did they know someone was trying to break into the mine?"

Cyn nodded. "As soon as they had Professor Braun on his way to the hospital, they went over and bagged up a detonator and the plastic explosive that had been placed at the mine entrance. They wanted to know if I knew anything about it. That was the first I knew about anyone trying to break in."

"Any idea who shot Hound Dog?" asked Mac.

Cyn shrugged. "Could have been one of the security people. Maybe they're on duty full-time at the ranch."

Mac looked at Skeeter. "What do you think? You think it was security?"

Skeeter shrugged. "Like I said, we couldn't see who was doing the shooting. Whoever it was seemed to know what he was doing with a gun. Fired shots into the ground around us, and then shot Hound Dog in the arm just as he was about to push the button on the detonator."

Mac thought for a moment. "Well, chances are it was security. There's no way they're gonna be able to trace anything to us, is there?"

"No way," said Skeeter. "We know how to cover our tracks."

Mac laughed and relaxed. "Yeah, I know that for sure. Why don't you go grab some chow? I need to talk to Cyn for a bit."

"OK, Boss," said Skeeter. He drained his beer can, stood up and reached for his coat.

"Thanks for looking out for my welfare," said Cyn. "I'm sorry things went wrong and Hound Dog got shot."

"All part of the job," said Skeeter as he went out the door.

As soon as the door closed behind Skeeter, Mac leaned across the table and said in a low voice, "So Braun's out of commission. Tell me, was that your doing?"

Cyn looked at him in surprise. "My doing? No! He really did have a heart attack, and I'm totally convinced now that he's not our leak. We can take him off the suspect list."

Mac leaned back in his chair again. "Yeah, I think you're right about that."

"Oh? What makes you say that?" asked Cyn.

"Well, for starters, we picked up some more communication that originated from the Air Base area today at 2:20." Mac reached into his shirt pocket and pulled out a slip of paper. He tossed it across the table at her. "See what you think of that," he said.

Cyn opened the folded slip of paper and read it. Her head jerked up. "You're kidding!" she said.

"Nope," said Mac. "That was on the screen when we got back."

Cyn looked down and read the message aloud. "Head scientist immobilized. Download delayed indefinitely."

"Now, who was at the Mountain at 2:20?" asked Mac softly. Cyn caught her breath and clenched her teeth.

"General Masters," she said in a voice barely above a whisper.

She and Mac sat staring silently at each other for what seemed a very long time.

* * *

MONDAY

4:30 a.m.

Cyn was fully clothed and pacing her room waiting for the call from Apparition Mountain. She kept glancing down at the cell phone in her hand. Suddenly it vibrated. She had a text message. She pressed a button and saw that it was from Jake in their old code.

She smiled as she read it. "Need you here. Video board working but there is a problem. The General has decided to go ahead with the download as soon as possible this morning. He'll be contacting you soon."

Cyn had just finished sending an acknowledging message back to Jake when the XJ14 cell phone lying on the bar counter rang. She glanced at the screen, saw that it was the General calling, and let it ring a second and third time before answering.

"Yes?" she said in a groggy voice.

The General's voice came over the line in clipped tones. "Cyn, I'm sorry to wake you so early, but I just got a directive from Washington to go ahead with the project without Karl. They don't want to postpone the download any longer. We'll have to rely on you and Jake to pull it off. Think you can manage that?"

Cyn smiled to herself. "Yes, Jeff. I'm sure I can with Jake's help, provided nothing goes wrong with the equipment."

"Good," said the General. "Get here as fast as you can. I'll get Dr. Graham over here from the Base to start prepping the candidate."

"I'm on my way as soon as I can throw on some clothes," said Cyn.

As soon as she disconnected from the General, she picked up her other cell phone and pressed Mac's number. He answered halfway through the first ring. "Yeah, Cyn?"

"I just got the call. The General's been ordered to go ahead with the download and wants me at the Mountain ASAP."

"Good," said Mac. "Your phone call to the Director worked fast. Keep me posted and watch your back."

"Will do," said Cyn. She pressed the "end call" button, placed both cell phones in her bag and headed out into the pre-dawn morning.

* * *

5:30 a.m.

"How soon can you be ready?" asked the General consulting his wristwatch. He was standing just inside the door in Jake's office with Cyn by his side. "I want to have this finished by the time the rest of the staff show up for work at 0900."

Jake got up from his seat at the computer and stretched. "Everything's pretty well ready to go," he said. "I'd just like to have Ms. Hoover double check a couple of things with me before we start. How about an hour?"

The General nodded. "All right. If we start at 0630, that means we'll be finished by 0830?"

"For sure," said Jake. "Maybe sooner because we won't have to spend time figuring out how to view the memory like we did with Professor Latter."

"That's right," said Cyn. "We might be able to finish in an hour to an hour and a half—plenty of time before the others start arriving."

"Good. I'll go see Dr. Graham and tell him to start the sedative. I'm going to make sure he gives him a strong enough dose so there's no chance of him waking up before we're finished—like Professor Latter. I'll check back with you in about thirty minutes."

The General left and closed the door.

After the door was firmly closed Jake walked over to Cyn holding out his arms. She looked warily at him for a second, then sighed and placed her head on his chest. He wrapped his arms around her and rested his cheek on the top of her head.

"How are you, Cyn-Cyn? Did you get any sleep?" he asked quietly, breathing in the scent of her hair.

"Not much," said Cyn. "I did manage to doze for a couple of hours, that's all. What about you? Have you been here the whole night?"

"Yeah, but you know me. I don't need much sleep," he said.

They stood like that for several seconds before Cyn reluctantly pushed him away. "Well, I guess we'd better get to work," she said. "You said in your text message that there's a problem?"

Jake nodded. "Come over and sit down. I'll show you."

Cyn followed him over to the computer and laid her bag down beside her chair.

"What's the word on Karl Braun? Have you heard anything new?" she asked as she sat down.

"He had surgery and is back in ICU. It's too soon for them to know if he's gonna make it. Dr. Graham says if he gets through today there's a good chance of recovery, but it will be a long haul."

Cyn put a hand to her brow. "Oh, dear. I feel so bad about Karl. I was just getting to know him."

Jake reached over with one hand and patted her knee as he clicked the computer mouse with the other hand. "I know, Cyn. He's a really good guy. It was lucky you were with him. If he'd been in there by himself, he'd probably be dead by now."

"Well, I see the new board is working," said Cyn. The visual display had come up on the screen as they were commiserating about Karl.

"Oh, yeah, the board's working—no problem with that," said Jake. "But there's a problem with Harry Latter's memory. I can't access it at all. I can't get it to come up from the memory, and I can't find any backup files. I even tried to download it from Roswell like we were doing the other night, but nada."

"What? That's strange," said Cyn. "How could all that data just disappear?"

"I don't know. That's what I've mostly been working on all night. I've tried everything—even hacking into Roswell in case it got encrypted somehow—but I can't find even one sign of it anywhere."

"So, all we have is *our* memory of what was in Harry's memory….." said Cyn.

"Afraid so," said Jake. "That and the printouts of the formula for the E-Weapon."

"Which is the main reason we were downloading his memory in the first place," added Cyn. She thought about that for a second and frowned. "And the only person who had those printouts was Karl, and he must have given them to the General...."

"He did, but there's someone else who has a copy of them," said Jake.

"Oh?" asked Cyn raising an eyebrow. "And who would that be?"

Jake turned to her with a mischievous grin. "Who do you think?" he asked.

Cyn looked at him and began to grin. "Oh, Jake, really?" she asked.

"Really," said Jake. "First rule of computing. Always make copies in case of computer crash."

"And you have them where?" asked Cyn.

Jake shook his head. "Not here. In a safe place."

"Does anyone else know?" asked Cyn.

Again Jake shook his head. "Just you," he said.

"Well, let's keep it that way for the time being, OK?"

He studied her face for an instant, their eyes locked together. "I thought you'd say that," he said. "Now, shall we get down to the task at hand?"

Cyn nodded and turned her attention to the computer screen where the familiar countdown clock and biometrics meters were on display.

* * *

7:30 a.m.

"That's it," said Jake as he watched the countdown clock come to a halt on the screen. "We've got his memory downloaded, Sir."

"Good," said General Masters as he glanced at his watch. "And in record time, too. There's still an hour and a half before the rest of the staff show up for work."

"Oh, no! Not again!" cried Cyn. She was still seated next to Jake watching the computer monitor.

"What?" asked the General. He strode over and peered at the screen over her shoulder.

Cyn pointed to the biofunction screen.

"I see what you mean!" General Masters quickly pulled out his cell phone and pressed a button. "Shut down and get him out of the chamber, NOW!" he yelled.

"It's just like what happened with Professor Latter," said Cyn. She was still staring at the monitor where the biometric meters indicated the subject in the chamber was not breathing.

"At least we got his memory downloaded before it happened," said Jake. "Maybe they can get him out of the chamber in time to revive him."

"If not, who cares," remarked the General.

Cyn and Jake looked up at him in surprise.

"This is hardly like losing Harry Latter. Jazar is a known terrorist and deserves to die after what he did. The only reason we were keeping him

238

alive was to find out what he knows about Mario and the Damascus Road. We've got his memory now, so who cares if he dies?" The General's voice was harsher than Cyn had ever heard it.

"I see your point," said Cyn. "Still it would be better to see him stand trial so the whole world knows what he did."

The General shrugged. "So he can grandstand and win the sympathy of Arabs everywhere? No thanks. I'd just as soon see him die now. Save the taxpayers a lot of time and money."

There was silence for a moment and then Jake announced, "The program was shut down at precisely 0734. What do you want us to do next, Sir?"

"Go ahead and prepare it for viewing. I'm going down to the chamber to see what's happening. Then I'll come back and take a look at his memory. I know the dates and times we're interested in, and I can take it from here. You two can go home and get some sleep. I'm sure you need it."

Cyn didn't say anything until she was sure General Masters was out of the room and well away from the door. Then she turned to Jake and placed a hand on his arm. "I don't trust him," she whispered, leaning over and saying it in his ear.

Jake raised an eyebrow and drew back to look at her face. "What makes you say that?" he asked.

"He was the only one at the Mountain at 2:30 yesterday, was he not?" whispered Cyn.

Jake nodded.

"Then I have reason to believe he's been leaking information to the terrorists, possibly even Mario," Cyn whispered.

Jake crossed his arms and leaned back in his swivel chair. "I think you're barking up the wrong tree," he said quietly.

Cyn waved a hand at him. "Well, there's no other tree left to bark up," she hissed.

"Are you sure of that? I think you're overlooking something."

"Like what?" asked Cyn forgetting to speak in a whisper.

"I'll tell you later," said Jake turning back to the computer. "Let's get this memory translated into visual form so we can get out of here."

Cyn stared at him in frustration for a second. Then she shrugged and turned her attention to the computer screen.

Jake was tapping rapidly on the keyboard. The screen remained blank. He clicked on the mouse a couple of times. Nothing. He leaned back and stared at the screen for a moment. Then he leaned forward and attacked the keyboard again. Again nothing happened.

"What's going on?" asked Cyn.

"Nothing is what's going on," mumbled Jake. "It appears the entire download has vanished. It's no longer on the computer."

"You're kidding," said Cyn.

"Afraid not. See for yourself." Jake shoved the wireless keyboard over in front of her.

Cyn frowned and began tapping on the keyboard. "That's odd," she said. "You can't even bring up the system files or anything."

She thought for a moment. "I know," she said snapping her fingers. "This computer must have an immense backup system, right?"

"Right," said Jake.

"Well, then, reboot the system and see if we can call up the backup files."

Jake complied and sat back to watch as the computer shut down and then restarted. After a few moments the start-up screen appeared. Jake went to the computer search function and tapped in the extension for backup files. The computer went to work and a list of files began to appear on the screen.

After the computer had listed all the backup files, Jake moved the cursor slowly up and down the list as he and Cyn read the file names.

Cyn looked at Jake in astonishment. "Not a trace," she said shaking her head.

"That's what I was telling you earlier about Professor Latter's memory files. Notice there's no mention of them in the backup files either," said Jake shaking his head.

"Oh, God, now what?" said Cyn. "We don't have Jazar's memory, and what if he died down there in that chamber? That means this mission has failed. At least we were able to get what we wanted from Professor Latter's memory before it disappeared."

"That's right," said Jake. Incredibly, he was casually leaning back in his chair regarding her with a huge grin on his face.

"What?" asked Cyn.

"You'll see," said Jake. He quickly turned back to the computer when the door swung open and in marched General Masters.

"Jazar is dead," he announced. "It is exactly the same as what happened with Professor Latter, right down to the mummification. At least we have his memory on file."

"I'm afraid there's some bad news," said Cyn as she turned to face the General.

* * *

8:45 a.m.

"Maybe the General's in league with someone at Roswell," said Mac as he poured Cyn a cup of coffee. She had just arrived from Apparition Mountain and was sitting across the table from him in the bus.

Cyn took the cup of coffee and frowned down into it. "I don't know. We hacked into Roswell and still couldn't find a trace of Harry Latter's memory, let alone the one we downloaded this morning. It's like they just disappeared into thin air."

Mac deposited himself in the seat across from her. "That is strange," he said. "It would take a genius to siphon off such large data banks and conceal them. I mean whoever did it would have to have a computer bank as big as NSA's, and to our knowledge there's no match for the NSA computer."

"I think the General is behind all this," said Cyn. "He was the only one who had the printout of the E-Weapon formula from Harry Latter's memory. And he was the only one at the Mountain when that message was sent about the Professor being out of commission. On top of that, he called off the download, using the Professor's illness as an excuse. The only reason he went ahead with it was because of pressure from Washington that I generated with the call to the NSA Director."

Mac leaned back in his chair and regarded her for a moment. "Yeah, I think you're right...." he said. "I wouldn't seriously have suspected him at all if it hadn't been for that intercepted message yesterday—I mean with his rep and all."

242

"What more perfect cover could you have?" asked Cyn. "Just think of it: his reputation as a hero from the Iraq War, his recent promotion, and his position in the NSA. He is in the perfect position to get away with anything."

"True," said Mac with a frown. "Still I hate that it's him. Hell, if you can't trust a man with a reputation like his, who in the hell *can* you trust?"

"I know. It's sad," said Cyn shaking her head. "Are you going to report it to the NSA Chief, or shall I?"

Mac studied her for a moment before responding. "I don't think we should report it just yet, Cyn...."

Cyn raised an eyebrow. "Oh? And why not?"

"Well, if he thinks he's gotten away with all this, he may let his guard down and get a little sloppy with his communication. If we keep tabs on him, he'll probably lead us right to Mario."

Cyn leaned across the table. "Yes, I see what you mean. We can pretend that our mission is over, now that the download was unsuccessful and Jazar died. I can tell him I've been called back to Washington at the end of the week."

"Yeah, and meanwhile, you can stay here and help with the monitoring. We have to leave tonight. We have a gig on Wednesday at the Blue Mesa in Albuquerque, but that won't be a problem. We can still stay in touch and still monitor calls going in and out of the Mountain. In fact, it'll throw him off his guard 'cause he'll think we finished our job and have gone on to something else."

Cyn nodded. "Yes, that's a good plan. The General is the only one who knows you and your team are part of the NSA, and I can tell him you've gone on because there's nothing more for you to do here."

"It's a plan then," said Mac. "We'll leave for Albuquerque just as soon as the rest of them get back from the coffee shop. What's next on your agenda?"

"Brent Jacobson," said Cyn.

Mac raised an eyebrow. "Oh yeah?" he asked with a grin.

"It's nothing like that," said Cyn. "Get your mind out of the gutter! He's coming by in about an hour and we're gonna go over the events to make a report for the Professor and General Masters. That will give me an excuse to stay in touch with the Mountain. It's possible Jacobson knows something that may lead to the General's involvement in all this."

"You think Jacobson's in cahoots with the General?" asked Mac.

"Oh, no, I don't. I have good reason to believe he's above-board with everything, but he might have accidentally observed something that would confirm the General's involvement."

"OK, Cyn. You know what you're doing. Keep in touch through the usual manner. I'd like to hear from you at least once a day, and I'll call you if I discover anything new."

"Will do, Mac," said Cyn rising from the table. Mac walked with her to the bus door and opened it.

"So long, Cousin Barb," he said. "It's been real."

"Yes, it has," said Cyn, grinning. "Thanks for all the entertainment."

"Think nothing of it. Maybe you'll show up at our next gig in Albuquerque."

"Could be," said Cyn. "You never know what's going to turn up in this business."

She stepped down from the bus and turned to look back.

Mac gave her a mock salute, and that was the last she saw of him in Roca Grande.

* * *

10:35 a.m.

"The General didn't seem terribly upset that we lost Jazar's memory," said Cyn, raising a cup of coffee to her lips. "That makes me even more suspicious of him."

She was facing Jake across the small dining table in her room at the Inn. He had come in from the Mountain in his Durango.

Jake regarded her for a moment and slammed his cup down on the table. "Come on, Cyn. There's someone you need to meet." He rose from his chair.

"What? Who?" asked Cyn.

"You'll see," said Jake. "Get your stuff and let's go. You're riding with me."

Cyn looked at him. He maintained a stone face. "Oh, all right," she said as she stood up and grabbed her bag. "I know you well enough to know that you're not gonna tell me anything until you're ready."

"That's right," said Jake putting a finger under her chin when she walked over to him. He lifted her chin and before Cyn had time to think about it, he was kissing her, and...*she* was kissing back.

Finally Jake leaned back and looked at her. "Some things never change," he said in a low voice.

"Whew! You've got that right," thought Cyn. She was too flustered to speak.

Jake turned and opened the door and she went ahead of him. As Cyn opened the back door, she noticed that Mac's bus was gone. She smiled to herself as she climbed into Jake's Durango.

* * *

11:10 a.m.

They were headed back through the town of Roca Grande when Jake suddenly took a left-hand turn at the deserted gas station. Then he took a hard right and came to a stop in a swirl of dust behind the Dos Amigos Cantina that Cyn had noticed on her first trek though Roca Grande.

When the dust settled Cyn saw that they were in a barren lot that was invisible to passers-by on the main road that went through Roca Grande.

"What are we doing here?" asked Cyn.

"You'll see," said Jake still maintaining his mysterious aura.

Cyn sighed. "I wish you'd quit saying that and actually show me something," she said in a huffy tone.

Jake laughed as he unbuckled his seat belt. "Still the impatient one," he said. "Come on. We're going in the back door over there."

Cyn looked to where he was pointing and saw a narrow low door on the far right-hand side of the rundown log cabin. "Why the back door?" she asked.

"Because the Mercantile is right across the street, and we don't want that busybody Shirl knowing our every move, do we?"

"No, I guess not," said Cyn with a chuckle. "I'd almost forgotten about her."

As they walked to the back door, Cyn asked, "Who owns this place anyway? They surely don't get much business here?"

"You'll see," said Jake again as he pushed open the back door. He laughed at Cyn's frustrated grimace. "After you, Madame. Soon all will be revealed."

With an exasperated snort Cyn charged past him through the open door and stopped short. She could see absolutely nothing. The air felt warm and muggy and smelled of cigar smoke mixed with something else like a combination of chili powder and mothballs.

"I can't see a thing. Where are we?" asked Cyn. "And if you say 'you'll see' one more time, I'll belt you!" she added.

Jake chuckled. "We're in the storage room behind the bar. Take my hand and I'll lead you until your eyes adjust to the darkness."

He moved in front of her and Cyn held onto his hand as he led the way to another door and opened it. Now her eyes were adjusting and she could make out the dim shapes of boxes in the store room. Coming through the door in front of them was a flickering light like that produced by candles or a fire.

When she walked through the door, Cyn saw that it was the latter. There was a roaring fire in the beehive fireplace along one wall. A strong aroma of burning mesquite assaulted her senses, causing her eyes to run. She looked around and saw that there was a bar running along the length of the room. There were enough barstools for four people at the bar and two small tables under a set of antlers mounted on the wall by the front door. All in all, Cyn estimated the place would accommodate a grand total of ten people.

Jake said something in Tiwa as he led her up to the bar. As she climbed onto the stool a tall figure emerged from a room behind the counter. Jake struck a match and lit a candle in a glass jar. The figure behind the bar said something in Tiwa, and Cyn caught her breath as he came closer. She thought he must be at least 6' 5"—maybe more. He was huge with a face that looked as if it had been chiseled out of rock, and he had long jet black hair tied into a braid with rawhide strips. The braid reached down in back almost to his waist.

Jake said something again in Tiwa and then turned to Cyn. "Cyn, I want you to meet my Uncle. This is Tom Fleetdeer, my mother's brother."

The giant reached out and grabbed Cyn's hand. "I am glad to meet

Halcon's friend at last. I have heard much about you." He squeezed her hand causing her to wince. "Sorry," he said. "I forget my strength. What will you have to drink?"

"A Dos Equis for me," said Jake. "How about you, Cyn?"

"Do you have Negro Modelo?" asked Cyn.

Tom nodded and reached into a cooler behind the bar. He uncapped the two beers and set them in front of Jake and Cyn. "Glass?" he asked looking at Cyn.

"Yes, please."

As he put a frosted glass mug in front of Cyn, he asked, "So what brings you to Dos Amigos, *Halcon?*"

"I want you to tell Cyn about General Masters," said Jake. He tilted his bottle up and took a long sip.

"What you wanta know about JAM?" asked Tom looking at Cyn suspiciously. "I served under him in Iraq."

"I just want to know a little more about him. You know, what made him such a hero, how he treated the men under him, that kind of thing," said Cyn trying to put him at ease.

"Well, I'll tell you this. They don't come any better than Jeff Masters. He saved my hide on more than one occasion. We were in the thick of things over there before and during the war—we were doing dangerous stuff." He raised a hand before Cyn could say anything. "Stuff I can't talk about, so don't ask."

"I understand," said Cyn. "I don't need to know the exact details of what your unit was doing. All I want to know is about the character of General Masters."

Tom put both hands on the bar and leaned across until he was nearly in Cyn's face. When he spoke she could smell his breath which had a faint redolence of garlic and something else that she couldn't identify.

"General Masters put together a very elite top-secret special forces unit back in 1999. I am privileged to be a member of that group. I have served with General Masters in Afghanistan. We were there on special assignment two years before the 9/11 attack on the World Trade Center.

"By the time the regular troops came to Afghanistan after 9/11, we were already in Iraq. I tell you there's no one I trust more than JAM. He didn't just command our unit; he was right in there with us taking the same risks. He even got himself captured to carry out one of our missions. He didn't send one of us in—he did it himself."

Tom straightened up and jabbed at the bar in front of Cyn with his index finger. "You want to know about his character? There's no one with greater integrity, loyalty and honesty." He leaned back slightly crossing his arms in front of his chest. He smiled slightly with a nod toward Jake. "And you should know that we Native Americans are not taken in by false character."

Cyn smiled. "Yes, I do know that. Thank you for the information. It sets me at ease."

"If you're working with the General, you should be at ease. You can trust him with your life. I do. And there's something else. This unit JAM put together is unique in another way."

"How is that?" asked Cyn.

Again Tom glanced at Jake with a slight smile. "All of us in this unit were born and raised in the Taos Pueblo. In fact, you can't get into the unit unless you were raised in the Pueblo."

Cyn blinked and sat up straight with her hands on the bar. "That *is* unique. But why?"

"*Halcon* can tell you later. I've already said enough."

The front door banged open, and Cyn and Jake turned in their bar stools to look.

Jake grinned. "Hello, Bean," he said to the large man who had just entered.

The man walked up to the bar and stared at Cyn with piercing dark eyes. Then he looked at Jake.

"It's all right. This is my friend Cyn Hoover. You can trust her," said Jake.

The man took off his black Stetson hat and placed it on the corner of the bar. He had long black hair streaked with silver. He took off his Levi jacket and draped it on the back of a barstool. Then he walked behind the bar and joined Tom.

"This is my partner, Bean," said Tom. "The other half of Dos Amigos."

"Pleased to meet you," said Cyn.

Bean only grunted at her.

"It's Bean's turn to bartend," said Tom. "You want another drink?"

"No, thanks," said Jake rising from the barstool. "We have to go. Just wanted to stop in and say hello."

Cyn followed Jake back through the store room to the back door. She held her tongue until they were back in the Durango. "Who is this Bean?" she asked. "Is that his last name?"

Jake laughed as he started the engine. "He is Taos Indian like us. His Indian name means 'bean,' and that's what he's always been called. I'm sure he must have a last name, but I don't know what it is."

Jake put the Durango in gear and drove through the undeveloped land behind the cantina and a couple of other houses that lined the main road that ran through Roca Grande. He glanced at Cyn. "Bean is in the special forces, too."

"All right," said Cyn. "I think it's time you tell me what this is all about. Why is the unit made up of only Taos?"

"Because they—the ones raised at the Pueblo—are the only people on earth who speak Tiwa."

Cyn frowned and thought for a moment. "So I assume their mission has something to do with top-secret communications...."

Jake nodded as he drove slowly up the road in the direction of the Air Base and Apparition Mountain.

"So is that what you were doing when you and your cousin at MIT were exchanging messages in Tiwa?" asked Cyn abruptly.

Jake didn't answer. He simply glanced at her with a slight grin and then looked back at the road in front of them.

"Didn't you say your cousin's name was Fleetdeer? Is he Tom's son?"

Again Jake just glanced at her with his enigmatic grin.

"And what are two Taos Indians doing running a cantina in Roca Grande?"

"That's their cover," said Jake without looking at her.

"Their cover? Aren't they out of the service now?"

"Oh, no," said Jake. "They are still on active duty."

* * *

12:15 p.m.

About two miles before they reached the Air Base Jake glanced in his rearview mirror and suddenly took a hard right turn onto a rugged country road that ran through sagebrush-dotted open range.

"Where are we going?" asked Cyn.

Jake glanced over at her. "I think it's time we took a look at that download, don't you?"

Cyn looked at him in surprise. "What do you mean? I thought you said it was lost."

"It *was* lost…at least at the Mountain," said Jake. He glanced at her again and smiled when he saw the look of frustration on her face. He reached over and patted her knee. "Come on, Cyn. Surely you don't think someone as astute as Karl Braun wouldn't have planned for all contingencies?"

Cyn gave him a blank stare. "I did think it was odd that he wouldn't have allowed you to order backup equipment, but now I know that was part of his ruse to check me out."

"That's right," said Jake. "But there's a lot more to it than just checking *you* out."

"I don't understand…." began Cyn. The ringing of a cell phone interrupted her. She frowned and fished the XJ14 out of her bag.

"No! Don't answer that!" Jake reached over and grabbed her hand.

Cyn froze and Jake removed his hand. After four rings the cell phone went silent. She glanced at the caller ID screen. "It was Charlie Denton," she said. "I wonder what he wants."

"Did he leave a message?" asked Jake as he swerved sharply to avoid a rock in the road.

Cyn pressed a button. "Yes. There's one message in my voice mail box. Should I listen to it?"

"Go ahead," said Jake. "Just don't return his call, at least not right now."

Cyn nodded and accessed her voice mail. After listening for a bit she pressed a key to save the message and put the phone back in her bag.

Jake glanced at her with a raised eyebrow.

Cyn shrugged. "He said he has something for me and wants to come in and take me to dinner tonight at the Rancho Bonito."

Jake snorted. "Still after your bod, I see."

Cyn sighed. "I guess so now that Veronica has gone on with the band to Albuquerque. He was becoming a real pest before he met her."

"Can you get away without returning his call for a while, or will he get suspicious wondering where you are?" asked Jake.

"As far as he knows I'm in my room catching up on my sleep. If I call him later I'll just tell him I had the volume on the cell phone turned down."

"Does he have any way of tracking you?"

Cyn shook her head. "No—except for the Grand Cherokee, and it's parked at the Inn."

"What about the keys?"

"I thought about that, too," said Cyn. "I left them in the room."

"Good," said Jake.

"Now do you mind telling me where we're going?" asked Cyn.

"You'll see when we get there," said Jake. He looked at her and grinned. "I just wanted to show you some of the country around where I grew up. Thought you might be interested."

Cyn smiled. "Great. I've never been in this part of New Mexico before."

She settled back in her seat to enjoy the view knowing that Jake was not about to tell her anything more until he was good and ready.

* * *

1:15 p.m.

The stacks of gold ingots gave off a mellow glow when the lights came on in the vault—the vault that Cyn had visited only twenty-four hours ago. Was it possible that it was only yesterday when she had stood here with Karl Braun? Cyn shook her head and touched one of the gold bars as she paused again to admire Karl's handiwork.

"This is really incredible, isn't it?" she asked, but there was no answer.

She turned and saw that Jake was walking toward the other side of the vault.

"Come on," he said over his shoulder. "We've got work to do."

Cyn wondered how many more surprises Jake had in store for her. They had arrived at the back entrance to Karl's mine about ten minutes ago after taking a series of rugged back roads that meandered through wilderness areas north of Santa Fe and eventually headed in a southeasterly direction through the Santa Fe National Forest.

High in the mountains east of Santa Fe, Jake had at last turned right on a narrow unmarked gravel road that curved to the left losing itself in dense thickets of pines. Within a quarter of a mile the road was blocked by a six-foot high chain link fence crowned with razor wire. Attached to the gate ahead of them was a huge metal sign that read "RESTRICTED. GOVERNMENT PROPERTY. TRESPASSING IS A FELONY PUNISHABLE BY A $20,000 FINE AND A FIVE-TO-TEN YEAR PRISON SENTENCE."

"Wow! That should keep the riff raff out," murmured Cyn. Ever since the cell phone call from Charlie Denton she had remained largely silent throughout the journey other than to comment on the scenery. "I hope *we're* not trespassing," she added.

Jake glanced at her and shook his head. He reached up and pressed a button on what appeared to be a garage door opener clipped to the windshield visor. The gate slowly swung open.

After he had driven through, it automatically closed behind them.

Now the road continued its winding course uphill through the scrubby pines and boulders that composed the landscape on the east side of the mountains. After another mile or so the road dead-ended in a small clearing at the base of a mountain. Ahead of them was a dilapidated old log cabin that looked as if it had been there since the 1800s—something a mountain man might have built.

Jake drove the Durango behind a huge boulder and cut the engine. Motioning to Cyn to follow him, he grabbed his rifle, got out of the vehicle and headed toward the cabin. Shouldering her bag, Cyn jumped out of the Durango and ran to catch up with him. She anticipated going in through the front door but hesitated when she noticed the sagging old door. It looked as if a whisper could cause it to fall off its hinges and even bring down the entire structure.

"Are you sure it's safe   " she began but saw that Jake had walked on around the corner of the building.

She followed and soon discovered that the cabin was a façade like the boarded up entrance she had gone through with Karl the day before. The cabin appeared to have only three sides with the rocky mountainside serving as its back wall. As Karl had done the day before, Jake pressed his palm on a rock and stepped back for her to do the same. A door slid open in what appeared to be the back of the cabin where it joined the mountainside.

She followed Jake through the door and it slid shut behind them leaving them in total darkness.

"Give me your hand," said Jake. "I'll show you how to turn the lights on."

He took her hand and guided it to the stone wall on the left of the entrance they had just come through. "Feel that?" he asked. "It's the third rock to the left at shoulder height."

Cyn could feel the cold jagged surface beneath her fingers. Jake pressed her index finger on a sharp edge that jutted out further than the others. They were immediately bathed in an incandescent glow.

Cyn blinked and looked around. They were in a narrow rock-lined room.

"What happened to the cabin?" she asked.

Jake was grinning at her. "It's on the other side of this wall." He placed a hand on the rock wall to Cyn's right. "I guess you could say this is a false back making the cabin look like it's built right onto the mountain. Pretty ingenious, huh?"

Cyn nodded and ran a hand over the wall. "I take it this is the back entrance to Karl's mine?"

"That's right," said Jake. "This is where the gold is shipped out when we get a call for it."

"So, I take it there's a way to get into the mine over on that other wall?"

Again Jake nodded. "It's the same as the front entrance from here on in. You use the same process to get through all the security doors until you come to the vault. Let's see how much you remember. Think you can find the panel to open the door?"

Cyn studied the rock wall for a moment and then pointed to a fairly smooth rock at eye level just to the right of the middle of the wall. "Is that it?"

"Bingo!" said Jake. "Your memory is as good as ever. Now, do you remember how to open it?"

They both walked over to the rock panel and Cyn paused. "Let's see. You say the sequence is the same as coming in the front entrance?"

Jake nodded.

"Then this is the door that dispenses the nerve agent," said Cyn. "What if I get it wrong? I haven't been vaccinated yet."

"I have every confidence you remember the process, but just to be safe, tell it to me before you try it. We'll have to have Dr. Graham take care of the vaccine as soon as we get the chance."

"OK," said Cyn. "You press your palm on the rock, and if everything's

OK, you apply slightly more pressure with your…ah, little finger. If there was someone holding you at gunpoint, you would apply more pressure with your index finger to dispense the gas. Right?"

"You're right on. Go ahead and open the door."

On their way to the vault Jake had Cyn open all the doors to test her memory of the codes. She never faltered, and within ten minutes they were in the vault.

Now Jake was waiting for her to open the last door—the door to the command center where the computer systems were housed.

* * *

1:20 p.m.

Inside the command center Jake went directly to the computer on the left side of the room and booted it up. Cyn followed and pulled up a chair next to him.

Just as she began to sit down the XJ14 cell phone rang again. "Now, what?" She scowled as she pulled the phone out of her bag and looked at it.

"What is it?" asked Jake.

"It's a text message from Charlie Denton. It just says 'Urgent! Call me right away!' Do you think I should call him back?"

Jake shook his head. "No. Wait until we're finished here."

"You're right," said Cyn. "Whatever is so urgent can wait until we've taken a look at Jazar's memory and are back at the Inn. I still want him to think I was sleeping and had the phone in mute mode."

Jake turned his attention back to the computer. Cyn looked at the text message again and read the last line to herself—the part she hadn't read to Jake. 'You're in danger!' She saved the message, thought for a second and remembered what Charlie had told her about emergencies. She surreptitiously pressed *33 before returning the phone to her bag.

As she sat down next to Jake, he finished typing in commands on the keyboard and leaned back in his chair with his arms crossed to look at the large flat panel monitor mounted on the wall ahead of them. "Here's where we stopped this morning at precisely 7:34," he announced.

"Why can we see it here when we couldn't pull it up at the Mountain?" asked Cyn.

"This is my backup system," said Jake with a chuckle. "I transmitted everything here that we downloaded at the Mountain for safekeeping in case anything went wrong."

"You mean even when you were also transmitting it to the NSA computer at Roswell?"

"That's right."

"Then why didn't you say anything when the video board blew? Does anyone else know you have it here?" asked Cyn.

"Look!" exclaimed Jake ignoring her questions. "Look at the clock. It's still going forward just like it did with Professor Latter's memory download."

Cyn looked at the monitor and sure enough the clock had moved forward. It now read 7:39 a.m. and there was the same spinning three-dimensional five-pointed star they had viewed at the end of Harry Latter's memory download.

"Translate that star into the visual the same way we did with Harry's memory," said Cyn, but Jake was already tapping on the keyboard.

An image came up. Now they were viewing Jazar's body from ceiling height, just as they had with Harry's. Again there was a brilliant flash and the screen went black.

Jake fast-forwarded the clock to the present time, and sure enough a signal was still coming in nearly six hours after Jazar had died in the chamber.

"It's the same thing all over again," commented Cyn.

"Yeah. I'd like to take a look at the view from where we left off with Harry, but we don't have time for that right now. Maybe we can do that after this mission is complete."

Cyn nodded. "Do you know where to start looking in his memory?"

Jake frowned and rubbed his chin. "I assume we want to go back to the day Jazar ambushed that patrol on the outskirts of Baghdad and find out how he got away."

"That sounds logical. Let's see. That was on June 19, three years ago, wasn't it?"

"That's right," said Jake. He began tapping on the keyboard.

Cyn watched as the clock spun back to the appointed time. A picture began to form on the screen.

There was a great cloud of dust and black smoke and the sound of automatic weapon fire and voices shouting in Farsi. They were looking down the barrel of an AK 107 Assault Rifle through Jazar's eyes. Then the gunfire stopped and the AK 107 dropped down out of sight and they saw Jazar's right hand waving in a forward motion. Three men dressed in Arab garb with black masks on their faces rushed forward into the dust.

As the dust began to settle they saw a Humvee turned on its side on the dirt road ahead of them. An American soldier lay crumpled face down in a pool of blood beside the wrecked vehicle. Another soldier was dragging himself along the road toward his fallen comrade, while a third one sat in the road with his back against the upturned Humvee wheel. He was rubbing his left arm and appeared to be in shock. He looked up in stunned silence, his mouth agape, when one of the Arabs ran up to him and viciously kicked him in the side. He slowly raised his arms over his head, and the Arab prodded him with his gun. He got to his feet, and the Arab grabbed his arm and dragged him over to where the other two Arabs were dealing with the soldier who had been dragging himself along the road.

After kicking him into submission, the Arabs each grabbed an arm and jerked him to his feet. After cuffing the two soldiers' arms behind their backs, they turned their attention to the dead soldier. One of the Arabs turned him over roughly with his boot and drew a long scimitar from the belt at his waist. He grasped it by the hilt with both hands and raised it high above his head.

"Stop!" cried Cyn closing her eyes. "I don't want to see that!"

"Neither do I," said Jake through gritted teeth as he quickly tapped a key and the screen went blank.

He looked at Cyn and patted her arm. "It's OK. You can open your eyes now. I've turned it off."

Cyn took a deep breath and slowly opened her eyes. "We know what happened after that. Those two little Iraqi kids found the head two weeks later when they were playing in that rubble heap ten miles away."

"Yeah, and we know what happened to the other two as well," said Jake shaking his head. "Tortured, dismembered and finally killed...."

"I know. I know. Don't remind me," said Cyn. "Now it doesn't bother me one bit that Jazar died during the download. My only regret is that he died so peacefully, but then he is still our only link to bigger fish. Move forward a couple of hours and see what he was up to."

Jake complied and another picture came up. He leaned back in his chair, arms crossed, studying the image on the screen.

"What are we looking at?" asked Cyn, squinting at the screen.

"I'm not sure," said Jake with a frown. "He's either got his eyes closed or he's in a very dark place."

"Listen," said Cyn raising a hand.

"Sounds like he's inside a truck or some kind of motor vehicle," said Jake after a moment.

After a few seconds, they heard the squeal of brakes and the growl of an engine as gears shifted down. Then there appeared to be just the rumble of an idling engine. Suddenly they heard voices from outside and then a very loud clang quite near. There was a distant circle of light as if they were looking up from the bottom of a well. Another clang and the light disappeared. There was another distant exchange of words they couldn't understand and then the roar of the engine as the driver changed gears and stepped on the accelerator.

"He seems to be inside something that's being transported on a truck, and now the truck is moving again," muttered Jake.

Cyn nodded. "They must have just gone through some kind of checkpoint."

"Maybe the Syrian border?"

"Could be," said Cyn. "Let's move ahead again a couple of hours."

Jake tapped on the keyboard and the clock spun forward. When it stopped, they were watching an oil tanker moving away from them with increasing speed and throwing up a cloud of dust. As the tanker disappeared over a rise in the distance, the dust cleared, and through Jazar's eyes they saw only a barren landscape with a one-lane dirt road cutting through it.

"Wow! So that's how he got away. He must have been down inside one of those oil tanks," said Cyn.

"Looks like it," said Jake. "What's he doing now?"

"Looks like he's squatting down," said Cyn observing the shift in view of the surrounding landscape.

Now they could see Jazar's hands and the sleeves of his garment. They were smeared with oil, and he was holding something in his left hand.

"It's one of those Thuraya satellite phones," said Jake.

"Yes, I see that," said Cyn. "Remember, that's why we couldn't track Taheri or the others. They were too smart to use regular cell phones."

"Yeah, I remember. The only way they discovered Taheri's whereabouts was through an informant. This ambush that Jazar participated in was purportedly in revenge for Taheri's death."

"He must be calling someone to pick him up," said Cyn as the hand holding the phone disappeared from view. All they saw was the barren land and the sky deepening to a dark violet on the horizon. They heard the low growl of a voice coming over the phone, but they couldn't comprehend any of the words.

After a few seconds the satellite phone came into view again as Jazar lowered it and turned it off with his right hand. Then it disappeared and they were staring at a point on the horizon again.

"Move ahead a little," whispered Cyn as if she was fearful Jazar could hear her.

Jake did as she asked and spun the clock forward a half hour. When he stopped, they saw the same landscape, the sky considerably darker now.

"Do you hear that?" asked Cyn.

Jake nodded as they heard the sound of engines in the distance. Through Jazar's eyes they focused on the distant rise in the road. As the sound of the engines increased to a roar, two vehicles crested the rise and sped toward them.

"Motorcycles," commented Jake.

There were two cyclists dressed identically in black leather, their faces obscured by the shields on their black helmets. Jazar watched as they approached but did not move from where he was sitting on the ground by the side of the road.

The cycles screeched to a stop directly in front of him. As the lead cyclist put his feet on the ground and revved his engine, the other cut his engine, put down the kickstand and dismounted. Without looking at Jazar, the second cyclist jumped on the back of the lead motorcycle. The driver gunned the engine and within seconds they had disappeared into the deepening dusk.

Jazar did not move until there was only silence and the faint light of a lone star on the horizon. Then he got up slowly and approached the abandoned motorcycle. Cyn and Jake watched in silence as Jazar boarded the bike, turned it on and pushed up the kickstand. He revved the engine, turned the bike around and headed up the road in the direction from which the cyclists had come.

"Where do you think he's going?" asked Jake.

"Three guesses," muttered Cyn.

"The infamous ,,Damascus Road"?"

"Literally, I'd guess," said Cyn. "Who knows how far out he is. Let's move ahead a couple of hours and see where he's at."

Jake complied and when the picture came up on the screen they saw that Jazar was still on the motorcycle, but now he was headed up a dimly lit palm-lined lane. After a few moments, the headlight of the bike revealed a massive intricately carved wooden gate set in a thick ten-foot-high white sandstone wall ahead of them.

The sound of the cycle's engine diminished to a low growl as Jazar pulled up to the gate and stopped. For a time the only vision they had was of the gate ahead of them, and then it slowly swung open. Jazar revved the engine and roared in through the gate. He appeared to be racing at breakneck speed toward another gate—this one made of white wrought-iron. Just as Cyn and Jake were sure he was going to crash into the gate, Jazar abruptly turned the cycle, nearly laying it on its side, and screeched to a halt.

As he dismounted, an apparition materialized ahead of him. When Jazar focused on the apparition, Jake and Cyn could see it was a man dressed in a white abaya. As he approached, they could see him motioning in the customary Arabic-style greeting and heard him say something in Arabic.

"Who's that? Do you recognize him?" asked Jake.

Cyn shook her head. "No. He must be some sort of underling."

They watched as Jazar followed the man through the iron gates into a sumptuous courtyard tiled with mosaics and dotted with palms, fountains and serene pools. Jazar's guide did not pause until he reached an open doorway hung with a silk curtain. He lifted the curtain and turned to Jazar, motioning for him to step inside.

Now they were looking around at a lavish apartment with richly-hued Persian carpets covering the floor. The guide appeared in front of them again speaking in Arabic and motioning first to a tiled Jacuzzi pool and a white abaya laid across the foot of a huge bed, then to a low table across the room on which resided several bowls of food.

"Apparently he's being told to clean up and eat," said Cyn.

"Yeah, but he must not be going to bed if he's going to change into those clothes," said Jake. "How about we jump forward about an hour?"

"Okay," said Cyn. "Now, maybe we'll find out who's behind his escape."

Again Jake fast-forwarded, and when the picture came up they were looking directly into the eyes of someone they recognized immediately.

"Abdul Assef al-Ahmin!" exclaimed Cyn.

"Yeah! He's the guy that took over leadership of al-Qaeda in Iraq after Taheri was killed, wasn't he?" asked Jake.

Cyn nodded. "Yes. He's the one who ordered the brutal torturing of those two soldiers in revenge for Taheri's death."

"What's he saying?"

"He's speaking in Arabian Gulf dialect, I think. I only know a few words," said Cyn.

"No problem. I'll activate the translator."

Jake froze the clock for a moment while he typed in a few commands on the keyboard. A white rectangular space appeared at the bottom of the screen. He activated the clock again.

As they watched, al-Ahmin waved a hand and called out. His words appeared in English at the bottom of the screen: "Farid, come here, please." The man who had ushered Jazar to his apartment appeared at his side. "Yes, Sir?"

"Farid, please inform our guest that we are pleased to meet with him," said al-Ahmin.

264

"Yes, Sir," said Farid. He disappeared from view.

Al-Ahmin turned his attention back to Jazar. "We will soon see, Tarique, how you will disappear so that you may be of service to our cause in later years. I trust your escape from Iraq was without incident?"

There was a pause during which Jazar must have been giving his reply. Al-Ahmin smiled. "It is as I thought. Our friend is very good at arranging these matters—as he should be, for the price we pay him."

There was another pause and Al-Ahmin looked to the left and extended his arm.

"Ah, there you are. Come sit with us."

Jazar turned to followed al-Ahmin"s gaze. A large man dressed in a black abaya had entered the room. Cyn and Jake saw him in profile as he approached but could not see his face. He wore a black kaffiyeh secured by a black and white agal. The kaffiyeh hung loose down to his shoulders obscuring his face, and he wore thick black-rimmed sunglasses.

"Welcome, Mario," said al-Ahmin. "I trust you have made accommodations for our friend Tarique?"

The man did not speak. He simply nodded as he sat down on an ottoman between al-Ahmin and Jazar. He did not look at Jazar, and the only view they had of him through Jazar's eyes was in profile.

"Mario!" gasped Cyn. "We're actually seeing him!"

"Yeah, but we can't really see him with all that garb and sunglasses," said Jake.

"Shhh! Maybe his voice will give him away," said Cyn putting a finger to her lips.

Mario produced a leather packet from somewhere in the depths of his abaya. He handed it to al-Ahmin.

No words were spoken as al-Ahmin opened the packet and removed a passport and a couple of other documents. Laying the other documents aside, al-Ahmin opened the passport and looked at it carefully, occasionally glancing up at Jazar.

"Very good," he said, handing the passport over to Jazar. "Learn your new name, Tarique."

Jazar's hand reached out and took the passport. His eyes focused on a picture of himself dressed in a Western business suit, wearing steel-rimmed glasses, and without a beard. The name on the passport was Rahim Akbar al-Hamad, a citizen of Saudi Arabia. There was a home address in Riyadh.

"That's where Jazar was finally captured," said Cyn. "An anonymous informant tipped off the Saudis and they arrested him and turned him over to us. He was posing as a resort developer and had actually gone in and out of the country several times."

Now Jazar was looking at al-Ahmin again. Al-Ahmin glanced at Mario who had not moved.

"You will remain here for a week to learn your new identity. Then you will drive a rental car to Beirut. After concluding a business meeting there, you will fly home to Riyadh. Mario has provided a movie of your new home that you will study before you leave. Mario has thought of everything you need to know. All the documents—driving license, bank accounts, and credit cards—are in this pouch," said al-Ahmin.

He reached down and picked up a titanium case sitting on the floor by his chair and turned to Mario. "Everything is more than satisfactory, as usual. Here is the agreed-upon amount in South African Krugerands as you requested."

Mario took the case from him, laid it on his lap and opened it. The case was filled with gold coins. He picked up one of the coins and held it between his thumb and forefinger holding it up to the light. He nodded, put the coin back in the case and snapped the case shut.

"So much for trying to recognize his voice," muttered Cyn. "He hasn't said a word."

"Yeah, and we haven't been able to get a head-on glance at his face either," said Jake.

Now al-Ahmin was looking at Jazar again. "This concludes our meeting, Tarique…rather, I should say, Rahim. You should rest now and in the morning begin the studies of your new life. Farid will show you back to your apartment. I have further business with Mario."

"Oh, rats! I suppose that's all we're going to see of Mario!" exclaimed Cyn as Jazar rose from his seat and began walking toward the door.

"Looks like it…." Jake began. "Wait! Look at that. He's turning around."

Sure enough, Jazar had stopped just before opening the door and turned around. Both al-Ahmin and Mario were looking directly at him. Then he turned and opened the door and left the room.

"Stop!" shouted Cyn. "Back it up and freeze that frame!"

Jake was already ahead of her. Frozen on the screen was the view of the two men looking directly at them from across the expanse of the large palatial room.

Cyn and Jake stared at the screen for a few seconds without saying anything.

"You still can't see much of his face," said Jake.

"You're right," said Cyn, disappointment registering in her voice. "Wait a minute. What's that?" she asked pointing at a spot on the screen.

Jake squinted at the spot. "I don't know. Looks like the light is glinting off something. I'll zoom in and see if we can figure out what it is."

Mario's face filled the screen. His mouth was slightly open, and just below his upper lip was a spark of light.

"There's still nothing discernible about his face," said Cyn with a sigh.

* * *

2:15 p.m.

Cyn paced around the control room deep in thought while Jake fiddled with the close-up of Mario's face attempting to get the best resolution possible before printing it out.

A blinking gold light on the monitor that displayed the location of Karl's gold caught her eye as she passed by. She turned back and looked more closely. The view was still of New Mexico where Karl had left it the day before. There was one light. She glanced over at Jake and saw that he was still preoccupied with the image of Mario's face and had his back to her.

She casually walked over to the control panel, studied it for a second and pressed a key on the keyboard. The image zoomed in, and she caught her breath in surprise when she saw that the one gold light in New Mexico was in Southwest New Mexico moving along Highway 26 toward Deming.

"That's the best I can do," announced Jake as he hit the print button.

Cyn quickly pressed another key and the image zoomed out to a map of the world. She walked back to where Jake was sitting and watched the photo as it emerged from the printer.

"Still doesn't ring any bells. I'll send it to headquarters. They can analyze it and see if the facial structure matches anything in our files," she said.

"Good idea. Be my guest," said Jake. He saved and closed the download program and got up from his chair.

Cyn quickly sat down and established a link to NSA. Then she scanned the photo, enclosed it in an encrypted message and pressed the "send" command.

"How long do you think it will take to get a reply?" asked Jake who had walked across the room in order not to view her security access codes.

Before Cyn could answer, the alarm began to sound.

"Oh, no!" cried Cyn. "What's going on now?"

"Someone must be trying to get into the mine!" yelled Jake. "Over here!"

He raced over to the monitor that provided the views outside the mountain. He flipped a switch and a view of the mountain filled the screen. He tapped a key and the view shifted to the mine entrance.

"For Pete's sake! It's Charlie Denton!" cried Cyn as the image came up. "What's he doing?"

"He's feeling around on the front gate, apparently trying to figure out how to get in," said Jake.

They watched as Charlie stepped back from the entrance and scratched his head. Then he stooped and picked up a hammer and a crowbar lying on the ground.

"He's going to try to pry off those boards. If he gets in, he might discover there's more to the mine than that old shaft, and we can't have that," said Jake.

"He must have somehow figured out I'm here," said Cyn. "You stay here. I'll go out and see what he wants and try to steer him away from the mine. I'll just tell him I came here to finish the bit of prospecting Karl and I were doing yesterday."

"Well, all right, but be careful," said Jake. "I'll stay here and keep an eye on him through the monitor."

Cyn grabbed her bag and raced out of the door. Jake looked at the monitor for a moment after she left. Then he pressed a couple of numbers on his cell phone and engaged in a few seconds of rapid text messaging. He quickly disconnected and raced over to pick up his gun where he had left it just inside the control room door. He grabbed the rifle, snapped off the safety, and rushed out of the control room.

For the second time in twenty-four hours Cyn found herself racing out of the mine having to remember all the codes in reverse order. By the time she reached the outer cavern, Charlie was banging in earnest on the iron gate and had already ripped off a couple of the boards.

"Stop!" yelled Cyn as she ran to the gate. "What do you think you're doing?"

"I have orders to come and get you. You're in danger," said Charlie as he dropped the hammer and stepped back from the gate.

"What danger? I just came back to finish some of the prospecting I started with Professor Braun yesterday," said Cyn.

"Come on out of there and I'll tell you," said Charlie.

Cyn sighed and opened the gate. She walked through and turned to close it. Suddenly, Charlie's arm was around her neck, his hand clapped over her mouth. "Not a word," he said in a low menacing tone into her ear. "Unless you want your head blown off."

He brought his other hand around and waved a semi-automatic pistol in front of her eyes. Then he crammed it in the base of her skull.

"Not a word, understand?"

When Cyn did not respond, he jabbed her neck harder with the pistol.

"Understand?" he asked again.

This time Cyn nodded to indicate that she understood. He slowly removed his hand from her mouth and wrenched her bag from her shoulder.

"I'll take that," he said. "No, don't turn around!" He jammed the gun into her back between her shoulder blades.

"Now, you and I are gonna take a little tour of this mine," he growled.

Cyn did not move. He pushed her violently almost shoving her to her knees. Again he ground the gun in her back. "Move!" he yelled.

This time Cyn complied. She walked to the back of the mine shaft and stopped.

"Come on," snarled Charlie. "I know there's more to this mine than that. Open the door!"

He jabbed her again, and Cyn slowly went up to the panel that opened the first security door. She hesitated again.

"Come on. Quit fuckin' around and open it!" he yelled, jabbing her even harder.

Cyn placed her palm on the panel and very slowly, very deliberately applied as much pressure as she could with her index finger.

* * *

2:45 p.m.

Cyn felt as light as a soap bubble. She was hovering above a gruesome scene. On the rock floor below her Charlie Denton lay sprawled on his back, a ghastly expression frozen on his face. His eyes were wide open staring sightlessly up at her. They made her think of the stuffed bear in her father's den when she was a baby. She had always cringed beneath the stare of those glass eyes that never blinked, never let her out of their sight.

Near Charlie was another body. She couldn't see it clearly because someone was leaning over it. Someone with a gun. The person stood up and pulled a cell phone from his pocket.

"Why, it's Brent Jacobsen," thought Cyn, "and that body looks like me, but it can't be me because I'm up here."

She hovered and watched as Jake looked up quickly. Then he began to run, and she decided to go with him. She reached the iron gate at the same time he did. It was ajar and he quickly pressed the panel. As the gate slid shut, he crouched down and began firing through the bars at something outside.

"I've got to go," thought Cyn. She was totally unconcerned about the scene taking place below her. Without another thought, she simply drifted through the bars of the gate and floated upward in the New Mexico sky.

A great euphoria engulfed her. She was free, free, free! There were no restrictions—no weight, no gravity—nothing to hold her down. As she rose, she observed two figures dressed in black firing at the mine from behind nearby boulders.

"Why, it's Veronica and Skeeter," she thought. She felt sorry for them. "They're earthbound. They aren't free like me."

Floating even higher she encountered a helicopter. She went right through one of the open doors, hovered a bit, and floated right out the other side. In the copter she saw General Masters and Dr. Graham and Tom Fleetdeer and Bean, all wearing grim expressions. "Look at me! I'm flying, too," she wanted to say but knew she had no voice.

Another helicopter zoomed by her on her way up, and then she seemed to gather speed. Now she could see New Mexico spread out below her like a map, then the rim of the earth, and then the earth spinning below her, and finally there was only blackness as if she were floating upward through a long black tube.

Then she saw the light. It wasn't like any light she had ever seen. It was brilliant, yet mellow; intense, yet soft; fiery, yet tranquil. It appeared to be at the top of this long black tunnel through which she was floating. She wanted nothing more than to reach that light, to bathe in that blissful glow. Upward, upward. Now she was nearly there, could nearly feel the warmth....

"Cyn, come back."

A voice was speaking to her from somewhere down the long dark tunnel.

"But I'm almost at the light," she thought. "I don't want to come back."

"Cyn, come back...come back...come back. It will be all right," the voice continued.

As compelling as the light was, Cyn found that she did not have the power to resist the urging of the voice. She no longer felt weightless. Something was tugging at her, and so she began to spiral down, down, down through the interminable blackness.

* * *

FRIDAY

10:20 a.m.

"Cyn, can you hear me?"

A voice spoke again, but this time it was a different voice—distinctly a male voice. Cyn had been drifting down the long black tunnel for what seemed both a very long time and just an instant. Now the blackness lightened and she seemed to be in a light gray fog.

She opened her eyes. A face was peering down at her—a face she knew. Now, who was it?

"Cyn, can you hear me?" the voice asked again.

"Dan?" she asked. Her voice came out in a croak.

The face broke out in a relieved grin and a hand touched her forehead.

"Cyn, thank God! You're still with us."

"Where…where am I?" Cyn coughed to clear her throat and struggled to sit up.

"No, don't try to sit up. I'll raise the bed. Just relax."

Dr. Graham pressed a button on a remote control and the top half of the bed began to rise. When Cyn was in a half-seated position, he pressed another button and the bed stopped.

"Where am I?" Cyn asked again. She tried to turn her head to look around, but her head seemed to be in some kind of vise.

Dr. Graham touched her forehead again and shook his head. "Don't try to move, at least not yet—not until I am satisfied that you are recovered. In answer to your question, you're in ICU at the Roca Grande Air Base hospital, and you've been here for almost four days."

"Four days!" repeated Cyn. "But I can't have been here that long! I just came out of the tunnel."

Dr. Graham cocked an eyebrow. "Tunnel? You mean the mine shaft?" he asked.

"Mine shaft?" Cyn looked confused. "No, no. I was way up in outer space, and I was heading toward this light, and then I heard a voice telling me to come back, and I didn't want to come back because I wanted to get to that light, but I didn't have any choice, and I had to come back down this pitch-black tunnel."

"I see," said Dr. Graham looking at her closely. "Do you remember anything from before you went into outer space?"

Cyn wrinkled her brow, closed her eyes and tried to think. "Well, let's see. Before I entered the tunnel, I remember seeing the Earth below me. It was just like those photographs they send back from the Space Shuttle. So beautiful...."

"And before that?" prompted Dr. Graham softly.

"Before that I remember seeing the rim of the Earth...and before that the whole State of New Mexico laid out below just like a geographical map."

"So, I take it you were going up?" asked Dr. Graham.

Cyn smiled, her eyes still closed. "Yes. I was always going up, and it was such a wonderful feeling—no weight, no restraints. I felt just like a soap bubble."

There was a moment of silence and suddenly Cyn opened her eyes and looked at Dr. Graham, still smiling. "I saw you on my way up."

"Me? How did you see me?"

Cyn smiled more broadly when she saw the incredulous expression on his face.

"I floated right through the helicopter you were in, and I saw you and General Masters, and Tom Fleetdeer and Bean."

"Impossible! How could you imagine that? And how would you know Tom Fleetdeer and Bean?"

"I met them earlier in a bar."

"Unbelievable!" exclaimed Dr. Graham shaking his head.

Cyn looked at him in alarm. "What do you mean? Are you saying you weren't in that helicopter? I know what I saw."

Dr. Graham smiled at her and his voice resumed its reassuring tone again. "I didn't mean to question you. What you saw was true. We *were* all in that helicopter exactly like you said."

Cyn relaxed slightly, but she looked away. "I know what I saw...." she murmured.

Suddenly she looked at him again with a frown. "By the way, what were you all doing in that helicopter anyway?"

"We were coming to rescue you," said Dr. Graham in a low, gentle tone.

"Rescue me?" Cyn looked puzzled.

"Don't you remember?" Dr. Graham prodded in an even softer voice.

Cyn gazed at him for a moment and then closed her eyes.

A few moments of silence passed. Dr. Graham leaned toward her wondering if she had fallen asleep. Suddenly, her eyes flew open and she bolted upright straining against the headband that secured her head to the bed.

"Whoa!" said Dr. Graham in alarm. "Not so fast!"

"What the hell is this?" asked Cyn clawing at her forehead to see what was holding her down.

Dr. Graham grabbed her hand and pulled it away. "It's a head restraint. I don't want you rolling around and hurting yourself."

"Well, take it off!"

"Only if you promise not to try to get up," said Dr. Graham. He was still holding her hand in a firm grip.

For a bit they had a staring contest and finally Cyn relented. She looked down and Dr. Graham could feel the tension going out of her arm. He released her hand and she looked at him again, this time with the hint of tears in her eyes.

"What is it, Cyn?" asked Dr. Graham. His voice was gentle again.

"It's just that...I remember...." Her voice trailed off.

"Remember what?"

The expression in her eyes hardened. She clenched her jaw. "I remember why you were coming to rescue me."

"And?" prompted the doctor.

Cyn swallowed hard and spoke in a voice hard as nails.

"You were coming to rescue me from Jake," she said.
Dr. Graham's mouth fell open as he stared at her in amazement.

* * *

11:05 a.m.

"She thinks it's Jake," said Dr. Graham. He was in his office at the Air Base hospital talking on the phone to General Masters at Apparition Mountain.

"Why does she think that?" asked the General.

"Apparently, she had one of those after-death experiences that you hear about. She was describing it to me and what she saw. She claims she saw us in the helicopter and wanted to know what we were doing. I said we were coming to rescue her and she asked from what. I was trying to find out how much she remembers, so I said, 'Don't you remember?'

"She closed her eyes and thought for a while. When she opened her eyes, there were tears in them, and then she became very agitated and angry. She told me she remembered why we were coming to rescue her—we were coming to rescue her from Jake. She didn't say why she thought that. She was so agitated I thought it best to give her a sedative and let her rest for a while. When she wakes up again maybe she'll be able to tell us more. I do believe she's going to be all right. I don't think there's any permanent brain damage, but we'll know that for sure in a day or so."

"Well, that"'s good news anyway. When will she be awake again?"

Dr. Graham glanced at the clock on his wall. "The sedative should wear off in about four hours, so I'd say she'll probably be waking up about three o'clock."

"All right. I'll come over about three and see what she has to say. Meanwhile, how are your other patients?"

Dr. Graham shifted the receiver to his other ear and leaned back in his swivel chair. "Professor Braun is out of the woods. We moved him out of ICU and to a private room this morning. He's eating a bland diet on his own now, and we've started walking him twice a day. I think we'll probably be able to release him sometime next week, but he'll have to take it easy and mind his Ps and Qs for at least six months."

"That's good to hear. I'll make sure there's no undue stress placed on him from my quarters. What about Jake?"

Dr. Graham frowned and sighed as he stared out his window. "Jake's a different matter. It's still very touch and go. Taking a bullet through the arm is one thing, but when you take another one through the chest it's an entirely different matter—especially when it shatters a rib and pierces a lung. The only thing I can say is he was lucky it missed his heart, which it did by only a hair, and that it came out clean on the other side."

"God! How well I know." The General sighed as scenes from Iraq flashed through his mind. He cleared his throat before continuing. "Has he been conscious?"

"No. We've been keeping him under heavy sedation and pain meds. The pain would be too great and would impede the healing process. We'll see how things are coming along this afternoon. When I took X-rays this morning I saw that the humerus is beginning to knit. The chest wound appears to be healing, but a rib takes a lot longer. Provided there are no setbacks I may be able to move him out of intensive care on Sunday or Monday." Dr. Graham swiveled back around, leaned an elbow on his desk and wearily cupped his forehead in his hand.

"Well, hang in there, Dan. You've got your hands full. Try to get a little rest, and I'll see you this afternoon. When this is all over I'll see to it that you get an extended leave. You're long overdue for some R and R," said the General.

"Thanks, Sir. I appreciate that," said Dr. Graham. He hung up the phone and got up from his desk.

After pacing about the room for a bit, he went over to a couch and lay down. He crossed his arms over his chest and closed his eyes. He tried to doze off but found that the events of the last week insisted on replaying in his mind. He kept seeing Harry Latter's mummified body over and over and then Jazar's.

At last he gave up. He sprang up from the couch and left the room.

* * *

3:15 p.m.

"She's awake and a lot stronger," said Dr. Graham. "You can go in now, but try not to be longer than fifteen minutes."

General Masters nodded and patted the doctor's shoulder. "I understand."

Dr. Graham opened the inner door to the intensive care unit and led the General past a curtained-off bed.

"Jake is in there," said the Doctor in a low voice as they passed.

The General nodded and followed the Doctor past two empty beds until they came to another curtained-off area at the end of the room.

"Just a second. I'll tell her you're here," said the Doctor. Again the General nodded, and Dr. Graham disappeared inside the curtain for a moment.

He soon re-emerged and held back the curtain for the General. "Go on in, but remember—fifteen minutes, OK?"

"All right," said General Masters. He walked through the curtains and stopped to survey the scene in front of him.

Cyn was propped up to a seated position in the bed. A sheet was drawn up to her waist, and above that the General could see that she had on a light blue hospital gown that tied in the back. An IV line ran from her right hand to a bottle hanging on a rack at the side of the bed. Other lines snaked out from beneath her gown and were attached to an assortment of monitors mounted on a shelf behind her bed.

Her head was secured to the bed by a headband that ran across her forehead, and a line ran from that to another monitor on which lines danced up and down in an array of colors. "Brain waves," thought General Masters.

Her dark auburn hair was dull and tousled, in need of a wash. Her face was pallid, but her eyes were bright. She was looking directly at him.

"Hello, Jeff," she said with a weak smile.

"Hello, Cyn," he boomed, breaking out into a huge smile. "Man, am I glad to see you," he added as he pulled up a chair beside her bed and sat down.

"I'm sure I've looked better," she murmured.

"Well, let me just say you look a hell of a lot better than the last time I saw you," he said with a grin and then instantly regretted it because the smile quickly faded from her lips.

There was an awkward pause as General Masters looked down at his hands and then back up at her with a more somber expression.

"Cyn, Dr. Graham says you remember us coming to rescue you, is that right?"

"Yes," she said softly. Her eyes were moist.

"Can you tell me why we were coming to rescue you?"

He looked intensely into her eyes. Her eyes rolled away and focused on something above his head.

"It was Jake," she said very slowly. "You were coming to rescue me from Jake."

The General put his hand over hers and pressed it gently. She looked at him again. "Cyn, why do you think it was Jake?" he asked in a low voice.

"Because of what I saw," she said.

The General patted her hand again and leaned back in his chair, arms crossed.

"Tell me about it," he said.

Cyn gazed at him for a moment, then closed her eyes and began to speak.

She told him how she had seen Jake hovering over her body with a gun and Charlie Denton's body lying nearby. She told him about Jake shooting through the iron gate and how she had seen Veronica and

Skeeter shooting at him from behind the boulders. She told him how she had actually floated through the helicopter he was riding in. By the time she finished speaking, tears were rolling down her cheeks from under her closed lids.

The General waited for a moment and then leaned forward and pressed her hand. "Cyn, look at me," he said.

Cyn slowly opened her eyes and stared at him.

He squeezed her hand again. "Cyn, I know that what you saw was real, don't get me wrong. It's your *interpretation* of what you saw that is wrong, do you understand?"

Cyn's eyes widened. She continued to stare at him with a puzzled look.

"Now think back. What were you doing before you saw Jake hovering over you?"

"I was…uh…I was going to find out what Charlie Denton wanted. He was trying to tear down the gate to the mine shaft," said Cyn hesitantly.

"And what happened then?" prompted the General.

"And then…uh…then Charlie told me to open the gate and come out—that I was in danger. And when I opened the gate he…uh…he grabbed me and pulled a gun. He forced me to take him to the back of the shaft. He wanted to get into the mine. Said he knew there was more to it than the abandoned shaft." She stopped.

"And what happened then?" asked the General.

Cyn opened her eyes and looked at him. "I can't tell you," she said.

"You mean you don't remember?"

"No, I remember. It's just that I can't tell you."

The General leaned back and looked at her in exasperation. "Can't tell me? Oh, I get it. The top-secret business." He looked around and leaned forward and said in a whisper. "It's OK, Cyn, I know all about Karl's mining operation, the gold, the tracking system, the computers, the whole she-bang."

"You do?" asked Cyn. She looked skeptical.

"Sure. And I know the codes to get through the doors. If you don't want to tell me what happened when Denton had the gun on you, I'll tell you. You put your palm on the panel and applied more pressure with your index finger. That triggered the nerve gas that killed Denton and very nearly killed you."

"So you *do* know?" asked Cyn. "How long?"

"Since the beginning, Cyn. You see, it's fairly widely known that I head up the NSA's Advanced Spectrum Division, but what is not widely known is that I am in charge of all intelligence gathering ops in the Middle East. To that end I employ vast numbers of people including engineering geniuses like Karl Braun and technical gurus like Brent Jacobson."

"And what about Taos Indians like Tom Fleetdeer and Bean?"

The General grinned. "Them, too. Great guys aren't they? I know you met them."

"Yes, but what is their role in all of this?" asked Cyn.

"Primarily communications."

"Communications? Then Mac must know about them since he's head of Worldwide Mobile Intelligence?"

The General shook his head. "No. No one knows about my special communications force except for a very elite few of which you are now a member."

"But why Taos Indians?"

The General leaned in close. "Because of their language that is not written down but has been passed verbally from one generation to the next."

"You mean Tiwa?" asked Cyn.

"That's right. We use them to send messages from certain informants that we've cultivated in the Middle East. No one understands the language, and even if they did, my guys have developed a code which only they are able to translate. That is how we were able to get Jazar. A certain Saudi prince passed the information to us through one of my guys who is posing as his grandson."

"I see," said Cyn. "This supposed grandson wouldn't happen to be attending MIT, would he?"

"Very good, Cyn," said the General with a grin. "I see your mind is functioning as well as ever despite the nerve gas."

Cyn sighed and closed her eyes. "Well, that explains one thing," she said, remembering the voice message Mac had intercepted. "I'm still confused. Didn't you send Charlie Denton to warn me about Jake, and isn't he the one who called you in to rescue me?"

The General's grin faded as he touched her arm again. "No, Cyn. Look at me," he instructed gently.

Cyn opened her eyes and tried to focus on him.

The General was shaking his head. "No, Cyn, I did not send Charlie Denton to warn you. Don't you remember? He pulled a gun on you and tried to force his way into the mine."

"Oh...that's right. Well, if you didn't send him, why was he trying to get into the mine?"

The General stared at her intently. "You know the answer, Cyn. Think about it."

Cyn swallowed hard and said nothing for a moment. Random thoughts were racing through her mind refusing to join forces. She closed her eyes again and tried to concentrate. Suddenly her eyelids snapped open. "Oh, I get it now," she croaked.

"What?" asked the General.

"Charlie Denton was in cahoots with Jake! They were the ones leaking the information from inside the Mountain!"

The General leaned back in his chair, crossed his arms, and stared at her in exasperation. "No, Cyn, you don't get it," he said in a disgusted tone just as Dr. Graham opened the curtain and walked in.

"But...but...what else could it be? Mac sent his crew to rescue me. I saw them shooting at Jake! And...and...Mac must have called you in." Tears were flowing from her eyes and she was clawing at the headband again.

"Can't you get this damned thing off my head so I can think?" she sobbed as Dr. Graham walked over and gently removed her hand from the headband.

"It's OK, Cyn. You need to rest for a while and then you'll be able to think," said Dr. Graham. He glanced at the General and shook his head.

The General got up from his chair and watched as Dr. Graham plunged a syringe into the IV line out of Cyn's line of vision.

Her eyelids began to droop and she was soon floating without weight and without care in the long black tunnel.

* * *

3:40 p.m.

"So, what do you think, Dan?" asked the General.

He was seated on the couch in Dr. Graham's office sipping a cup of coffee and looking at the Doctor's back. Dan Graham had been pacing about the room as the General told him about his recent conversation with Cyn. Now he stood gazing out the window, absent-mindedly plucking at his earlobe with the thumb and forefinger of his right hand.

The General waited. At last Dr. Graham turned and extended his arms outward in a sweeping motion. "I think she is going to be fine," he said. "It was fortunate we were able to get to her with the antidote when we did."

The General took a final sip from the mug and put it down on the coffee table in front of him. "I sure hope you're right, Dan. She seems pretty confused about what happened, and she never once mentioned Mario."

The Doctor waved a hand in dismissal. "That doesn't worry me. She's got a little temporary amnesia, which is to be expected. Hell, you would, too, if you'd been in a coma for four days! No, I'm convinced it will all come back to her and she'll be as sharp as ever. It will just take a little time. Right now, she's stressing out trying to remember, plus trying to make sense of what she saw in that after-death or out-of-body experience or whatever it was that she had. I think when she wakes up again she'll remember even more—maybe everything."

"Well, it makes me feel better to hear you're so confident about her recovery, Dan." The General flicked a piece of lint off his sleeve and stood up. "I've got to get back to the Mountain and call the Senator with an update on her condition."

Dr. Graham raised an eyebrow. "The Senator. I nearly forgot about him. What does *he* think happened to Cyn?"

"He thinks it was a mining accident, which is partially true," said the General with a shrug. "I told him Cyn had gone off on her own prospecting in an old abandoned mine and was overcome by a pocket of methane gas. Said she was able to call us on her cell phone and tell us where she was before she passed out. Be sure to remember that for the public record, Dan."

"Of course," said Dr. Graham. "I'll write up an 'official' report right away in case it's needed in the future."

"Good," said the General. He glanced at his wristwatch. "What time should I come back? At about twenty hundred?"

Dr. Graham glanced at the clock on the wall. "Make it about nine o'clock. I want to see if we can get her to eat something when she wakes up."

"Twenty-one hundred it is, then," said the General reaching for the door knob. "I hope she'll be able to tell me what she knows."

"Well, if she can't, I suppose there's always the memory download," said the Doctor in a bitter tone.

The General stopped short and turned to look at him. "You can relax about that, Dan. I've made a recommendation to the powers-that-be, and if they agree, as soon as Karl is released from the hospital, I'm going to have him dismantle and destroy that whole operation. It's served its purpose and that's enough. No more cracking heads. We don't need any more deaths."

A smile flitted across Dr. Graham's face. "And I, for one, am very happy to hear you say that. In fact, I am delighted."

"I thought you'd be pleased," said the General matter-of-factly. He gave a small salute as he opened the door to leave.

Dr. Graham stood gazing at the door for a moment after it had closed behind the General. Then with a satisfied smile on his face he pulled off his lab coat and hung it on a hook, rolled up his sleeves and sat down at his computer to write his official report on Cynthia Hoover's mining accident.

* * *

9:05 p.m.

"She's waiting for you. You'll be surprised to see how much better she is," said Dr. Graham as he opened the door to the ICU.

"Great," said General Masters. He followed the Doctor to the curtained-off area at the end of the room.

When the Doctor opened the curtain, he saw that it was true. Cyn was propped up in the bed again, but this time the head restraint was gone, and her hair was glossy. She had more color in her face, and she smiled as he entered the room.

"Well, Cyn, you're certainly looking good. How do you feel?" asked the General as he drew the chair up to the bed and sat down.

"Much better, thank you," said Cyn. "I had soup and a cheese sandwich, and Betsy gave me a sponge bath and washed my hair. That makes a lot of difference, plus Dr. Graham removed that head band. He says I only have to wear it when I'm sleeping from now on."

The General beamed at her. "Good, Cyn! Your voice is better, too— not so hoarse."

"Yes," Cyn agreed. "My mouth and throat aren't nearly so dry. Betsy said that was caused by the medication in addition to not having any oral liquids. I think I drank about a gallon of water when I woke up."

"Have you been out of bed yet?"

Cyn shook her head. "No, not yet. Dr. Graham says we'll try that tomorrow if I'm still doing better."

"Good. Are you ready for another memory test?"

Cyn nodded. "Yes, I think so."

"All right then. Can you remember what you were doing at the mine?"

Cyn's brow wrinkled slightly as she thought for a moment. "Let's see. That was the day we did the memory download on Jazar...."

"That's right," said the General encouraging her.

"I remember we did the memory download, but then we couldn't access it. It was as if it had totally disappeared from the computer banks...."

"That's right," said the General again.

"And then...and then I went back to the Inn and...uh, let me see. Oh, yes, I met with Mac and told him what happened and then I...uh, went to my room and Jake came...." Cyn stopped and closed her eyes.

"And what did Mac do after you told him about the download problem?" asked the General quickly.

Cyn"s eyes opened and she looked at him again. "Nothing, really. He had to leave for Albuquerque because his band had an engagement there. He just told me to stay in touch and he would let me know if anything turned up on his end."

"Did you tell him you were going to meet with Jake?"

"Yes...I think so." Cyn frowned and thought for a moment. "Yes, yes, I did. I told him maybe Jake would know something about the loss of the memory download."

"You didn't tell him you were going to the mine?"

Cyn looked at him in surprise. "No, definitely not, because I didn't know we were going to the mine at that time."

"I see," said the General. "And then what happened after Jake came to your room?"

"We were talking and I said something about...." Cyn stopped abruptly, a look of apprehension coming into her eyes.

"About what?" prodded the General.

When Cyn did not respond, the General leaned in closer and placed a hand on her arm. "Come on, Cyn. You can tell me."

"Well...I hope you don't take offense, but I said something about not trusting you, and Jake said there was someone he wanted me to meet, and then he took me to the Dos Amigos Cantina and introduced me to Tom Fleetdeer. Tom told me how he had served under you in Iraq and what a great leader and person you are. Then Bean came in, and I met him, too. Jake later told me Tom and Bean are in some kind of special forces under your command." Cyn stopped again and looked at the General apologetically.

The General patted her arm and smiled. "I see. And what was it that made you suspicious of me?" he asked softly.

Cyn gazed up at the ceiling. "Let me think…it was after Karl had the heart attack. Ah, yes, now I remember. Mac intercepted a message that originated from Apparition Mountain—something to the effect that the head scientist was out of commission and the memory download would have to be delayed. The message was relayed at around two-thirty in the afternoon on Sunday, just after Karl had been flown to the hospital. Mac asked me who was at the Mountain at that time. Everyone else had been accounted for, and you were the only one at the Mountain as far as I knew. And then, sure enough, you did call off the download and didn't give the order to proceed until I got the Director to pressure you."

Cyn stopped speaking and looked at the General with a raised eyebrow.

He nodded at her reassuringly. "Yes, that's correct, Cyn. I was the only one at the Mountain at two-thirty that day, and yes, I did not want to proceed with the download without Karl."

"Then you did send that message?" asked Cyn with a frown.

"No, Cyn. I did not."

"Then who…?"

The General leaned back in his chair and shook his head. "You'll figure it out. Go on with your story. What happened after you went to see Tom and Bean?"

Cyn stared at him with a puzzled expression for a second and then shrugged. "Well, then Jake drove up the road toward the Air Base and suddenly took a right-hand turn on a rugged dirt road. When I asked him where we were going, he told me we were going to take a look at the memory download…said he and Karl had a backup system. Then we ended up at the back entrance to the mine and went in that way."

"You went in the back way? Then that accounts for why we couldn't find Jake's Durango," said the General almost to himself. "So, when you were in the computer center in the mine, you were able to pull up Jazar's memory?"

"Yes," said Cyn. "We saw how Jazar escaped to Syria from Iraq, and we saw him meeting with al-Ahmin…and Mario! We saw Mario! But we couldn't see his face because he had on dark glasses and a black kaffiyeh that hung down the sides of his face. He never looked directly at Jazar, and we could only see him in profile…until…until Jazar was leaving the room, and he suddenly turned and…uh Mario was looking straight at him. It was just for a second."

"But a second was long enough, wasn't it Cyn? What did you do next?"

Cyn looked puzzled again. "Well, even though we froze the frame and enlarged the picture, there was nothing discernible about his face…except…" Cyn's voice trailed off.

"Except?" prodded the General.

Cyn frowned. "Well, there was this…uh…this glint of light, and when Jake zoomed in on it, we discovered Mario's mouth was open slightly and the light was glinting off a gold tooth. That was the only distinguishing mark we could find."

The General nodded. "And what did you do then?"

Cyn thought again. "I had Jake print out the images, and then I relayed them to NSA hoping they might find a match in their files after analyzing the facial structure."

"Precisely," said the General with a huge smile. "And that is how we captured Mario!"

"You captured Mario?" gasped Cyn wide-eyed.

"Yes, thanks to you. We've already turned him over to the CIA," said the General, crossing his arms over his chest and smiling hugely.

"But where…when?"

"Heading for the Mexican border at the same time we came to rescue you," said the General looking at her closely. "He was going to cross at Palomas and get out of the country with the E5 formula."

Cyn's eyes grew even wider. "Mario was in New Mexico?"

"That's right. You know who he is. Think, Cyn."

Cyn looked bewildered. "Charlie Denton?" she ventured.

The General shook his head. "Nope, although Denton was in league with Mario and turned out to be the informant inside the Mountain."

Cyn still looked puzzled.

"Want a hint?" asked the General.

Cyn nodded.

"What did you do with that gold bar Karl gave you?" he asked.

"Gold bar...." repeated Cyn with a frown.

She looked questioningly at the General. He only gave her an intense stare.

Suddenly she sat straight up in the bed and smacked her forehead with the palm of her hand. She remembered Jake dropping her off at the Inn after the fiasco at the mine on Sunday. She remembered grousing to herself that no one was around and that Mac wasn't answering his phone. She remembered taking the gold bar out of her bag and admiring it. Then she remembered going out the back door and carefully planting it beneath the bus.

"It's Mac," she said.

* * *

SUNDAY

8:20 a.m.

Halcon was soaring. He had ridden the thermals over Taos, the Pueblo, the Rio Grande Gorge, the vistas of his youth. Now he was miles from there descending in slow lazy circles, down, down, down until at last he alit.

He opened his eyes and smiled. He was gazing at the face he loved most in the entire world. "Cyn-Cyn," he murmured.

Cyn's face lit up in a beautiful warm smile as she leaned toward him and stroked his forehead. "Oh, Jake, I'm so happy to see you. You're awake at last."

"Was I asleep?" he asked groggily. "Where am I?"

He began to struggle to get up and immediately went still when he felt the sharp stabbing pain that took his breath away.

"No, don't try to get up. Just lie still," said Cyn in a soothing voice, still stroking his forehead.

"I'll take it from here," said Dr. Graham, leaning in toward Jake from the other side of the bed. "Hello, Jake."

"Dan… What's happening?" asked Jake when Dr. Graham's face appeared in his line of vision.

"You've been out of commission for a while, pal, but you're going to be OK."

Dr. Graham looked at Cyn who was holding Jake's hand. "You'll have to leave now. I need to do a couple of tests and have Betsy in to give him a bath and then we want to move him out of ICU to a private room."

"All right, I understand," said Cyn.

She started to let go of Jake's hand, but he clutched it with surprising strength.

"No, don't go," he moaned.

She leaned over him again and touched his forehead. "It's all right, Darling. I'll be right outside, and I'll come back to see you just as soon as the Doctor says it's OK."

Cyn gently withdrew her hand from his and turned to leave the room. Jake looked pleadingly at Dr. Graham.

"Cyn can come back and have breakfast with you when you're settled in your new quarters," said the Doctor with a reassuring smile.

"What time?" asked Cyn pausing at the curtain.

The Doctor consulted his wristwatch. "I should think it would be about 9:30. We'll let you know."

"All right," said Cyn. "I'll see you for breakfast, Jake."

"OK," said Jake, the tension draining away as he watched Cyn leave.

"So, how bad off am I, Doc?" he asked when he was sure she was out of earshot.

"Well, you've got a broken arm, a broken rib, a chest wound and a perforated lung, but other than that you're fine," said the Doctor with a grin.

"That good, huh?" asked Jake with a feeble smile.

"Seriously, it was touch and go there for a while, but things are on the mend, and you're going to be OK. Do you remember what happened?"

Jake frowned and thought for a moment. "Yeah, I remember," he said through gritted teeth. "Cyn and I were in the mine and she got a call from Charlie Denton saying he needed to see her right away. She ignored it and we went on with our business. Then a while later Denton appeared at the entrance to the mine and was trying to break in. Cyn went out to find out what he wanted and see if she could ward him off.

"I thought there was something fishy about Denton showing up, so I called General Masters. He said he hadn't sent Denton, so right away we both knew something was wrong. I told him he'd better get there fast and to bring you along with the nerve gas antidote because I was afraid Denton would try to force Cyn to open up the mine and she would have no choice but to deploy the nerve gas. We hadn't had the chance to have her vaccinated yet.

"I grabbed my gun and went out, but I got there too late. Denton and Cyn were lying on the ground. Denton was dead, and I was afraid Cyn was, too, but before I could examine her any further, I heard voices outside. I ran to the entrance and saw a couple of people approaching the mine. I started firing and they took cover behind some boulders and started shooting at me. I remember taking a hit in the arm and trying to keep on shooting. Then I felt something slam into my chest and knocking me back. I must have passed out because that's the last thing I remember other than the sound of choppers overhead. God, I was so worried about Cyn."

Jake's eyes clouded and he closed them. "I thought I saw her here a while ago, but I must have been dreaming," he muttered.

Dr. Graham touched Jake's good arm. "Jake, look at me. You did see Cyn. It wasn't a dream."

Jake's eyes snapped open. "She's all right?"

Dr. Graham nodded with a smile.

Jake sighed and a smile crossed his lips. "Oh, thank God," he breathed.

"Yes, Cyn is fully recovered, and she owes her life to you, Jake. If you hadn't called the General when you did, I'm afraid it would have been a different story."

"Oh, thank God," said Jake again allowing his head to sink back onto the pillow.

"Now, let's get you cleaned up and moved. Then Cyn can tell you the rest of the story," said Doctor Graham.

Jake smiled. He was soaring again, but this time totally within himself.

* * *

10:00 a.m.

"One word pure and simple," said Cyn. "Greed."

She was seated across from Jake at a small table by the window in his hospital room. He was in a wheelchair, his right arm in a sling, guiding a spoonful of oatmeal to his lips with his left hand. She smiled to see how easily he did this with his left hand, remembering that Jake was ambidextrous. He had told her that part of the tribal custom was to train young people to be able to use both sides of the body with equal dexterity. "Otherwise, you're only half a man," his father had told him.

Jake swallowed the spoonful of oatmeal and lowered the spoon to the table. "So it was another case of money speaking louder than words such as loyalty and honor and decency?" he asked with a cocked eyebrow and a twinkle in his lapis-blue eyes.

Cyn's heart fluttered at this familiar gesture. She swallowed hard before replying.

"That's right, but Mac never had much training about anything other than greed when he was growing up, you know."

Jake pushed an errant strand of jet-black hair from his face and Cyn's heart fluttered again. "You mean being raised in a motorcycle gang?"

Cyn nodded. "Apparently, when he was in Afghanistan buying off warlords, that's when he turned rogue. He saw the way to make millions and eventually change his identity and disappear in the Middle East to a life of luxury. He was going to sell the E5 formula to Iran for 2.5 billion and then retire."

"So, Charlie Denton was his inside man at Apparition Mountain," mused Jake to himself. Then he looked at Cyn. "That doesn't explain how he was able to get hold of the formula because Denton definitely didn't have access to that."

"That's right," said Cyn. "Unfortunately, he got hold of it because of me."

"Because of you?" asked Jake in surprise.

"Yes," said Cyn. "You remember when the video board blew and we couldn't figure a way to view the memory?"

Jake nodded.

"Remember who came up with the solution?"

"You did," said Jake. "You suggested to the General that he get permission to upload it to Roswell."

"That's right," said Cyn. "But it wasn't my idea in the beginning. It was Mac's, and like the trusting fool that I was, I passed the suggestion on to the General. As it turned out, the uploads were going to Roswell vis-à-vis Mac's computer. He was able to see and keep everything he wanted as well as edit out anything he didn't want the NSA to see."

"Aha," said Jake leaning forward slightly. "That explains why we had those problems with accessing the data banks from time to time."

Cyn nodded. "Not to mention Jazar's memory download totally disappearing. That was something Mac definitely didn't want anyone to see. I could kick myself for not figuring it out earlier. In hindsight I remember several things that should have tipped me off. If I'd been on my toes, I'd have figured it out."

"Don't be too hard on yourself, Cyn. After all, you worked with Mac in the past, and he *was* the head of WMI. If he fooled all of NSA into trusting him, there was no reason you shouldn't have trusted him," said Jake in a soothing tone.

"Yes, but still…I feel such a fool to have been manipulated the way I was. He had me suspecting everyone from Karl Braun to you and even the General. I should have picked up on some things—like that supposed NSA scan he did of Karl's old MIT photo. And then it turns out his guys

Hound Dog and Skeeter were the ones involved in the first attack on the mine, and he explained that all away so glibly, and I believed him! He was using me to get his hands on the formula and to waylay the download of Jazar's memory. Because of my stupidity, you were very nearly killed."

"What do you mean?"

Cyn paused and stared down at the untouched oatmeal in front of her. "When I got that call from Charlie Denton in the mine...."

"You mean, when he said it was urgent that you contact him right away?"

"Yes, but I didn't tell you the whole message. He also said I was in danger," said Cyn. She still could not bring herself to look at Jake. "I pressed the panic button on the XJ14 that Charlie had given me when he set me up with all the equipment. That's how he tracked me to the mine. I thought...I thought the General had ordered him to get me away from you for some reason. I'm so sorry, *Halcon*."

Jake lifted a glass of orange juice to his mouth and took a sip as he continued to watch her in silence. A few seconds passed. He put down the orange juice and leaned back in his chair.

"Cyn, look at me," he said quietly. He waited until she slowly lifted her head and gazed at him with teary eyes. "It was because of *my* stupidity that *you* were very nearly killed."

She looked at him in surprise. "What do you mean?"

"For not making sure you were vaccinated against the nerve agent before we went to the mine," he said.

She started to protest, but Jake held up his hand.

"No, Cyn. Facts are facts and what's done is done. You have to quit blaming yourself and take credit for the fact that Mario would still be on the loose if not for you. Besides, you must have had some suspicions— otherwise, why did you plant that gold bar on Mac's bus?"

Cyn emitted a sardonic snort and waved her hand. "Oh, that! I did that as a sort of joke and a little test to see if the thing really worked."

"And what did you think when you saw it down near Deming when I was fiddling with the image of Mario?" Jake was looking at her with a sly grin.

Cyn's mouth dropped open. "How did you know about that?"

"Eyes in the back of my head, remember?"

Cyn smiled. "Oh, yes, I do remember."

"So, what did you think?" repeated Jake.

Cyn's smile faded and she looked down at her hands folded in her lap. "I wasn't sure what to think. I remember being surprised that it was not in Albuquerque where Mac and the band had supposedly gone for their next gig…and then when Charlie Denton showed up, I thought the General had sent him to rescue me from…from you. I'm sorry, Jake."

She looked up at him apologetically.

Jake shrugged. "It's all right, Cyn. I can understand how you got that impression. The important thing is that you know the truth now. Did you tell Mac about the mining operation and the gold?" asked Jake.

"Oh, no," said Cyn. "I didn't tell him anything about the mine, but it turns out Mac knew the data was being transmitted to the mine at the same time it was being sent to Roswell. That's why he tried to break into the mine the first time under the pretext of protecting me from Karl Braun. When they discovered my location through the XJ14 phone that Charlie Denton had programmed, they knew we were probably in there looking at Jazar's memory and they had to put an end to that at all costs. Mac sent Charlie, Skeeter and Veronica to get into the mine, destroy the data base, kill us and then join him and Hound Dog down in Mexico. Then they'd sell the E5 formula to Iran and all of them would simply disappear in the Middle East. I'm sure Mac didn't know about the gold, but imagine what would have happened if he'd discovered that!"

Cyn paused for a second to catch her breath. "No, Jake, I didn't tell anyone about the mining operation—not even the General, who, as it turns out, knew about it all along."

"That's right," said Jake with a grin. "I guess you know we all work for him, don't you?"

"So it seems," said Cyn with a wry smile.

"And don't you feel the slightest bit manipulated by him?" asked Jake.

The smile faded from Cyn"s lips. "Why do you say that?"

Jake continued to smile at her. "Think about it, Cyn. To catch a fish you've got to bait the hook."

"Meaning?"

"Meaning that the General baited the hook. For years we've suspected that Mario might be someone in our own top-level ranks because he was always one step ahead of our best efforts. He always seemed to know how to get around our latest most sophisticated surveillance technology, right?"

"Right...." said Cyn hesitantly.

"Well, if you let it leak out that (a) you're going to recover the formula for the most sophisticated weapon the world has ever seen, and (b) you're going to look into the memory of a man who's actually seen Mario, then it's pretty likely that the culprit's going to show his hand, don't you think?"

Cyn nodded.

"So, really, when you think about it, all of us were 'used' or 'manipulated,' or whatever you want to call it, in this mission to catch Mario, don't you see?"

"Is that why no one told me about the backup storage at the mine?" asked Cyn.

Jake nodded. "Exactly."

"I always did think it was very odd that neither Karl nor the General saw to it that there was plenty of backup equipment, especially something as basic as a video board," said Cyn.

Jake chuckled. "That was the thing I didn't think I could fool you with. I blew that board myself when you were across the room. We had plenty of backup boards."

"Really!" said Cyn huffily. "And what was the reason for keeping me in the dark? Did you all think *I* was Mario?"

"No, Cyn. The General simply wanted you to believe that it was blown so you would tell the truth as you knew it to the people you were reporting to. Remember, we suspected that Mario was high-up on the top-secret totem pole? The General wasn't ruling anyone out."

"But I don't see what he hoped to gain by delaying the process," said Cyn.

"Well, if you remember, we'd just printed out the formula when the board blew, but we had not yet discovered what went wrong with it, right?"

Cyn nodded.

"The General figured that would create some anxiety with anyone who was trying to get hold of the formula and get out of the country. He knew you'd tell your people, and he even leaked a bit out as well knowing that Mario would find out. He was quite interested to find out who would come up with a faster solution to the video problem than waiting for the supposed new video boards to arrive from IBM."

"And then I'm the one who suggested uploading it to Roswell, and in fact even convinced you to do that instead of saving it on DVDs," said Cyn with a bitter taste in her mouth. "I suppose I was really under suspicion then because I didn't mention that the upload was Mac's idea in the first place."

Jake shook his head. "No. The General figured that you had actually come up with that on your own. After all, that was part of your job here— to figure out the technical glitches that bumblers such as Karl Braun and I could not handle."

"Bumblers, my foot!" laughed Cyn.

"Speaking of bumblers, is it possible for this one to come in?" inquired a familiar voice from the doorway.

Cyn and Jake turned to look and simultaneously broke out in broad smiles as they saw Karl Braun wheeling himself through the doorway in his wheelchair.

"Professor Braun!" said Jake. "It's good to see you."

"Oh, come on. It's Karl, and it's good to see you up and about at last," said Karl as he wheeled himself up to their table.

"You're looking chipper, today," said Cyn. "Much better than when I saw you yesterday."

Karl nodded enthusiastically. "Yes. I just got word from Dr. Graham that I'm being released tomorrow. I'm feeling good and strong. I don't really need to be in this wheelchair, but the Doc wants me to use it in between my scheduled walks. How about you, Jake?"

Jake grinned at him. "They're starting me on physical therapy later today, and the Doc thinks I might be out of here within a week. They want to take this cast off before they release me and also give it a little more time for the rib to heal. Just seeing that both you and Cyn are all right is great physical therapy for me."

"I know what you mean. You both had very close calls. I'm sorry I wasn't around for the last procedure. I feel responsible for what happened to you," said Karl. He looked away for a second, his expression becoming grave.

"No, Karl, don't feel bad," said Cyn quickly touching his arm. "We were terribly concerned about you."

"So what's on the agenda after you're released from the hospital?" asked Jake changing the subject.

The smile returned to Karl's face. "Retire—but first, the General has recommended to his superiors that the memory download project be shut down. If they agree, the first thing I will do is dismantle the entire computer system and destroy all records and data. The General and I have talked about it, and we have come to the conclusion that it's just not the ethical thing to do even though we could certainly justify it under the provisions of the Patriot Act. In every instance, the subject has died, and I haven't figured out how to correct that. Just think. If it ever came out, there would be a huge hew and cry—we'd be branded with the same iron as terrorists or barbarians. It's comparable to beheading a person—only worse. In our case, we're literally gutting a person's mind and stealing his private memories. No, we can't allow that to go on."

Cyn patted his arm. "The Senator will be relieved to hear that. As you remember, he expressed concerns about the right-to-privacy aspects."

"Yes, I remember," said Karl. "As far as the Senator knows, the one download we did on Harry Latter accomplished the purpose of reviving the E-Weapon. He doesn't know about the download of Jazar's memory which remains ultra top-secret. So, end of story."

"And what are your plans for retirement?" asked Jake.

"First thing I'm going to do is rent a penthouse on the Queen Mary and cruise around the world for a year. Then after that we'll see. I might buy a place in Belize, and I'll continue to oversee Harry Latter's trust, which I can do from anywhere in the world."

"Trust?" asked Cyn.

Jake and Karl looked at each other and Karl nodded.

Jake cleared his throat. "Remember Harry's gambling fortune?" he asked looking at Cyn.

She nodded.

"Well, when Harry was working on the E5 project here in New Mexico he became very interested in the Taos Indians and realized that many of the young people had superior skills and talents but no means of developing them through higher education. He established a foundation to fund MIT scholarships for qualified Taos Indians. My cousin Allen Fleetdeer is going through MIT on one of those scholarships right now," explained Jake.

Cyn beamed. "What a great thing! And all along, I thought there was something shady about his money."

"Harry Latter was a very private person," said Karl. "Only a couple of us know about this Foundation, and the reason he kept his money in Switzerland was to avoid taxes eating up the proceeds that he wanted to preserve for the benefit of deserving students. Now you know, but please don't spread it around."

"I understand," said Cyn. "Some secrets are definitely worth keeping. I won't say a word."

There was a knock at the door and Betsy Mallory stuck her head in. "Professor Braun, it's time for your walking therapy," she announced.

"I've got to go get back on my feet, so to speak," said Karl with a grin. "I'll be back to see you before they release me tomorrow."

Jake and Cyn watched as he wheeled himself out of the room.

"So, Cyn-Cyn," said Jake after a moment's pause. "All mysteries cleared up?"

Cyn looked at him and smiled. "I think so, except for one...."

"And that is?"

"Professor Latte's slot machine formula. We never had the chance to search his memory for the actual formula, and now we'll never know because they're going to destroy the data bank."

"Yeah, I'd like to see that myself," said Jake somewhat wistfully. There was a pause as they gazed at each other. Then Jake asked, "What's next with you, Cyn?"

"Well, tomorrow I have to make a quick trip back to D.C. and help the Senator spiff up his funding recommendation for development of the E5.

Then I have a meeting with Jocelyn, and after that I'm on a six-month leave."

Jake's face fell. "You're leaving tomorrow? What are you doing on your leave?"

Cyn looked at him with a serious, almost stern expression. "Do you remember asking me to go to Las Vegas with you when this was all over?"

"You mean to test Harry's slot machine formula?" he asked cautiously.

"No," said Cyn very slowly.

Their eyes locked on each other for a long instant. This time Cyn did not blink.

"There's this wedding chapel in Las Vegas where my parents got married. I've always wanted to visit it," she said.

"With me?" he asked.

"You've got that right, *Halcon*," she said.

* * *

11:05 a.m.

Betsy Mallory quietly opened the door to Jake's room to tell him it was time for his first therapy session. She opened her mouth to speak but quickly shut it when she saw the scene inside.

Jake was standing up beside his wheelchair clutching Cyn in a passionate embrace.

Betsy quietly closed the door.

"Best therapy in the world," she murmured as she walked on down the hall.

The End

Benson S. Forbes is the pen name for co-authors and married couple John Benson and Shari S. Forbes. Benson grew up in England and worked for the British Ministry of Defense before immigrating to the U.S. For 25 years he headed up design engineering for several high tech companies including several that he started. Forbes grew up in Rush County, Kansas. She is an award-winning writer and editor, a former English and journalism teacher and a former editor of a nationally-distributed magazine. The couple currently lives in the country near Portland, Oregon where they draw on their combined experiences and expertise to collaborate on works of fiction. *Cracking Heads* is their third novel. Other published novels include *The Bottom Five*, published in 2003, and *Mad Cows Come Back To Bite*, published in 2004.